THE PERFECT HEIR

A DARK ROMANIAN MAFIA ROMANCE

MONIQUE MOREAU

Cover design by Steamy Designs
https://steamydesigns.net

MEET MONIQUE!

Join Monique's Newsletter (and receive goodies and release information) https://bit.ly/SteamyReadNewsletter

Join Monique's FB reader's group
Possessive Alpha Reads

Like her Facebook Page
https://bit.ly/MoniqueMoreaufb

Follow her on TikTok
https://bit.ly/MoniqueTikTok

Follow her on Instagram
https://bit.ly/MoniqueMoreauIG

Follow her on Book Bub
http://bit.ly/MoniqueBookBub

Learn all about Monique's books
MoniqueMoreau.com

1

TATUM

They did things differently in Cali, no doubt about it.

This was still my first thought whenever I sat down at the oval-shaped table in the long shadows of the Hagi library. It was typical to have *mafie* men like myself, Nicu, or Sebastian at the negotiating table. Same for the Hagi clan boss, Boian, or his *consilier* Grigore.

It was unheard of for a woman to sit at the table during negotiations between clans. But after spending weeks in LA, I'd quickly learned things worked differently than in the bastion of Romanian *mafie* power, New York City.

Might not have been a problem if Clara wasn't both drop-dead gorgeous and infuriatingly difficult.

She sparked like a firecracker at the other end of the table in the dusky library of their huge mansion, a room with floor-to-ceiling shelves crammed full of books and crowded with heavy mahogany furniture. The library's medieval castle vibe contrasted starkly with the crisp powder-blue Los Angeles sky framed by long, narrow windows.

We were in the middle of a tense discussion about opening their drug routes from Mexico to my clan. I snarled in response to Grigore's stonewalling tactics when Clara glowered at me from across the table and said, "Why don't you call off your goon?"

Addressing her insult to me, about me, this woman had the audacity to talk like I was some low-life criminal. The woman was nothing if not bold, and she took any chance to humiliate me. I was the Lupu *consilier*, for God's sake, not a mere soldier. And here this woman ran her mouth at me, insulted me, in front of my clan brothers and her own people?

Fury coursed through me. She was baiting me again. I rarely lost my patience, but if there was one woman on God's green earth who could manage the feat, it was Clara Hagi.

Why Boian didn't control his daughter was a mystery to me. Certainly made my fingers spasm with the urge to smack her plump ass into submission myself.

It was either that or fuck her.

Between my flushed body and twitching hands, I was about to lose control, and that was unacceptable. Without speaking a word, I made my displeasure known by slapping a palm on the lacquered tabletop, screeching my chair back as I rose to my feet, and stalking out.

I paced the richly carpeted corridor outside the library of the Hagi mansion, passing a window overlooking the Hollywood Hills. It was a canyon dotted with huge luxury homes like this one, interspersed with little bungalows clinging to bluffs. Marching up and down the hall, I halted for a moment to stare at the red walls. Who but the vulgar Hagi family would paint the walls of a hallway this godawful shade of red? Jesus, where were we? The Moulin Rouge?

Shaking my head, I resumed my walk of fury and tried to focus on *any*thing other than the woman I hated and shouldn't want; my mind naturally turned toward the worry constantly plaguing me.

My last, but most deadly, secret.

But let's back up for a second because for most of my thirty-odd years, I've held *three* secrets close to my chest.

The first secret was about our last şef and the second family he kept hidden from us. I found out as a kid, eavesdropping on my mother's gossip. The second secret was that our şef had treated his second son, Luca, worse than an animal because Luca wasn't his natural son. I'd found this out on my own when I discovered Luca locked in a closet, battered and bruised.

The last secret, though, was deeply personal.

At first, it was my father's secret, and if he'd been a real man, he would've taken it with him to the grave, but the bastard never could do the right thing. By extension, his secret became mine, tainting me and everything I touched.

A smooth as silk feminine voice reverberated through the door of the library, followed by a husky laugh, distracting me from my thoughts.

Clara.

As usual, my rage quickly turned into another kind of heat. Heart rate quickening, my stride picked up to match its pace, wearing a path on the opulent floral runner beneath my custom-made Italian wingtip shoes.

Burdened and tainted as I was by my secret, along with the mutual hatred we had for each other and the fugitive urges roaring through me, I made a point of keeping my distance. She hounded me by incessantly testing my boundaries and poking the demon inside me. She did it just to get a rise out of me, and most of the time, it worked.

Clara Hagi, the Virgin Queen. The story goes her father gave her the moniker to scare away men. I snorted. Ice Queen would've been a better fit. Despite an hourglass shape and a pair of tits that would make a grown man cry, the woman did everything she could to hone her sexuality into a sharp, brittle thing—

The door to the library swung open and out stomped Grigore, the Hagi *consilier*, and my nemesis. My hatred for him might only be topped by his for me.

He bumped his shoulder into mine as he stormed past me and disappeared down the hall. It took every ounce of control, and God knows I was endowed with an immense amount of it, not to bodycheck him into the wall. Wouldn't have been hard. The man might be tall, but I was huge, a frame of pure muscle.

Suddenly, the door slammed wide open, smashed against the wall, and Clara barreled out like an avenging angel, eyes alight with fury.

She didn't just wear makeup. No, she wore a battle mask.

She didn't just wear a suit. No, she wore armor.

And the worst of it was, despite applying layers of makeup that could rival a geisha's and wearing a power suit more structured than a man's, she taunted me with a hemline short enough to leave me salivating for a peek of that untouched pussy of hers.

Yeah, I was the sick bastard who fantasized about getting under her skirt. Or, better yet, bending her over that huge monstrosity of a desk in the library and baring her fine bubble ass to my hand.

Her eyes darkened and landed on me.

She stormed up to me and poked a refined finger in my chest.

"You," she spat out. "This is your fault. I know you're the one behind this fucking *insane* idea. Only someone as sick as you would come up with such a twisted plan."

She stood toe-to-toe with me, the top of her head barely reaching my collarbone.

My blood roiled at her baffling accusation, aggression, and conceit. But my cock stirred—oh, did it stir—at her display of spirit.

I fantasized about taming a strong woman like her. Any woman who became mine would have to thrive on my special brand of domination. I wasn't an insecure man; I didn't need to have the upper hand with a woman of Clara's caliber to boost my own self-worth. I would give my left nut for the privilege of providing for her every need and whim.

But I couldn't give her a clue as to how enticing she looked—a little dark angel trembling with rage in front of me, nudging me with her tiny finger. I cast a disinterested glance toward the open window, the scorching California sunlight making everything overly bright for a New Yorker like me, and then slid back to her.

Curling one side of my lips in a scornful smirk, I swiped her touch off me.

"Don't act like you're about to go toe-to-toe with me, little girl. Your lack of manners is nearly unforgivable."

"Un-un-forgivable? My *what*?" she sputtered out in a spitting rage. "Who even speaks like that?"

"Yes, unforgivable because they're uncouth," I growled back. "I'm the only one in this godforsaken place with the balls to call you on your behavior. You're the kind of spoiled brat begging for a man with a firm hand to take control."

"You're unbelievable, you arrogant di—"

My hand collared her throat.

Her spine met the wall.

"Don't finish it," I warned. "Watch what you're about to say to me, Clara." My forefinger and thumb hover in front of her eyes, an inch apart from each other. "I'm this close to losing my patience. I don't know what happened in the library, but it wasn't my doing. Sebastian and I have been at the negotiating table with you, Grigore, and Boian for weeks. *Weeks* of fruitless negotiations. It got to the point that Alex had to send Nicu to clean up this mess. I've been my *şef's* advisor for a decade, and yet he brought in his most inexperienced brother because I couldn't finish the job."

I edged closer, my mouth mere inches from her luscious lips. I wanted to bury my front teeth into those plump, pouty red lips and devour them. Devour her.

"Imagine the shame. And who should I blame for this, huh? Your *consilier*, for sure. But mostly, *you*. You're the reason for this clusterfuck because until you, I succeeded in everything I did."

Her eyes flickered, splinters of moss green bleeding through and invading the blue. My gaze flicked from one iris to the other and back, riveted, drinking in that beguiling color.

There was one other time I'd seen her eyes change color like that, but before I could conjure the memory, she interrupted me, "Get your fucking hand off me. Don't ever touch me without my permission."

I dropped my hand.

Stepped back.

She was right, of course. It wasn't a show of force, as she'd assumed. It was a show of dominance, a show of my diabolical urge to own her, worship her, drive my cock into her tight heat.

I'd been sent here to bring a small, but nasty little clan under control. Not only had I failed, but the object of my hate, my desire—dark humiliating urges—strained my epic self-restraint like nothing else.

Clara broke open the floodgates to drives I'd had on a tight leash until now. It hadn't been hard to keep my distance from women. Don't get me wrong, I liked to touch. I just didn't like to *be* touched. Every couple of years, I broke my self-imposed celibacy and went out on a bender to a club for very specific needs like mine. There, I could touch and torture to my heart's content with women who understood the rules, who ached for my brand of punishment if said rules were violated. And they were always violated. That was the nature of the game.

What I did was misunderstood and unacceptable in my society. So I only went when I was at my wit's end. Now might be a good time to hit up a club and work out my frustration on a willing woman because Clara had to be the most *un*willing female imaginable. She antagonized me at every turn. I didn't make mistakes. I didn't slip. I didn't lose my patience. Anything less than perfection was unforgivable, and yet with her, it happened at an alarming rate.

After the little show of power I'd displayed, after wrapping my hand around her delicate throat, feeling the pulse fluttering away under my fingertips, I craved more. But I could never have it. Never have her. We'd destroy each other.

Turning from her abruptly, I prowled the hallway like a caged tiger, returning to stop in front of her. "What happened in there?"

I swallowed down the undeniable urge to fix whatever upset her, a sensation I refused to pry into. The strain of chivalry pushing up right now, for *this* woman, was damned inconvenient.

She rolled her eyes at me and made an irritated huffing sound. "What does it matter. It's a done deal."

My teeth clanged loudly at the disdain in her expression, but before I could respond, the door opened, and Sebastian poked his head out. "Come on in. You'll want to hear this."

Hearing the warning tone in his voice and knowing it was best to turn away from Clara, I entered the library.

Nicu waved me over as I stepped inside the gloomy, cluttered room, Clara close on my heels.

"We've come to a decision," he cautioned. Holding my gaze with his glacial, light-colored eyes, he tugged the cuffs of his suit, covering his rose gold and diamond Cartier watch. He was antsy without access to his fleet of bikes and race cars to burn off his excess energy.

That didn't sound promising. I paused mid-stride.

Resuming my walk, my gaze flicked over to Clara. A high flush stained her cheeks red, and green slivers still dominated her blue eyes.

I remembered the time I'd seen her eyes change color. I'd stopped by the house unannounced one evening and caught her sitting by the infinity pool, overlooking the hills, wearing a bikini the same sapphire color as her eyes.

Caught out, she threw on a sheer cover-up that did nothing to hide her killer curves. Her shapely body could bring a man to his knees, begging for the chance to sin, to do anything to get between those smooth, lithe thighs.

She turned her sharp gaze on me, and I was captivated by green within her blue eyes, a shade that'd make the Caribbean Sea weep in envy. The shift in color spoke of lust, with a dash of submission, a deadly combination for me. If

I'd ever doubted it before, in that moment, I knew she was trouble.

Making my way back to my chair, I sat down smoothly, placed my elbows on the overly wrought arms of the chair, fixed my cufflinks and sleeves, and turned my full attention to Nicu. Clara resumed her seat in a big armchair to my left. Thankfully, Grigore hadn't come back from his huffy departure earlier.

"Clara has agreed to spend four months in New York with us. In my mother's house. To apprentice with the Lupu clan," Nicu pronounced, giving me a warning stare.

My brows shot up. My entire body stiffened, adrenaline coursing through my blood as a roar rushed through my eardrums.

Nicu had a girl he was itching to get back to in New York and wanted to wrap up these endless negotiations as soon as possible. He was taking the helm, and that was new for him, but at the same time, what the hell had happened in the last five minutes I was absent?

Giving him an accusatory glare, I said, "I see. Would you care to explain further?"

Pressing his lips tightly in a flat line, he gave a slight shrug as an apology.

I don't need an apology, brother. I need words.

"We're not getting anywhere here," he said in a clipped tone. "Clara doesn't trust us. Until there's trust, there's no moving forward. She needs to give us an honest-to-God chance to prove we're more than a bunch of dirty criminals. If, after spending time with my mother and grandmother, if after meeting our family and seeing how we work, she decides there's no going forward, then I promise to defend her position to Alex." He turned to her. "But it has to be an honest attempt, Clara."

Clara's beautiful blue-green eyes flashed.

And completely wasted on a woman like her, I know.

Her spine ticked up.

"Are you questioning my honor, Nicu?" she asked sweetly.

Sweet, with a side of salty.

He narrowed his eyes slightly. While Clara took out most of her aggression and frustration on me, he was getting a little taste of her whippy tongue. *Good luck, buddy.*

His face smoothed out. "Of course not. I'm simply making sure we're on the same page."

"We're on the same page," said Boian.

Aww hell. No wonder Clara was desperate. Her father agreed with this crack-pot plan. He wasn't much of a talker, so when he did speak, his word was law. His support explained how this madcap scheme had come to fruition in my brief absence. Clara might be a pain in the ass. Clara might be *mostly* in charge. He didn't tug the leash often. God knows, if he had, we would've been much further along resolving our issues.

But he'd tugged it now.

It was a done deal. My eyes flickered to her. Her high flush was present. Her eyes met mine, held, and glared, but I couldn't be angry with her. Her earlier raging made perfect sense. She'd been right; there was nothing I could do. Not without undermining Nicu in front of rivals, not without insulting Boian for agreeing to said plan.

Clara was coming to Sunnyside, Queens. Two doors down from the brownstone where I grew up, and where my mother and little sister still lived. Between visiting the Dacia Café, where Alex had his office, and looking in on my mother and my sister, I was there daily.

All I could say was, thank God she wasn't staying at my

mother's house. As *consilier*, I usually hosted in my penthouse in Manhattan. Since I was an unmarried man, she would've ended up living with my mother and sister, but Nicu had made sure to clarify she'd be with *his* mother and grandmother instead. Since I wasn't accommodating Clara in my family's home, I had little ground to fight this.

Grateful she wasn't my charge, I spread my arms wide and gave her the kind of smirk I knew would get under her skin. What I was about to do would wound her, but after the slip I had outside, I had to fan her hatred for me. Christ, I could barely wrap my head around four months of her flittering around New York in my clan.

Widening my grin, I taunted, "Welcome to New York, Clara. I'll do everything in my power to make you feel at home."

When hell freezes over.

Dear God, the next four months couldn't be over soon enough.

2

CLARA

"Why, Tata? Why?" I asked, with a bit of a wail in my tone as I sat cross-legged on my bed, surrounded by stuffed animals. I kept them around because my younger brother found comfort in them when he was in my room. I was in a rare moment of rest, wearing a pair of sweats and a crop top, my hair in a messy bun, my face scrubbed free of makeup. Picking up the violin my brother left for me, I began to tune it.

It sounded distinctly like a whine to my ears, but dammit, Nicu's plan was going to upend my life. He tried to tag on a so-called *apprenticeship* at the end; as if anything could validate this crazy-ass plan of his.

Even worse was when I found myself alone with Tatum in the near-empty hallway. It was a moment of baffling weakness. The feelings of rage and impotency must've provoked the desperate urges in my body when Tatum wrapped his fingers around my throat and growled at me. His huge dominating presence enveloping me, his spicy scent weaving its unholy sinfulness around me, his hand collaring my throat, taking control—all of it upended my self-control. I almost gave in to the urge to pull up my skirt, drag my panties down to my ankles, display my ass to him, and *beg* him to smack it.

I wiped a hand down my face.

Christ. What was wrong with me?

Sure, I read my lion's share of BDSM romance and watched porn. I mean, how else did a girl doing her best to stay a virgin get satisfaction but for her own hand, a drawer full of sex toys, and porn? I accepted that my tastes diverged from the average woman, but I'd never had them triggered by a man before. And for it to be Tatum, of all people, was unacceptable. Not only was I left feeling an achy pulse between my thighs, but I was infuriated by Nicu's plan, a plan my father gave his stamp of approval. I was forced to leave LA for some godforsaken, ugly East Coast metropolis. I'd never find a decent fish taco in that concrete jungle. And I might as well say adios to an In-N-Out cheeseburger. Ugh, I was so frustrated and angry and powerless I could've screamed.

I might be twenty-one years old, but I crossed my arms over my chest and huffed at my father.

Handmade bespoke British tailored suits were strewn across the floor of my chaotic bedroom. My father teased me because no other young Californian would be caught dead in one of my signature suits, but I loved them. They screamed boss lady, and I needed the ego boost when I accompanied my father on his rounds.

Every room in our spacious Spanish-style mansion was filled to the gills with furniture and *objets d'art*. Okay, that might be a stretch, but where some people saw bric-a-brac, I saw small decorative objects and mementos. I looked across my room as I tuned my brother's violin. At thirteen years old, he was better than I was at my peak. Even though

Adrian didn't share our father's genes, he was the spitting image of our father in every way that counted.

The same father who sat heavily on the bed and sighed. My heart twinged in sympathy. My father was my hero. I had witnessed the suffering he'd endured on my behalf, me and my clan. I had witnessed my mother's betrayal.

"We have no choice but to accept. Anything else would be an insult. Nicu may look like he's all brawn and no brains, but he's a Lupu through and through. Inviting you to his home was a high honor, and no matter how much we may distrust them, we cannot refuse."

"But I don't want to live in that awful city for *four* months. I don't want to be away from you and Adrian for *four* months. I don't want to be away from our clan for *four* months," I griped. "And for what? I'm not going to change my mind. I can't change my mind, even if they're the loveliest people in the world. I can't relinquish anything to those people."

I frowned. Could I be wrong?

No, not possible. First, because their attempt to change my mind was for the sole purpose of taking over my clan. *My clan. Mine.* Sebastian might be okay, but Nicu was a dolt, and there was nothing redeemable about Tatum.

Nothing, I thought as I plucked the string of the violin to hear whether it was tuned.

A shiver worked its way up my spine at the thought of *him.* The way he looked at me with his dark, inscrutable eyes. He might look like an oversized blue-blooded Anglo, but his eyes spoke of something wild and dangerous. They spoke of a wilderness teeming with wolves, boars, and savage animals, like the mountains of Moldova where my family originated.

If I didn't know better, I'd guess his eyes came from an

entirely different hereditary tree. They didn't match the rest of him. It was as if his Adonis features came from one place and his eyes came from another distinct place, and "never the twain shall meet."

Except in him ... in him, they came together with devastating effect. A man as gorgeous as Tatum had to be a player. For a quiet man, he still managed to ooze confidence, like he knew his worth and he didn't care if anyone else noticed. Just from the way he moved, it was obvious he was skilled in bed. Even a virgin like me could tell.

Fanning my face, I distracted myself by grabbing lip gloss from the makeup scattered across my night table and swiped my lips. It was best not to spend time thinking about a man as unattainable as Tatum Lupu. I pressed my lips together, smearing the lip gloss around, and then smacked them together. Even at home, without my bad-bitch makeup and my boss-lady clothes on, I had to slather something on my lips.

I know what people whispered behind my back. *Virgin Queen.* They used it as an insult, but I thrived on the title. I was given that nickname because everyone knew of my father's requirement: I'd never have a husband. My life was my clan. If I expected to take the mantle, this single most important condition must be met. Men would vie to marry me for the sole purpose of taking over, so he cut them off at the knees by prohibiting it, warning that if I got married, I'd never inherit the crown. But I knew the real motivation behind his decree: my mother's treachery.

It wasn't just Tatum, and the delicious emotions he drew out of me, that made me want to hide under the covers. I dreaded the thought of living in New York City. It was a dirty, filthy city. I hadn't escaped cold Romania and moved to paradise just to be thrust back into a grimy urban center.

New York was crowded and people were rude. What little that was quaint or picturesque would be gone by the time I got there in late October. All the pretty leaves will have fallen from the branches, leaving everything barren and drab.

"Can't we place this on hiatus until spring, at least?" I looked pleadingly at my father.

He shook his head, an indulgent smile on his lips.

Patting my hand, he said, "It's only a few months, *draga mea*. Look at it as an educational opportunity. You will be in the bosom of one of the most powerful families in existence. Learn from them. They are what we aspire to be. I may not want the Lupu clan to take over, but do not think I do not respect them. Alex is a genius, having built on his father's legacy and expanded across the country. Absorb as much as you can from him."

Again, it was obvious he wasn't budging.

Adrian sauntered into my bedroom and lounged over my bed with his long, gangly body, his doe-brown eyes on me. My heart gushed with overwhelming love whenever I looked at my beautiful brother. I'd protect him with my life.

I turned an accusing eye on my father. "I'm going to miss him. He's never been without me."

"He'll be fine," my father assured me with a dismissive wave of his hand.

I was like a mother to Adrian since our own mother vanished a few years after giving birth to him. He didn't come from my father's loins. He was the only good thing to come from her deceit, the affair she had with my father's *consilier* and best friend.

Adrian had been so-called "special" from a young age. Both my parents saw it as some sort of punishment. *She* felt it was castigation for cheating, and my father felt it was his cross to bear for neglecting his wife for our clan.

But not me. My brilliant, loving brother saved me and my father, even if Tata would never admit it. Adrian was the only pure thing in our sinning world, and I refused to let my parents' failings sully him or my love for him.

At first, my father kept my brother for two reasons: Adrian was a boy, and my father could never admit to being cuckolded. It was the same reason he allowed my mother to stay, despite the wrong she'd inflicted on him. Eventually, he came to love my brother. One couldn't *not* love my brother. Ironically, it was the adoration of a son derived from a horrible betrayal that stitched together the tattered pieces of his broken heart.

Adrian gently took the violin from my hands and played a sprightly country jaunt to test out my tuning abilities.

He gave me a lopsided smile.

I grinned back at him.

"Pretty good, huh?" I said.

He made a satisfied grunt, and I watched as he picked up the same tune and waltzed out my bedroom door. His music resonated throughout our large house. I loved when he came to me to tune his violin. He didn't like being touched. Touching and twisting the fine strings of his violin was the equivalent of hugging him.

My brother represented everything good and true in this world. It was up to me to protect him, and protect him, I would. With my last, dying breath.

As if hearing my thoughts, my father said, "You're doing this for him as much as for the Hagi clan, Clara. The stronger you are, the safer he is. And if you do this, I'll hand over any domestic problems within or between families for you to deal with. You prove yourself, and it will become your exclusive domain."

Whew, a double whammy. My father was no slouch when it came to setting up the stakes. Protecting my brother *and* getting the chance to have the final say on family matters? No doubt, it cinched my decision to stop arguing and go to New York. I'd do as my father advised and find out as much as I could about the Lupu to further my own ambitions. And if I learned a secret or two to use against them?

Even better.

3

TATUM

"You're going to be in charge of her," Alex declared as he tapped on his laptop in his office above The Dacia Café. We both shared a penthouse floor in The Time Warner Building, recently renamed the Deutsche Bank Center, in Manhattan, but we crossed the 59th Street Bridge into Queens almost every day. Sunnyside, Queens, nicknamed *Little Bucharest*, was the hub of our *mafie* world. Alex came to work above the café his family had owned since we were children. Me? I came to check in on my mother and sister, Starlene, or Star, for short.

Shifting my big frame on one of the oxblood leather armchairs facing his desk, I crossed one leg over the other in a futile attempt to make myself fit and stuttered out, "W-what?"

I swung my head toward Luca, the second Lupu brother, sitting beside me, a look of shock on my face.

That was some bombshell he'd dropped in my lap.

I was the negotiator, the peacemaker, the fixer, and my automatic response to any of his requests was always yes.

The reason for this circled back to my last remaining secret. The one that could never come to light.

Not if I wanted to live to see another day. Not if I wanted my little sister, an innocent in this entire mess, to marry well. Not if I wanted my mother to remain in the only world she knew, the only world that mattered to her.

If anyone found out, I'd either forfeit my life or be banished from the Lupu clan.

Even if I was Alex's best friend. Even if we loved each other like brothers and I was his second-in-command. Even if I was perfect ... nothing could save me or my family if anyone got a whiff of my secret.

The only pure, untainted thing in my life was my sister, and I'd never let any harm come to her. Like every seventeen-year-old *mafie* girl, she dreamed of marrying an important clan member, or, at least, an up-and-coming one.

Her future made this secret an albatross hanging around my neck, dragging me down.

Strangling ... always strangling me. It was the reason I walked around like a fragile vase, filled to the brim with filthy sludge, teetering on a pedestal.

One day, it would crash to the floor and spew waste everywhere.

I was that vase *and* its filth.

I worked every day to keep the looming chaos at bay. It was the reason I always said yes, always did a perfect job. For the first time, I found myself in the unenviable predicament of saying no.

I didn't contradict Nicu when he'd come up with this insane scheme precisely because I wouldn't have to deal with Clara. She tickled my dominance like no other. I had a sixth sense about these things, which meant she had a little subbie beneath that pain-in-the-ass mask she wore, and it was begging to come out to frolic and play.

The woman was impossible, and there was no way I could manage her *without* letting my dominant nature out, and once the beast was out, there was no stuffing it back in. It was imperative that I kept my distance.

Alex's fingers halted in midair; the abrupt end to the clattering keys left a ringing silence. He raised his bright green eyes to me, curiosity and humor dancing in them. He knew Clara and I clashed, yet he was doing this to me? Then again, I'd never once countered his request. I'd trained him to lean on me in all things.

He clarified, "The Hagi woman, Clara. This is our chance to bring her over to our side. Wine her. Dine her. Charm her. I don't have to warn you not to fuck her because you'd never cross that line, but anything else is on the table."

For the first time, I shook my head at him.

"I don't think that's a good idea ...," I hedged.

I turned to Luca, catching his gray eyes with mine, and silently pleaded with him to come to my aid.

To the outside world, Alex and I were the closest. We were the same age and did everything together, from school to running the Lupu empire. Despite appearances, my true comrade-in-arms was Luca. I took him under my wing the day I found him cowering, bound and gagged, in the closet of his home during a game of hide-and-seek with Alex.

Luca once harbored an ugly secret. Little had I known I would soon join him in the exclusive club of sons who held the secrets of their fathers. I knew what being betrayed by a father felt like. I knew how it ruined the very foundation of one's life.

Shrugging, Luca gave me a confused look, not under-standing my distress.

Alex frowned. "Why not?"

"She's ... she's impossible," I pounced, throwing my hands up. "More importantly, she doesn't like me. I don't think it will help our case to have me look after her. She trusts me least of all, for some reason."

Likely because my nature calls out to hers, and being a smart girl, she knows to run from a predator like me.

"Then, you'll have to work harder because we need to put our best foot forward. Nicu doesn't have the patience. There's no way Luca can do it, with his wedding coming up in a couple of weeks. I certainly don't have the time with the Bratva circling around us. We finally get the Popescu clan off our backs, thanks to Luca, look to expanding westward, and the Bratva come flexing their muscles. It's never-ending."

Goddamn the Bratva, source of my secret and bane of my existence. Alex wasn't lying when he said they were back to their old tricks, lurking around and sabotaging our ship-ments. Their interference came in waves. They messed with us, we fought back, and they retreated for a time, the cycle repeating itself endlessly. With other Romanian clans, there were options like negotiations or arranged marriages.

Not with the Bratva. With them, it was pure hate.

And I had reason to hate them, more at stake to keep them off our territory.

"And since when does someone not like you?" He raised an eyebrow challenging me. "Every virgin in a ten-mile radius sighs at the sound of your name, and Clara's the virgin of all virgins. She's the Virgin Queen, is she not?"

"She is ...," I replied carefully. "But we clashed during my time in Cali. She's ... something else."

Luca finally intervened, not used to coming to my aid.

I'd never needed backup before, but I simply couldn't watch over her. The woman was a menace. Worse still, she twisted me up inside. The heat that invaded my body when I was around her, the lust I felt for her, was unnatural, unhealthy. Certainly wasn't good for my mental health; I could testify to that.

Luca finally interrupted, "He's busy, Alex. Hasn't he done enough with the Hagi clan? Give this one to Sebastian."

Ignoring his younger brother by two years, Alex's voice turned hard. Hard like the *şef* he was, not the friend who loved me like blood. His wife, Nina, was the only person who never saw this side of him. With her, he was a pussycat, through and through.

"Sebastian isn't experienced or high enough on the totem pole yet. It'd be an insult to her. If she doesn't like you ... then make her like you. Surely you can do that much for me?"

With a weary sigh, he leaned back into his high-backed chair, reminding me of how much responsibility he carried on his shoulders. I pinched the bridge of my nose. Knowing exactly how stressed he was, especially with the Bratva—the same Bratva that had killed his father—I felt my resistance crumble.

As if knowing how close I was to succumbing, he went on, "I don't like to lose, Tatum. You're the fixer, so fucking fix this. I'm too busy for this shit right now. Nina and I are trying to start a family, so I need to focus on my woman. That Bratva scum, Ivanov, is up to no good, and I can smell their intentions like week-old garbage during a New York blackout. You're more than capable of taking care of this, and I need someone I can trust. I'm leaving her in your hands. End of story."

His rigid features softened a touch after laying it out like a hard-ass.

Tempering his tone of voice, he finished, "You haven't let me down yet. You succeed in everything you do. You can do this, too."

I swallowed down the retort hovering on the tip of my tongue. *You have no idea to what extent I've let you down, brother.*

But no. That wasn't a possibility. The image of my father the day his secret became mine shimmered in my mind's eye. He'd come home early, looking far too smug. My father was rarely happy, but there was no denying the self-satisfied expression on his face. He'd always been a liability to our family, and when he was in the shower, I stole his phone and checked the last person he called.

Ivanov.

No, no, no.

The Bratva boss.

Our *şef*, Alex's father, would've never engaged with the Bratva. There was no one he hated more than them. My father contacting the head of the New York Bratva was a rogue and dangerous move. The kamikaze move of a man on a suicide mission. Only later would I find out quite how perilous a move it was.

My father was Rudari, an ethnic group linked to the Roma that worked as mine workers and gold panners. That made sense for my father. He was always panning for gold in the shit that was his life. When he saw Alex stick up for me when I was bullied about my heritage in school, when he realized how close Alex and I had become, when it became clear to him I might become the next *consilier*, he decided to hurry things along by getting our *şef* killed by the Bratva.

For once, my unlucky father bet on the right horse. Our *şef* was gunned down in broad daylight, forcing Alex to take over our clan. The day Alex called me to his side as his *consilier*, my father was gleeful. In a drunken spree afterward, he crowed to me what I'd already suspected. He'd been behind the hit. The only good that came out of the Summer of Blood, as we dubbed the summer of retribution for our *şef*'s murder, was that my own father was eliminated by the same Bratva he'd conspired with.

I didn't feel an ounce of regret for his demise, even if it left me alone, saddled with his secret.

And that secret reared its ugly head anytime I wanted to bow out, to be imperfect, to be *human*. I lived a lie. I was the second-hand man of the most powerful *mafie şef* to exist, and at the same time, I was the son of his father's murderer.

Knowing that did something to a man.

Guilt wasn't my only motivation. I loved him like a brother but feared him as a *şef*. He was ruthless. I'd seen it in action during the Summer of Blood; the gifts of severed heads left on the doorsteps of the Bratva brass, taking a page from the book of our illustrious Romanian, Vlad the Impaler.

With all the heavy baggage weighing on my shoulders, I did what I always did.

I bowed my head and replied, "Yes, *şef*."

I didn't mess with women, and she was most definitely not a woman to mess with. She taunted and teased me every opportunity she got. She was a downright bitch at times. But I'd do what was expected of me. Out of guilt for my father. Out of love for Alex. Out of fear for my mother and sister.

I'd somehow figure out a way to make this work. I had no other choice.

4

CLARA

I took a deep breath and slumped back in my seat in the reception hall of the biggest *mafie* society wedding of the year. The Lupu clan hadn't spared any expense. There were hundreds of people in attendance in some over-the-top fancy Marriot hotel in Times Square. Every table had a monstrous bouquet of flowers as a centerpiece on top of linen tablecloths, and the guests ate off fine-bone Limoges floral dinnerware, trimmed in gold, no less.

I'd been to my fair share of weddings, and this one was both a statement of Lupu wealth and a celebration of the alliance between Luca and his bride, the princess of another strong family, the Popescus. *First comes feud. Then comes arranged marriage. Then comes baby in the baby carriage.* Only in the *mafie* world did the pendulum swing from one extreme to the other so abruptly.

Looking out at the huge dance floor from the dais, where I'd been seated at the tables for the two families as a courtesy, I watched the loving couple twirl around for their first wedding dance. Had to admit, the way they lovingly gazed into each other's eyes couldn't be faked. I stifled a little groan of lament, knowing I'd never have a first wedding dance. Hell, I'd never have a groom.

I hadn't been here long, but I'd quickly learned the Lupu clan was exceptional. This wedding was a prime example of their tenacity and cleverness. It was no small feat to kill a feud with an arranged marriage and manage to create a couple as lovely as Luca and Cat.

I wanted to hate the Lupu clan, I did, but I had to admit that since my arrival, Alex's mother and grandmother had been extremely kind to me. They poked and prodded my hips and waist, tsking about how skinny I was, and promised to fatten me up with good, homemade cooking. So far, they hadn't disappointed.

Alex kept his distance, as was expected. That was part of how a *şef* maintained his mystique, something I would use as well once I became *şef*. I observed him closely with his wife, Nina, during the party. By the looks of her, she was clearly an outsider, which was a rare thing indeed. He was extremely solicitous of her. Another rarity. Husbands usually ignored their wives in public. I know my father did. He ignored my mother in private as well, which is what led to her infidelity and the reason my father placed the virginity condition on my rule. Love and *şef*-hood couldn't mix. You could have one or the other, but not both.

Unlike Alex, there was nothing rare or precious in the way Tatum, my handler, treated me. Which was particularly grating since he was impeccably charming to everyone … except me. I rolled my eyes as yet another pretty, young thing stopped by our table to flirt with him.

I eyed him discreetly. *Ugh*, his attractiveness was irritating. He moved with a certain sleek grace, which was surprising considering how large he was. And speaking of large, I couldn't help but notice how his biceps bulged and stretched the fine wool of his dinner jacket. The width of his upper arm rivaled the size of my thigh. Okay, it might be an exaggeration, but not by much. Damn, now I was thinking about his arms and my thighs.

Lifting my gaze, I noted how his blond hair was coiffed just so, not a hair out of place. Made my fingers itch to ruffle his head and dislodge strands until they stuck out in every direction.

His dark eyes scanned and processed everything. He was always watchful, that one. It was unusual that he was still unmarried, given his age. In *mafie* years, a man of thirty-two was practically a dinosaur.

As the flirty girl took her leave, Tatum angled his head in my direction and murmured low for my ears only, "I know I'm handsome, but there's no need to stare."

My fingers curled into my palms, balling into fists to punch him with.

There it was.

His arrogance.

He only acted this way with me. With everyone else, he was solicitous as fuck, but with me, he brandished his condensation with rabid zeal.

"I want to ruin the *coif* you've spent a lot of time perfecting," I sneered. "It's always so perfect. You're always so perfect."

He stiffened beside me. I wanted to crow in delight.

"Don't you ever get messy?" I asked, rolling my eyes at him because I knew how much any show of disrespect irritated him.

His opaque black gaze turned on me and checked me out slowly. Disdain radiated from his inspection, but my skin pebbled with goose bumps, my pulse slowing under his careful perusal.

"I could ask the same of you," he replied casually.

I harrumphed. "As if I could ever be messy."

He and I weren't equals. As a woman, I had to be impeccably put-together. Moreover, I represented my clan. He could look however he wanted, and he'd automatically garner respect, whereas I had to earn it every single day of my life. First impressions were a necessary step in getting that respect. I couldn't afford to ever *get messy*.

I gave him a disgusted once-over. "What you said just proves how little you know me, fool."

He pulled back with a scowl on his drop-dead gorgeous face. Even provoked, he dripped arrogance and sensuality. His onyx eyes snapped to me. Tatum's eyes were guarded, and yet, they could burn me alive at the same time. He stared as if he wanted to lift me onto the table with one hand, tear my clothes off, and rut with me in front of all these people. It made no sense whatsoever because I knew for a fact, he couldn't stand me.

His chiseled jaw flexed, and his wide, generous mouth lifted in a snarl. Right then and there, I decided he looked even hotter enraged.

"No one calls me a fool. You, of all people, have no right to insult me. You know nothing about me."

I gave him a dismissive shrug. "I can read people, and I'm never wrong, so if the shoe fits ..."

"Oh, is that right? Then please, enlighten me as to how I'm an ignorant idiot."

I dragged my eyes down the line of pristine tuxedo buttons and back up to his gaze. "You've never looked beyond this insulated little world of yours. Before going to LA, I bet you've never dealt with a family you hadn't known since birth. I'm certain you've never once in your life considered what it's like to be a woman. And never as a woman in a position of power, like me. As *consilier*, you're the best at what you do, and you do it in a big enough pond that you don't need to consider any other person. Other family. Other clan. Other world."

I leaned in close. His gaze flicked to my breasts, showcased as if I were a heifer for sale in this stupid, stifling, bodycon dress. I grinned at his moment of weakness.

"That statement proves you don't know a thing about me," he countered.

Yeah, right.

"And which part am I wrong about, exactly?" I asked with a scornful chuckle, knowing it would get a rise out of him.

"I've thought of what it's like to be a woman," he pronounced.

I raised a dubious eyebrow and looked at him askance.

"Is that right?" I drawled. "I call bullshit."

"No need to sink down to using slovenly language," he chided, one side of his sculpted lips curled up.

I barely restrained myself from snapping at him. He was so damn perfect he rarely cursed, the sanctimonious prick. It made me want to get in his face and spit out, *fuck you, Tatum. Fuck your gorgeous, beautiful face. Fuck your big, hot body. Fuck your impeccable manners. Fuck your eloquent charm. Just. Fuck. You.*

Instead, I bit my tongue.

"I have a mother and younger sister," he went on. "I've often thought of how they live. Of how limited their lives are."

He rolled his eyes. Huh, he rolled his eyes like a petulant little boy. I almost laughed. He rarely broke character, especially the haughty pose he'd perfected oh so well. While he was charming, he always carried an air of being above the fray, of being above us lowly humans, certainly of being above *me*.

"Never mind," he muttered. "You wouldn't understand."

I pulled back in shock, catching a vulnerability I would've never imagined. For a moment, I almost believed him but quickly shook the compassion off as insane. He brought out empathy I only felt for my brother. But Tatum was nothing like Adrian. He was sitting on top of the food chain, a predator of the highest order. And he was so cold and haughty, peering down at us from his high horse, he must get a crick in his neck.

I barked out a short, bitter laugh.

"Riiight, you think about what it's like being a woman until you step into a strip club and have your fun. God forbid you refrain from playing with women like they were in a harem made especially for you."

His eyes turned flat as obsidian. "I don't have that kind of fun. In fact, I don't have fun at all."

He straightened his already straight-as-a-rod spine. "I'm *consilier* of the Lupu clan, and I'm the head of my family. I have no time for mindless stupidity. As evidenced by this moment. Here I am, at the wedding of a man who's like a brother, and I'm stuck babysitting *you*."

His heated gaze burned a path down my body, making me squirm with rising lust. He looked at me with disgust, and yet, every time he looked at any part of my body, it went up in flames. I didn't know what it was about his icy, condescending glare that made me want to hate-fuck him. Jesus, I was sick. That was what happened when you were still a virgin while every *mafie* woman your age was popping out babies, I thought bitterly.

He stood up abruptly, his chair screeching a little even in the loud hum of the festive room.

"I wouldn't expect you to understand. Engaging with you is only marginally better than squandering my precious time at a strip club," he said in cold fury. His insult stabbed me like a stake in the heart, taking my breath away.

"Excuse me," he snapped with condescending formalness, even going so far as to give me a mocking little stiff bow before stalking away.

My mouth dropped open.

His sharp answer and curt exit left me burning with shame. It churned and roiled in my stomach like acid.

Watching him slip out of the reception hall, it hit me that I'd been too judgmental, too harsh. I'd gone too far. Having left my father, my brother, and everyone I knew, having been forcibly plopped down into this cold, hostile city with this foreign clan, I was on the defensive. To be fair, that was generally my go-to attitude. Despite Alex's mother's and grandmother's kindness, being around Tatum amped me up, and I'd taken out my frustration and homesickness on him.

Unfair, I know. I tortured him any chance I got, like some sort of high school bully. It was infantile of me.

Remorse sliced through my chest.

Even a blind man could see I'd been handed to Tatum against his will. He avoided me where he could and when required to be with me, ignored me as much as possible. Besides his arrogance, his avoidance behavior pricked my pride. There was no doubt it still got me into trouble.

Letting out a weary sigh, I dropped my chin to my chest. There was no denying it. I'd been undeniably rude, and I owed him an apology. I had four months to go in this godforsaken city. I didn't need to antagonize him further.

Pushing my chair back, I slapped my hands on my lap and stood up to go find him.

5

TATUM

God, I had to get away before I did something unforgivable. It was infuriating to run away, but I didn't know whether to yank her by the hair and punish her with hard swats to her ass or crush my lips to hers and smother her with a kiss. Either would've worked if only she'd shut up.

Of course, I could do neither. My sense of powerlessness when it came to her drove me to the brink of my sanity. I had a little dominant demon that lived in my gut, and nothing could rile it up like Clara and her sharp tongue.

Stalking out of the reception area, I blindly turned left, then right, then left again. In front of me was a glass door leading out onto a deserted rooftop terrace. I threw it open and stomped out.

Crisp late-autumn air whipped against my face, cooling off my anger. One side of the empty terrace was lined with sectional couches facing toward me, interspersed with coffee tables, each with a trio of glass-covered white candles flickering in the soft glow emanating from lights along the building. This late in autumn, there were a few desolate yellow and brown leaves clinging to small apple trees in planters. Other than that, everything was bare and dormant.

The door swung shut behind me, and I was blessedly alone. Taking in deep breaths, I stared up at the two or three twinkling stars above me in the inky night sky, visible despite the light pollution of the city.

I unclenched my hands and shook them out, attempting to shake off the rage gripping me by the throat.

I could never do anything right with that woman. All night long, she was enticing as hell in a backless dress that clung to her wicked curves like a second skin. Her eyes blazed with fire, even beneath the layers of makeup she'd applied. I wanted to hate-fuck her so bad my cock was stiff and torqued in the trousers of my tuxedo. *Get down, you bastard.* I gave it a hard squeeze to teach it some manners.

Swish.

I heard the door behind me. Twisting around quickly, I came face-to-face with Clara.

Goddammit.

"What are you doing here? Get back inside. It's freezing here."

Ignoring my command, she scoffed, "Please, Tatum, don't act as if you care."

Motioning between the two of us with her hand, she commanded, "Let's stop pretending and get this out of the way."

"Who's pretending? What's there to get out of the way?" I asked, incredulous. Because really, when did this woman pretend to ever like me or even tolerate my presence?

"I came here to apologize for how I acted, but seeing you again just makes me realize how much I loathe you," Clara professed, eyes glowing a liquid blue and hands fisted by her sides.

I was at the wedding of a man who was like a brother to me. I should be joyous. At the very least, I should be drunk. Instead, I was fuming. Between the anger and the months of sexual frustration I'd suffered with this woman, I was at a breaking point. I knew she detested me, and the feeling was more than mutual, but somehow it upset me to hear her say it.

The hurt poured gasoline on the flames of fury already burning in my gut. Her hissing at me like a wet cat broke the seal over my control. I wanted to turn her around, flip up her dress, and pound out my frustration into her tight, unused pussy, only heaping more kindling onto my blistering wrath. Hell, at this moment, I was so twisted up over her, I ached to bring her down a peg.

It was petty of me, but, for once, I didn't care how it made me or the Lupu family look. I didn't care if I had to get up close and personal to make her feel an ounce of what she made me feel.

Payback was in order.

Stalking her, I backed her against the wall right by the door. Slapping a hand on the brick beside her head, I penned her in.

Her eyes blew wide with fear—and something else.

I angled my head to the side, narrowing my eyes at her. Bright light from the corridor streamed in through the glass door to illuminate her face. I reached for her, curling my hand around the silky skin of her delicate neck, and bringing it to rest.

Thrusting my face into hers, I growled, "You hate me? Sure about that?"

Her eyes rounded wide. She shuddered out a soft breath that coasted over my skin, soft as a feather. I expected to be inundated with expensive perfume, heavy and syrupy, something sultry and dripping with power. Instead, I got a whiff of something clean and bright, like ... laundry detergent without the additives? No, no, that wasn't right.

Beach.

Yes, her scent evoked the sensation of hot sand sliding between wiggling toes, of waves lapping over outstretched legs.

I stepped closer, bending my head until my lips were inches from hers. Before she had a chance to do or say anything to piss me off further, I pressed my lips over hers.

She made a strangled sound.

Gripping her delicate jaw, I flicked my tongue against the seam of her lips. She gasped, giving me access to lick my way inside, and fuck if the taste of her didn't hit me hard. It was as surprising as her scent—like crisp blades of grass on a summer day. Smooth, cool, and surprisingly addictive. If innocence had a taste, this would be it.

The dark demon inside my gut uncurled from its sleeping position, lifted its dark head, and sniffed the air. He'd caught her scent.

Clara jolted in shock, and in that instant, I knew that at twenty-one years old, she had never been kissed.

I was her first. The realization took me aback, but not enough to stop me.

On the contrary, I pressed my advantage.

She jerked back a little, but firming my grip on her jaw, I tilted her head for better access and claimed her wickedly sarcastic mouth again, the same mouth that had spewed comebacks and snippy insults at me for months.

I plunged deep, but in that moment, her hot, silky tongue swept over mine. I shuddered. Her taste was delicate. Innocent. Pure. The antithesis of everything I thought I knew her to be. It beguiled me, and I couldn't stop from delving deeper.

I never thought I'd be in this position because nothing, *nothing* was crazier than the reality of Clara yielding to me. By now, I'd expected her to scream bloody murder and punch me or run for dear life. Instead, she'd timidly placed her hands on my chest. It expanded with pride beneath her soft touch.

Clara's elegant fingers spread open, exploring me haltingly, shyly. I waited with bated breath to see what this innocent, inquisitive creature would do next.

She leaned in, pressing her full tits against me, and tentatively, but decisively, licked into my mouth.

Good Lord.

I groaned at the inexperience and bravery of it.

Sinking my fingers into the back of her neck, I pulled at the base of her mane and yanked her closer, eliminating any space between us. I wanted to *inhale* her.

I wrestled with myself because I wasn't the type of man to do this to a pampered *mafie* virgin princess. This kind of behavior was for the Lupu brothers. They could do whatever they wanted because they were both heirs.

The thing was—I hadn't expected to meet innocence in tasting this sassy little bitch, but that was exactly what I'd gotten.

Which was why I should stop.

I'd made my point.

It was time to pull back.

Only ... I couldn't. I found myself in a struggle between the good son, who prided himself on his reserve, and the bad man, who hungered to devour this woman. My inner demon rattled his chains at me, mocking my effort to fall on the side of the righteous in the skirmish between good and bad.

With superhuman force, I shoved myself away. Problem was that she moved with me, not allowing an inch of space between us.

Clara was like a Lupu, taking what she wanted when she wanted, and for once, I wanted to do the same. Christ, I was tired of being flawlessly perfect. I wanted to indulge. For once, I was greedy.

I smoothed my hand up the side of her torso and cupped her plump breast. Talk about luscious, *Jesus*. My gaze had been glued on her tits more than once, and I'd had to drag my eyes away before she caught me, although I'm almost certain she'd sensed it.

I thumbed her nipple, feeling it peak. She moaned into my mouth, the vibration shuddering down the length of my body to my cock. Fuck, my balls grew heavy at the sweet moans she made. So needy, those sounds. They drove me wild, pushing me to take Clara right then and there.

I couldn't do that; I couldn't hoist her up, push her thighs wide, and plunge my demon cock into what was surely the tightest pussy ever known to man. Demon because, like the rest of me, it was oversized. It wasn't the kind of thing I could just whip out without prepping her for it beforehand.

I instinctively knew she was wet, and I wanted to feel her silky flesh on my fingertips. I needed the knowledge of how much she wanted me. Sliding a hand down, I caught the hem of her dress and yanked it up. My fingers glided over her panties. The heat coming off her pussy scorched me. I felt her juices through the silk.

She was drenched. Soaked.

For me. It was a heady thought.

"Spread your legs," I directed in a voice I barely recognized.

She shifted on her feet, tilting her pelvis to give me better access. I loved how she instinctually responded to my command. I pushed a thick finger in deeper, but the gusset of her panties prevented me, and like a heat-seeking missile, my finger needed more. It demanded that tight, wet flesh be parted.

Prodding her panties to the side, I pushed inside.

Motherfucker. Slippery *and* tight. The perfect combination. Too bad she had such a nasty little mouth. The thought of putting her on her knees and making use of that mouth for good instead of evil was tempting. My cock jerked in my pants.

Dirty girl that she was, she writhed on my hand, her hips twitching as she worked herself on my fingers. It was just how I imagined it because, yeah, I'd fantasized about her many times. This put those fantasies to shame. Her tight muscles sucked me in. She was a sensual woman; I'd give her that. The sensation of her walls clamping around my fingers was close to divine.

I moved my mouth to her ear. "You say you hate me, but your tight pussy is greedy for my touch. Tell me you want it, little girl. Tell me, and I'll give it to you."

With a decade between us, it seemed only right to call her "little girl." For the first time in any of our interactions, I undoubtedly had the upper hand. Finally. Because Clara undermined me every chance she got.

Not now, though. Now I had something she wanted, something only I could give her.

My brow furrowed. She could get it from her idiot of a *consilier*, Grigore. The thought of that bastard touching her goaded me to start stroking.

Unhinged, I let out a low, deep growl. "You want something, you come to me. Only me. I'm the only man who will ever satisfy you, you hear. You will never go to any man but me." The vow fell from my lips, unrestrained as I cupped her pussy. "I'll be the one to take this, to fuck this tight channel, and burst through your cherry. You'll bleed all over my cock."

What the fuck?

I didn't talk like this.

I didn't act like this with an innocent.

Yet, the words spilled from my mouth like an oath. Like a curse.

I stumbled back, pulling my fingers out of heaven. My cock strained against my tuxedo pants, my nuts feeling like they were about to burst, wanting to spray come all over her face and inside her womb. To mark her. To breed her. To make her forever mine.

What in the ever-loving fuck is happening?

I couldn't have this woman.

I shouldn't even *want* this woman.

She was toxic.

We hated each other.

I scrubbed a hand down my face, scenting her fragrance. Even her pussy smelled fresh. I wanted to thrust my fingers into my mouth and suck until there wasn't a drop left, until I'd absorbed her juices.

I dragged my hand over my face, tugging at my chin to stop myself.

My lungs heaved.

Face distorted with horror, I rasped, "Fuck, *that* was a mistake."

She inhaled sharply. The glaze over her eyes vanished as she recoiled in disgust.

"A-a mistake? The first kiss of my life, and such an incred —" I strained to hear what she was about to say, but she cut herself off, pressing her full lips in a tight line. Shame flushed her supple skin a bright shade of pink right to the tips of her ears.

Covering her chest with her arms, she turned on me with fury in her eyes.

"A mistake, you say?" she spat out, pulling her hand back and letting it fly across my face with a resounding *crack* that echoed off the walls of the buildings surrounding the terrace.

My head snapped back, skin aflame from the impact of her hand meeting my cheek.

"You arrogant bastard," she hissed, her eyes twin blazes of midnight blue. The green had vanished.

I rubbed the imprint of her palm on my skin. Damn, she was made of pure fire. A fissure cracked around my chest, vicious, vindictive pride spurting through like lava. She was right to call me a bastard for pilfering her first kiss. Not only that, but she got more than she'd bargained for. I was the first man to fondle her pristine, untried pussy.

I was fucking *proud* of that, and I realized with a ruthlessness that startled me that if the opportunity ever came again, I'd take it in a heartbeat.

Which is why I was thankful for my insult. A kiss like the one we shared, a break in my control like the one I'd allowed, was dangerous. If anyone happened to come upon us, we'd be at the altar with our wrists bound together and crowns placed on our heads by the end of the week.

She couldn't want that, could she?

I shook my head. No, definitely not. Every single moment she was in my presence, she used it to challenge or undercut me, to establish how much she despised me.

Did she, though?

She didn't hate me quite as much as she pretended because there was no way Clara, even with our age difference, would allow a man to touch her if she didn't want it. I may have started it as a challenge or simply to shut her up, but she'd kept it rolling.

Shoulders back, chin up, she spewed out, "Oh, it was a mistake, alright. You should be so lucky to ever touch or kiss me again. Don't for an instant think this changes *anything* between us."

Her voice was a mixture of injury and rage, yet neither of us believed a word she'd said.

Even so, she was a proud woman, and I didn't like the distress on her face. Superiority, smugness, disdain. Those I was used to.

But hurt?

That, I could not stand.

I lifted my hand, about to reach for her, to comfort her, but she faltered, stepping to the side as if my touch would burn. Before I could say or do anything to try to make things right, she spun on her heel and stormed into the restaurant, positively enraged.

She was fucking glorious.

Not only did I have the incredible taste of her still on my tongue, but I'd turned her against me even more. Panic flooded my heart.

For the first time in my life, I wanted more from a woman.

A woman I'd lost any chance of ever having.

6

CLARA

Embarrassment. Humiliation. Degradation. That was how the first man I'd ever kissed made me feel.

I HATED him.

Fleeing from the terrace, I ran down the corridor, as far away from Tatum as I could get. Spotting a sign for the bathroom, I threw the door open and slammed it so hard it shuddered in its frame, giving me a twisted sense of grim satisfaction. If I could only tear it down. Tear down the whole building. This whole city.

Gritting my teeth, I slammed my palms on one of the white porcelain sinks. As I dropped my head, hot tears escaped from my clenched eyes. My fingers curled around the sink, and I let out a rage-filled screech.

I glanced into the mirror and gave out a startled cry. Someone was in there with me. A woman I recognized from the party stepped out of one of the bathroom stalls. Her frightened hazel eyes met mine in the mirror and widened. I winced in pain. I'd probably terrified her. My gaze shifted away from her back to me, and my face crumbled again. Red blotches made my face look like a target-practice board. My eyes were bloodshot, with big black circles where my mascara had smudged, tracks of black makeup running down my cheeks.

God, I hated that man. I hated him for reducing me to this crying, hot mess of a woman. Crying over a bad kiss was so below me.

My shoulders slumped inward. And yet, here I was.

The woman—girl—really, because she wasn't much younger than I was, her modest satin pink dress advertising her as an unmarried debutante—rushed over to me.

"Are you okay?" she asked, her hands coasting over my shoulder and arms, checking for injuries.

After assessing that I was unharmed—*girl, the injuries are all internal*—she wrapped her arms around me from the side and gave me a surprisingly tight hug. My eyebrows rose high on my forehead from shock. I was not used to having such an instantaneous, determined stranger come to my aid.

"He's not worth it," she said forcefully. "Whoever he is, he's not worth it."

I huffed out a half-laughing, half-choking sound. "What makes you think it's a man?"

"Oh, please. Unless someone's died, only a man can reduce a woman to your state."

I pushed out my bottom lip. "Thanks a lot."

"I'm sorry, I didn't mean to insult you. Even the strongest of women can be brought down and reduced to shit. I should know." Her eyes cast down. "I've seen it happen over and over again."

I frowned down at her as she busied herself by rummaging through her purse and pulling out a surprising array of makeup accessories. That was an odd statement to make. She was too young to have experienced love, much less heartbreak, so she must be speaking of someone close to her. Maybe her mother?

"I'm Gabriela, by the way," she politely introduced herself, pulling a sheet from a small package of makeup remover wipes.

"I'm Clara," I replied.

She had to lift onto her toes to reach my cheeks with the wipe because she was a petite, doll-like creature.

Dabbing and wiping away the ugly black streaks on my skin, she said casually, "I know who you are. Everyone knows who you are."

My brows puckered together. "You do?"

"Of course. The *mafie* scene in New York is filled with the most notorious gossips this side of the Atlantic. And how could we not be curious about a woman who comes to represent her clan all the way from California?" she asked matter-of-factly as she tossed the dirty wipe in the trashcan beneath the sink and grabbed another.

"Who upset you?" she demanded. "I'll tell my sister, and if it's a girl, she'll take care of the little bitch for you. She's the baddest of the bitches, my oldest sister is." I almost smiled as she puffed her chest with pride, sweeping long, thick ropes of dark hair over her shoulder.

I snorted. "If it was a girl, I could take care of her myself. No, your instinct was right. It's a man. The worst bastard I've ever met and *consilier* of this awful clan, of all things. Sorry, I didn't mean for that to come out as an insult, but you'd think he'd know how to behave, the fucker," I finished vindictively.

"Tatum?" She pulled back, her hazel eyes turning round with disbelief. "I'm shocked. Never heard a whisper of anything bad about him. He's always a perfect gentleman. With his height and blond hair, he's, like, every girl's dream.

Everyone has a crush on him. Not me," she hurried to add. "But he's very popular. And no one's ever seen him run around with women, Romanian or otherwise. He's considered a prince."

"He's so *not* a prince," I fumed. "He's as far from a prince I've ever met. Ever seen." I ground down on my back teeth and clenched my fists. "He's a pig. A heartless prick who takes a kiss and then slings insults."

"Okay, okay. Shush. There's no need to work yourself up again. Tonight was way out of character for him. He probably drank too much, with Luca getting married. You see, Tatum is Luca's close friend. He's younger than him and already married. Everyone wonders why Tatum doesn't have a wife yet. Any girl would marry him in an instant. Not me, but any other girl. You'll see. By tomorrow, he'll wake up with the worst hangover, apologize, and leave you alone."

"Oh, he made it more than clear that he wanted nothing to do with me, acting as if he's too good for the likes of me. I'm the Hagi se—," I swallowed down the rest of the word before I got myself in trouble. "I-I'm stuck with him. He's my keeper, and there's no way I can explain what happened. I can't exactly say, 'Oh, Tatum kissed me, and I don't want to be around him any longer.'"

"No, no. Of course not," she confirmed in a horrified tone.

One kiss did not create an engagement where I was from, but in New York, things were way more traditional. The Lupu family certainly had no hold on me, although who knew how far those conniving bastards might go to destabilize me and my clan. I supposed I should consider myself lucky because if I had kissed anyone but Tatum, it could be used to blackmail me or my clan. By the way he'd reacted, there was no fear of another kiss. God, he'd behaved as if he'd kissed a troll. Now, I may not be the sexiest girl in a room, but I *knew* I was no troll. Rage-filled adrenaline surged into my bloodstream, and I seethed with fury.

Either way, I couldn't risk any kind of scandal. I couldn't let word of our kiss get back to LA.

I gripped Gabriela's hand. "Please, please, for the sake of the sisterhood, do not tell anyone. I was stressed out and let my mouth run away from me, but if it got out, it would ruin me."

"I would never! I know everything about sisters," she whispered harshly. "Your secret is safe with me, but you cannot tell another soul. I can't guarantee that anyone else will have your back. Like I said, the women here are vipers. You can't trust anyone. You're lucky I'm the one who found you."

She pulled out her eyeliner and mascara, wielding them like weapons. "Now come on, let's get you fixed up. If you go out there like that, they'll know something's up. After I'm done, you'll look so good, he'll be eating his heart out."

I seriously doubted that. Tatum made it painfully clear what he thought of me and my so-called assets. But I was grateful for Gabriela's help.

"Sit still," she warned as she swiped mascara on my lashes. I stared at the fierceness on her otherwise sweet, innocent face. The strain around her eyes and the corners of her mouth were real.

"Why would you help me?" I couldn't help asking. "I'm not even a Lupu."

"Please. The women may be horrible bitches, but men are the absolute worst. Granted, I didn't expect this from Tatum. He's always had a good reputation, but that only goes to prove my point. Even the best of them can't help themselves. They're animals. Beasts. Lupu or not, you're a *mafie* woman, and there's no way I'm throwing you under the bus over one ill-advised kiss, clan allegiance aside."

I wasn't sure how I felt about what she'd said. As a *şef*, I'd consider her statement a travesty. Nothing was above clan and family, but these were Lupu men we were talking about. Considering how untrustworthy Tatum had proven himself to be, and he was considered the cream of the crop, I could only imagine what the others were like. I certainly couldn't blame Gabriela. The level of ferocity in such a young girl didn't come from nowhere. I might not know the details, but this girl had certainly witnessed some ugly stuff.

Checking over her shoulder instinctively, she turned back to me and suggested, "I'll tell you a secret about my family. That way, you'll have something on me, and we'll be even."

I gave a little shrug. She tutted me for moving as she swiped on an extra bit of eyeliner on the outside of my lids.

"My sister is married to one of these monsters. You know, with arranged marriages as they are, she was paired off with a guy who was considered a catch. My father was the former *consilier*, but he'd been killed during the same hit that took out our old *şef*. Without my father around to protect my sister, her husband tortured her." She leaned in close and confided in a harsh whisper. "But we're about to get our revenge."

My eyebrows raised up to my hairline. Fuck, this was some serious shit.

"There. Now you know," she said with a satisfied look.

"Don't do something irrational or stupid, but if you need my help, just ask," I offered. I didn't know where that came from or what kind of hot water it might get me into, but this girl was courageous, and I couldn't let that go unrewarded.

She shook her head. "I couldn't possibly get you involved. Anyway, the fewer people who know about it, the better. We're going to disappear and never be found again."

"What?" I gasped.

I stared down at this tiny, young girl with new respect. Escape from a *mafie* clan? Especially one as well-connected as the Lupu? That was a near impossibility.

She stepped back and tilted her head to the side, examining her work. Pulling out a bright red lipstick, she smeared it thickly on my lips.

"Shh. No more talk," she chastised me severely. Her eyes shifted left and then right. "There are ears everywhere. Just consider yourself lucky for having escaped with one measly, unwanted kiss."

I sighed inwardly. If only it had been measly. If only that wretched kiss had been unwanted. What I would do for that to be true … But I wasn't about to humiliate myself further by divulging my feelings on the first kiss I'd ever had with a man. My lips still stung from the force of his mouth on mine. The feel of the crisp, smooth cotton of his shirt, and the hot, chiseled flesh of his muscles underneath as I touched his chest. Dear God, I was getting hot thinking about it, and I hated the guy. I bit down my groan of despair.

Gabriela turned me toward the mirror so I could inspect her work.

Hmm, I looked even better than before. The red shade of the matte lipstick made my full lips stand out more than usual. I fluttered my eyelashes, the thick black outline of liner and mascara making the blue of my eyes pop.

I looked good.

I pulled my shoulders back. My ego survived an epic battering, but I could do this. No man, and certainly not Tatum the Stupid, was going to get the best of me.

"Go out there and show him what he's missing. Stay close to him, but flirt outrageously with every man in his vicinity. I don't care what he says ... he's going to regret whatever he did to you," she forecasted.

"I will," I swore bleakly, but I knew the truth.

Tatum wasn't interested in me. I'd salvage my ego, but he'd have to care to get jealous, and he didn't care for me in the least. The truth stung so badly that my nostrils burned, but I swore if I let one rogue tear escape, I would scratch my eyes out for my purebred stupidity.

Snapping my spine straight, I stifled the tears, stuffed down my feelings, and wrapped my strength around me like a mantle, like an Amazon's armor.

He doesn't want me. He hates me.

It was a brutal reminder, but it was real. I'd already let myself slip into fantasy once before and look what had happened.

I glared at myself in the mirror and swore to myself, *never again.*

7

TATUM

I avoided Clara like the plague, picking her up and dropping her off wherever she needed to be with little more than the barest of greetings.

It was hell.

I felt like a grade-A bastard, and on top of that, I ached for her like an addict. Grimly, I reminded myself it was for the best. Best for her, best for me, best for my family. Best for everyone, I repeated to myself ad nauseum.

Things were manageable ...

Until the hurricane.

The night of the hurricane changed everything.

Hurricane Augusta made landfall in Louisiana and barreled to the northeast coast to drown the city in a deluge of epic proportions. It battered Manhattan, and like a wrathful god, it tore through the boroughs. The flooding, along with the tornado warnings, almost drove me to the brink of insanity as I lay in my luxurious penthouse, unable to leave my building and race over to Queens to take care of the ones I loved.

Strong wind gusts blasted sheets of rain against the glass

wall of my apartment as I wore a groove into the parquet floor pacing, up and down, up and down. The city implemented a travel ban until 5 a.m., a nail-biting experience rivaling the Titanic.

Cell reception was intermittent, but Star kept in contact when she could. Thank Christ, in the end, our house was spared. It was sheer luck and nothing else because Alex's mother's house, a few places down from my mother's, was flooded. Part of the roof was torn off, and some of the siding was missing. Windows were blown out. Power was out for the whole neighborhood.

I let out a hushed curse when Alex alerted me to the situation. He and I were texting incessantly. There was a good hour of sheer panic as his house in Queens held out against the hurricane-turned-tornado, the women trapped inside.

Icy terror flooded my veins.

Clara.

I should've been there, or she should've been here with me. By my side. In my arms. *In my bed.* Safe with me, dammit. This was my fault. All of it. Regardless of how much she hated me, I should've dragged her over to my place the moment I'd heard about the hurricane. It wasn't like I hadn't lived through Hurricane Sandy in 2012. It was after Sandy that I had our basement flood-proofed. I may have only been twenty-one years old, but I was the head of my family, and I'd be damned if I didn't protect my mother and sister.

I stopped by Alex's penthouse next door and told him to evacuate the women to my mother's house the moment it was safe enough for them to venture out into the streets. Those turned out to be a rough few minutes as they braved the elements to find refuge. The rain was still coming down hard, but they made it safely to my mother's doorstep with the clothes on their back and nothing more.

Once the rain had dissipated enough for the city to lift the travel ban, I took off in the Range Rover. I drove through the flooded streets, swirling with debris, bringing what supplies I could with me. As I slowly crept across the Queensboro Bridge at a snail's pace, I glanced down at the East River. It roiled beneath me like a cauldron from hell.

Once Queens-side, I slowly swerved around fallen trees and made it five blocks away from Mama's house before I was forced to abandon the car.

Throwing the door open, I grabbed what I could and waded through the rushing river that came up to my hip. Rain pounded down on me like buckets thrown down by an angry Thor or Zeus. Their wrath reflected my inner turmoil; I was furious at myself for having been so far away from the women during this waterlogged apocalypse.

Anticipating my arrival, Star flung the front door open as I dragged myself up the flight of stairs to Mama's house. Squinting my eyes against the rain, I made out Star's slim silhouette. Eyes wide like a panicked horse, she covered her open mouth with her hand, as I took the last few steps in the torrential downpour, drenched to the bone.

"Oh my God, are you alright? I can't believe you drove through this," my little sister said in a panicked rush.

I stripped off my drenched sweater as I stepped through the door and dumped it on the floor of the foyer along with the bags of supplies I'd carried with me.

Grabbing her to me, I held her tight.

I didn't do touching. It was even rarer for me to go into a full hug, but I was desperate to feel her under my fingertips and make sure she was alive.

Caressing her hair, I pressed for information, "How is everyone?"

"Fine, Tatum. We're fine. Mama is with Alex's mom and *Bunică* in the kitchen. And Clara's here, of course."

"Clara," I murmured and felt an odd pricking sensation on my nape.

As if I'd conjured her up, I looked over my sister's shoulder, and there she was, leaning against the wooden column flanking the entrance to the living room.

Our gazes clashed.

Jesus, she was as gorgeous as ever. More so, even.

Wiping dripping water off my face, I quickly stepped away from my sister.

"Let me go there and get you a couple of towels to dry off," suggested Star and skipped up the stairs to the second floor, leaving me alone with Clara.

Left alone with Clara, I was riveted on her. It was the first time I'd seen her in anything but a perfectly tailored suit and full makeup. She was barefoot, wearing leggings and a long-sleeved T-shirt that she'd likely borrowed from my sister. Thick waves of light brown hair, streaked with lightning bolts of blond, cascaded down the sides of her face, ending at her nipples.

She looked so achingly young and vulnerable. I hurt with the possessive urge to wrap those long tresses around my fist and tug her to me. Crash my lips over hers and taste her exceptional, sun-drenched taste to assure me she was alive.

Our one kiss was seared on my brain, and the memory of her pouty lips against mine reared its head, thickening my cock.

I asked in a hoarse voice, "Are you okay?"

She nodded; her sparkling eyes larger than when she circled them with her raccoon makeup.

From fear?

No, I didn't like that idea. It jangled the demon inside me. It'd been howling to be freed for hours now. He railed at me to touch her. Hold her. Crush her to me and inhale her until we were fused into one.

I took a step closer.

Then another.

I was so close I could reach out and touch her, so I did, cupping her warm cheek and breathing her in. It was soft. Jesus, was it soft. Her cheeks turned a pretty shade of pink. The same pink I imagined the imprint of my hand would leave on her buttocks when I jerked off to fantasies of her in the darkness of my bedroom.

"You okay?" I asked gently, my heart in my throat as I awaited her answer. On the radio, I'd already heard of one woman drowning in her basement in Jamaica, Queens, only a few miles from here. If anything had happened to Clara, I wouldn't have been able to live with myself. She was mine to protect.

Realization jolted through my body.

She wasn't just mine to protect. She was mine, period.

Her eyes widened further, tears brimming in the wells. Not a single one fell, but it didn't have to. I cursed under my breath, loud enough for Star to make another gasp of surprise.

I stepped closer.

Images of Clara's beautiful body floating facedown in a pool of cold, dark water in the Lupu basement assaulted me.

"You should've been with me. I should've taken care of you. I'm so sorry, Clara." My tone was stark. "I will never fail you again."

A tear dropped. Then another. Her plump bottom lip quivered.

"I was scared. Really scared," she choked out in a wheeze.

My heart felt like it had been gouged out with a carving knife. I took her by the shoulders and squeezed her tightly to my chest. Feeling her soft curves against my hard frame, her rapidly beating heart against mine, was a fantasy come to life.

Her tears wet my skin. Her breath puffed over my exposed chest. The combination was erotic, tempting me to do something bad. Very bad. My nipples hardened at the contact between us.

Her hands braced my flanks. They may have been cold as ice, but her touch burned me. She inhaled sharply and pushed to get away. I tightened my hold on her, crushing her to me. My cock dug into her soft belly, but I didn't care. She hated me; I knew that. *But. I. Didn't. Care.* Let her know what she did to me. Let her know where my cock would one day be.

I'd been up all night, watching the torrent of rain outside my window, watching the news as a deluge as ancient as the Great Flood from Genesis traveled across the city. I knew in my bones that I could've lost her.

I'd tried to keep my distance and look where that had landed me. With her at death's door.

Lesson learned. I'd never let her get far from me again.

A shiver rippled through her body. Her teeth chattered. She was in shock from what she'd been through. At one point during the worst of the hurricane, the house shook so hard that the glass windowpanes had shattered.

I scanned her face and neck.

No marks.

"Are you hurt?"

She shook her head, but her gaze darted away.

Clara never averted her eyes.

Never.

"What is it?" I demanded.

Eyes glued to the floor, she licked her dry lips.

My tone turned hard. "Tell me."

"It's nothing," she answered too quickly. Lying. She was lying.

"It's not nothing. Where does it hurt?"

I grabbed her arms. She hissed in pain.

"Your arms?"

"I'm fine," she insisted.

"Take off your shirt," I ordered.

At that moment, Star came down the stairs, holding a few towels. Hearing what I'd said, she tutted me from behind.

"Tatum, she can't take off her shirt in front of you," reprimanded my sister.

I twisted my head over my shoulder. "She damn well can and will. I'm taking care of her."

Afraid to touch her arms, I took her nape and bent down until we were face-to-face, her gaze on me. "Where are you hurt, Clara? Tell me. You should've told my mother. You may need a doctor. Where, Clara, where is it?"

Her eyes attempted to flee again, but I adjusted my glare so that she had nowhere to escape.

She let out a little huff. "There are cuts on my arms from when the windows shattered. We ran to the basement, but the water was rising. We ran back upstairs, but the house was shaking. I was near one of the windows as we rushed around trying to find a safe place to hunker down. I was only wearing a nightie, and glass blew into me as I passed by one of the windows. I covered my face, but my arms and hands got the worst of it."

My chest cracked open like an abyss. Rage, pure rage, spewed out of me.

Trembling, I took her hands. Her fingers felt brittle and ice cold. I turned them over. Sure enough, small angry red slashes stood out against the perfect peach cream of her skin. My vision tunneled, the edge red with wrath and help-lessness.

"Take off your shirt." My voice dripped with danger.

"No," my sister intervened. Her hand landed on my back. I shrugged it off. I didn't want anyone but Clara to touch me.

Ignoring my sister, I demanded, "Take it the fuck off."

I curved my back until I loomed over her like a monster. My cursing and aggressive posture must have convinced her I wasn't playing around. Clara's face paled, but she grabbed the hem of the shirt.

Good girl. I liked it much too much when she followed my orders.

Star gently wrapped a hand around my biceps.

Again, I wanted to shake her off, but she pleaded, "Stop. Tatum, I know you're upset, but she can't do that in front of you. I'll go to the bathroom with her." She pointed to the couch, where there was a first aid kit. "I'll take care of her."

My head was shaking in denial. No, I took care of her. No one but me. I'd failed her once. I could never allow it to happen again.

"You *can't*," Star maintained. "I know you feel some kind of claim over her, but she's not your wife. She's not even your fiancée. I'm here. I'll take care of her."

"No," I growled.

My sister gently turned my head until our eyes met. "Don't you trust me?"

"I already failed once," I choked out. My throat closed up.

"You can stay outside the door, okay? I'll tell you everything I see."

"I want pics. Take photos of them. I need to make sure."

"Fine," she acquiesced.

Clara's eyes darted from me to Star, volleying back and forth with our negotiation. We spoke about her as if she weren't there. That, and the fact that she didn't have anything to say, was more proof that she was in shock.

Star slipped her hand into Clara's and slowly led her away from me. My demon screeched in protest as the distance grew between us. Clara followed her passively. Panic gripped me by the throat like a tightening noose. I'd never seen her behave meekly, and it made me want to shake her until she was her normal, sassy, rude self again. Guilt crashed through me. If she'd been with me, she would've been safe. If she'd at least been at my mother's house, she would've been safe. But I'd rejected her advances and then kept her at arm's length until she almost *died*.

Star slipped her hand in Clara's and slowly led her away from me. My brain screeched in protest as the distance grew between us. Clara followed passively, head down. Panic gripped me by the throat. I'd never seen her behave meekly like this.

Swiping up the first aid kit, I dogged them to the hallway bathroom.

As Star went to close the door, I put my palm against it.

"Leave it open a crack," I ordered as I handed her the kit.

Through the gap in the door, I could see most of Clara's reflection in the mirror.

My sister dragged the T-shirt off her. I inwardly cursed at the expanse of beautiful creamy skin speckled with little cuts. I seethed inside. Adrenaline pumped through my blood. If the hurricane had been mortal, I would've gutted it like a squealing pig by now.

Carefully, Star dabbed iodine on every cut, clucking gently like our mother would have. Clara's shoulders slumped forward as my little sister took care of her. My heart cracked open further. Then, Star applied antibiotic ointment on each tiny wound. She snapped discreet close-up pics of Clara's arms, hands, and collarbone. I felt my cell phone vibrate in my back pocket as the texts poured in.

Vibrating with rage, I stood stock-still as I watched. The desire to murder tore through me, but I was powerless. It was the same inane sense of helplessness I felt as when my father disclosed his sick secret to me, but a hundred times worse. I'd become semi-obsessed with Clara since our one kiss, but I'd stupidly thought I could stay away from her and smother my feelings.

The realization that she could've died and I'd failed to protect her drowned me in remorse and self-recrimination.

There was only one way to make this right.

I swore to myself, to my clan, to my God, I would never fail her again.

I'd be so up her ass, she'd wish that hurricane had never hit New York City because she'd never be rid of me.

8

CLARA

A few days after the night of the hurricane, I was in the dining room, just sitting down for breakfast— a soft-boiled egg and toast that Alex's grandmother had prepared for me. Sunlight poured in from the tall windows, each flanked by thick, blue-velvet curtains. A large swath of light fell over the long, dark walnut dining table, set with placemats and dishes for two, which meant one of them was for …

Tatum.

Humph.

Tatum kissed me, rejected me, then a hurricane hit, and he thought he could have a change of heart and everything would be alright? *I don't think so, buddy.* I wasn't a gullible little girl. I was a boss lady, an up-and-coming *şef*, I was the so-called "man," and I wasn't about to get fucked over again.

I tapped on the delicate eggshell with the bottom of my spoon.

An uncomfortable thumping of my heart nagged at me. It was the look of sheer terror on his face when he'd walked through the door, drenched to the bone. He'd been legit scared for us women, for me specifically.

I gave myself a mental smack, desperately hoping it'd whack out the stupidity stubbornly clinging to me. I couldn't afford to weaken around a man who'd already managed to make me feel so fragile.

His new attentiveness was disturbing, as was the moment he'd pulled me into his chest and hugged me tight the night of the hurricane. It felt so warm and delicious to be wrapped by his thick arms. The thumping of his heart against my ear had lulled me into the first moment of calm since the hurricane hit. My body had melted into his as I absorbed his heat and the feeling of safety and protection. Then, the way he got protective over me when he realized the windowpane had shattered on me. He was panicked, solicitous, and possessive at the same time. At that moment, I wanted him. And I wanted more with him.

I mentally smacked myself again. Viciously, I hissed to myself, *Remember, Clara, he said our kiss was a mistake. Those were his words.*

I revived the humiliating aftermath of that spectacular kiss to resurrect the walls the past two days of his intense attention had eroded. I had to admit, I'd been spooked by the hurricane. He'd caught me in an intensely susceptible moment in the aftermath, I reasoned, being away from the comfort of my family and home. After days of this, it was time we returned to hating each other the way we were supposed to. That's all it was. Nothing more.

I squeezed my eyes shut. Who was I kidding?

Tatum's constant care had been an unexpected solace I'd clung to over the past several days. Especially when I woke up at night screaming in my bed. Before I got a chance to gain full consciousness, the lights in my room flicked on, and Tatum was by my side, taking my hand in his.

He'd leave and return with a glass of water, which he made me sip before carefully placing it on the nightstand and tuck me back in bed. Once I was settled, he'd caress my hair until I fell asleep. Normally, I would've batted his hand away and tersely ordered him out, but I'd been vulnerable. I'd never felt that for anyone other than my father. Each morning, I woke up to my bedroom door open and the hall light on, verifying it hadn't all been a dream.

Before I could finish my pep talk, Tatum sauntered in, looking ridiculously sexy in a simple long-sleeved shirt and joggers, his golden hair tousled and eyes still heavy with sleep. A pang of conscience hit me. How long had he been by my bedside last night, petting me until I fell asleep? I was sure it had been quick, but he didn't look like he'd slept.

"Hey," he greeted me casually, his voice rusty and unused. He may have been sleep-deprived, but as they always did now, his pitch-black eyes sharpened instantly, focused entirely on me. Before, he'd averted his gaze every chance he got. Now, he couldn't take his eyes off me.

A shiver coursed down my spine. *Ignore, ignore, ignore.* My fingers gripped harder around the spoon in my hand as I forced my pulse down to normal.

I nodded brusquely and returned my focus to my food.

He swung the door to the kitchen open, and I heard him greet Alex's grandmother. She asked what he wanted to eat and he requested an omelet. They chatted for a few more minutes as I tried to inhale my food to get out of there before he returned.

Dammit, I didn't finish in time, and I couldn't leave a morsel of food on my plate for fear of insulting Alex's grandmother.

"Hey gorgeous," he said as he returned. "How was the rest of your sleep?"

I froze at his endearment, spoon suspended halfway to my mouth.

He sat beside me and leaned in close. I got a whiff of his natural oaky scent and inhaled it greedily. Dammit, I shouldn't have done that. It left me slightly light-headed and a lot turned on, a combination that served to irritate me more. I couldn't risk my crown for this guy. As traditional as the Lupu were, I couldn't even consider simply fucking the living daylights out of him and then cutting it off because we'd end up married. A shiver coursed down my spine. I blinked. That wasn't a shiver of fear. It was a shiver of arousal. Did the thought of marrying him turn me *on*? Oh, hell no.

Thrown off my game, I continued staring down at my plate, choking my spoon with my grip. At least I remembered to bring the spoon up to my lips. Opening my mouth, I stuffed it full and chewed to avoid having to reply to him.

After swallowing, I glanced over to find him waiting for my reply.

"I'm not your gorgeous anything," I snipped as a response.

"Hey." His tone pitched low and hard.

The inner muscles of my pussy clenched. Fuck. Whenever he used that domineering tone, it only agitated me more.

I ignored him.

"Clara," he demanded, his voice commanding my attention.

There was a long moment of silence. His hand wrapped around mine, forcing me to drop my spoon. Then, he pushed my chair back and turned it around until I was facing him.

A finger dipped under my chin and raised it up.

Serious, jet-black eyes inspected me. A lock, streaked blond, fell across his forehead. He looked so boyish in that moment. Before the hurricane, I'd never seen him in anything less than a perfectly fitted and pressed suit, with a tie, cufflinks, and an expensive watch to match. His hair never had a strand out of place.

After the hurricane, it was like Tatum was suddenly unspooling in front of my eyes, looking less and less like the robotic, haughty man I knew him to be. In the moments when I caught him laughing or got a glimpse of him relaxed, like now, I melted like an ice cream cone on a hot summer day.

Despite the gooey and warm feeling spreading through me, I made sure to harden my face and glare at him. It wouldn't do for him to know how I really felt.

His eyes softened. "Did you not sleep well after I left? Did you have another nightmare?"

I didn't answer.

"What's with the attitude, little girl?"

His jaw clenched as if the thought of me having a nightmare or waking up made him angry.

"I'm not a little girl," I snapped back. "I'm a powerful woman—soon to be the head of my clan, in case you've forgotten—so it's none of your business if I've had another nightmare or how I've slept."

He wrapped his large hand around my throat and drove me into the back of the chair.

Thrusting his face into mine, he said, "Baby girl, I don't care what you are to the outside world. To me, you're *my* gorgeous girl. My smart, sassy little doll. My pretty *mafie* princess with an attitude hiding a generous heart. You can't hide from me anymore. I see the way you treat *Bunică*, my mother, Star. I see you—"

"Will you stop?" I pleaded.

Oh, God, his words gutted me, but he was surely messing with me. Why would he say these things when he hated the one and only kiss we'd ever shared? I mean, sure, I didn't have any experience, but I'd certainly melted. Instead, he'd called it a mistake. How could he say what he just said when he hadn't even wanted to kiss me before?

My eyes slashed away from him. I didn't appreciate this little game he was playing. It cut me to my core. He had no right to say what he'd said. As sexy as he sounded, his words were meaningless.

His head canted to the side. "What's going on in that beautiful head of yours?"

"That, right there," I accused him, poking a finger in his chest. "Will you stop *that*? Calling me gorgeous and sexy like you mean it when we both know you don't. Anyway, those things mean nothing. Being tough is what matters in this world, especially for a woman like me. Or being strong and shrewd."

"I called you smart and sassy."

Was he purposely dismissing what I was saying? I swallowed hard, pressing into his fingers around my throat. "I don't know why you're toying with me, Tatum."

As painful as it was, I forced myself to lift my gaze and painfully hold his soulful, dark eyes. They turned stormy at my words.

"You've made it abundantly clear how you really feel about me," I said sullenly. Sheesh, I didn't think I'd ever have to bring up the delicious, awful kiss again.

He got closer until his breath whispered over my lips as he asked, "What the hell are you talking about?"

Oh my God, how dense could one man be? I huffed and waggled my head to throw off his hand, but he only secured my throat more firmly, not allowing any movement.

Fine, if he was going to make me say it, I'd say it. Rip the bandage off and go back to the way things were before. "I'm talking about the kiss that was a *mistake*, that's what I'm talking about. Or did you forget what you said afterward? I certainly didn't."

Another sharp incision notched itself on my heart at having to speak of that awful moment.

He blanched. "Clara, I didn't mean for it to come out the way it did. It wasn't the kiss that was a mistake. Your kiss *gutted* me."

I inhaled sharply, my heart in my throat. I'd gutted him? The idea was fantastical and also incredibly enticing.

"It was me taking your first kiss that was the problem," he explained. "I violated your honor and that of the Lupu clan by touching you."

There goes that annoying Lupu traditionalism rearing its head again. These Lupu people were obsessed.

"Oh, please, Tatum, I'm not a wilting wallflower virgin," I retorted.

"Perhaps not a wilting wallflower, no. But you are a virgin. Your clan dubbed you the Virgin Queen. We already know how important that title is and what your father's intentions are."

My eyes sharpened on him. He knew? No, no, he couldn't know. No one knew for sure of my father's intention of handing the kingdom over to me. It was an exceptional move, a delicate time. It wouldn't do for his plan to come out before everything was set in place, before my own clan accepted me as queen.

"Anything between us would be ... complicated," he concluded with a frustrated sigh. "Impossible."

I flinched. *Touché.* There was no denying that.

His lips swept over the corner of my mouth down to the edge of my jaw and back up again. "Don't think for an instant that I didn't want you then or that I don't want you now. Even though I tried to convince myself I hated you, I want you every moment of every day. Don't even get me started on the nights ... thoughts of you sleeping nude in your bed torment me. Tortures me. Why do you think I'm so sleep-deprived?"

"I thought you didn't sleep because of my nightmares," I whispered. "And I don't sleep nude in this house."

I did at home, but that was none of his business.

"Your nightmares wake me up, of course, but I don't need you to sleep naked for me to be tormented by fantasies of you doing that and more. So much more," he murmured against the shell of my ear, giving my earlobe a nip that had me biting down on my lips to suppress a strangled groan.

My heart rate picked up, and he could feel it underneath his fingers. I squirmed in my seat because his husky voice was doing things to me that I had no business allowing, but my body had a mind of its own when it came to Tatum.

"I'd said anything between us was impossible, but the night of the hurricane—not knowing if you were dead or alive—changed everything. *Everything.* I blame myself. You should've been under my roof, where I could watch over you. You should've been in my bed, with me balls deep inside you."

My head was shaking emphatically. I placed my hand

over his soft lips to shush him before he went on because anything between us was still impossible. Wasn't it?

He gently pushed my hand off and continued, "Now, sweetness, now the world has tilted on its axis. What was once impossible will become reality. The ball's in your court. You decide what you want but know this: I'm at your beck and call. Just say the word, my queen, and I'll give it to you because I'm all in."

The walls I'd erected against this man were crumbling fast, leaving me helpless, but I couldn't lower my defenses. Not only was he giving me whiplash with the fast turnabout, but I'd worked too hard to get to where I was. My father and family depended on me. He'd blasted away the anger of our first kiss, but I still didn't trust him. What if this was a ploy to get me to go easy on the Lupu clan, to let them in, and once in, they would take and take until we were but figure-heads and nothing more?

These Lupu men were wily, and while I believed the authenticity of his concern, it didn't mean he couldn't exploit my feelings for him. Erode my suspicions, wheedle himself into my heart and then, *pow*, manipulate me to give away too much of the Hagi power, leaving the Lupu clan to rule over Los Angeles like they did New York City. Even if he was completely genuine, I still had to focus on my goal, which was a smooth transition to Hagi *şef*hood. I'd worked too hard to get to where I was and wasn't about to renounce my crown for him.

As much as my body clamored for him, as much as I ached to open my heart up to him, I couldn't allow anything to happen.

"No," I said, placing my hand over his securely collared around the base of my throat and attempting to push it off. "You were right to call it a mistake. It was."

His grip tightened for half a second before he allowed me to remove it. Just in the nick of time since Alex's grandmother walked into the dining room carrying his plate of omelet.

Tatum unclenched his jaw and turned to thank *Bunică*. Coward that I was, I took the opportunity to slip out of my seat. I grabbed my empty plate, hurried to leave it in the kitchen sink, and then took the long way around through the living room and sped up the stairs to hide out in my bedroom.

Twisting the lock closed, I leaned back against the door. Regret bled into my aching heart, but I'd done the right thing. He was right when he said it was an unnecessary complication. My ego had smarted after our kiss, but in retrospect, I had to admit he'd made a wise move.

While Tatum hadn't looked happy downstairs, he'd accept my decision.

I chewed on my lower lip.

He will accept it, won't he?

Knowing Tatum, anything could happen.

9

TATUM

I heard shrieks coming from Star's bedroom and stormed down the hall in fight mode, only to find Clara and Star rolling around on the floor in a fit of giggles, throwing fake money at each other.

I did a double take as fierce longing ripped through me. I'd laid out my feelings to Clara, and she'd turned me down. I had only myself to blame for being such a stubborn idiot and suppressing my true feelings for her.

Not going to lie, though, it was a bitter pill to swallow.

I couldn't blame her. After the months we'd spent sparring and the deep level of suspicion she had over all things Lupu, I hadn't done anything to establish trust between us. As hard as it was, in the end, I'd backed off and respected her wishes because I knew myself. If I got my hands on her and burst through her tight channel, I'd never let her go. It would never work between us. She was obsessed with her clan, and I couldn't leave mine. If I took her virginity, hard choices would have to be made.

Seeing Star acting silly didn't surprise me. Clara, on the other hand, I almost didn't recognize. But the two of them together, appearing so carefree and relaxed, cracked my heart in two. My sister was shy and reserved. She didn't open up to just anyone. And Clara ... Clara's life was relentlessly demanding. She was constantly interrupted, taking calls from her people in Cali, making decisions for her people, and proving she was so much more than a pampered little princess.

Clara kept people at arm's length, and Star was a bashful introvert, yet they'd found something in each other. Needless to say, family meant everything to me, and seeing Clara with my sister disarmed me. If I hadn't fallen for her before, this clinched it.

Blinking down on her, I barely recognized her.

Gone were her stiff, structured suits. Gone were the caked-on layers of makeup. Gone was her perfect hair. She was dressed in yoga pants and a shirt that rode up to expose her tiny waist and slightly rounded belly. Her pants rode dangerously low enough for me to lust over her flared hips. All her fair, peach skin displayed for my lips and tongue to worship.

Clara popped up and her thick tits jiggled in a way that told me she wasn't wearing a bra. Dear God, I hoped no one noticed my cock lengthening in my pants. Her hair was in a messy bun on top of her head. I'd never seen her glow like this before; she was slightly flushed from laughing so hard. She'd never looked more stunning in all the months we'd spent together. It took my breath away.

The lust and pleasure on her face when her eyes swept over me stirred my blood to a boil. After catching her unguarded expression, there was no way, I mean *no way*, I could take her resting bitch face at face value again.

Her eyes dropped as if she couldn't hold my gaze. I'd won every staring contest between us, but ever since I'd begun my campaign to win her over, she couldn't look me in the eye long enough to challenge me.

I'd unmoored her, and I loved it.

"Hey, Tatum," my sister said breathlessly, breaking the spell.

"I thought something happened. You two were screaming like hyenas," I griped, expressing the residual irritation that had quickly evaporated after seeing them on the floor laughing.

My sister rolled onto her back and gazed up at me from the floor. "There's no internet, so we were whiling away the time. After we watched every makeup video Clara had saved on her phone, she did a makeover," she said with a flourish of her fingers toward the smoky eyeshadow around her eyes.

My brows lifted. My kid sister looked like … like a grown woman. At seventeen, she was blossoming, and I made a mental note to watch over her more carefully.

"We got bored," Star continued, "so I pulled out this old game."

My eyes flicked to Clara, who gave me an almost shy look from beneath her lashes. She fiddled with the fake cash and started organizing it by denomination, her shoulders hiking up as if expecting me to mock her. We'd been at each other's throats for months, and she still wasn't used to our new reality. *Have no fear, little one, I'm a patient man.*

"That was sweet of Clara, and the eyeshadow looks good on you," I praised my sister, who scrunched her nose at me in response to my compliment.

Clara guardedly lifted her gaze to mine.

"You, on the other hand, are more beautiful without makeup. I can see you better," I said.

A flush rose high on her cheeks. She got my message. I didn't see her *better*, I simply saw her as she was at her core.

Now that I had my eye on her, she wasn't safe behind the makeup and clothes she hid behind.

She wasn't safe from me, period. It was fine that she wasn't ready. To be honest, I wasn't ready either. I wanted her, there was no question about that, but our situation was delicate, and I was nothing if not a cautious man.

Star, who would've been blind to not see a shift in me, patted a place by her side and said, "Sit and play with us, Tatum."

"No," Clara instantly said. "H-he's too busy."

Star made a little scoffing sound. Throwing me a wide smile, she said, "My brother's never too busy for me, isn't that right, Tatum?"

"That's right," I replied, dropping beside her.

I'd already discarded my jacket, but suddenly feeling stifled by my tie, I whipped it off and placed it carefully between Clara and me. Stretching out my long frame, I propped myself up on my elbow and caught her gaze bouncing from my body to the tie and back. Hmm, already guessed she had a little kink to her, but this solidified my suspicions.

Her interest wasn't helping me keep my cock under control, either. Crazy ideas bubbled in my head, ideas I had no business conjuring. Ideas of using my tie to bind her to the white metal bars of the headboard of her bed, her naked body writhing beneath me. Or skimming the tie lightly down the center of her torso, teasing her with the edge. Or better yet, spreading her legs open for me and taunting her clit with it. The possibilities were endless.

I picked out a token from the board game as Clara licked the tip of her thumb and counted out fake money for me. Each time she flicked her pink tongue to her thumb, I stifled a groan. I didn't know if she was taunting me on purpose, but hell if it didn't have me imagining her tongue swirling around the crown of my cock. Or whether the color matched the lips of her pussy. Having had the privilege of touching her cunt, I already knew what it felt like while thrusting my fingers into that tight wet hole. I just hadn't seen it yet.

Christ.

We began playing, tossing the dice and moving our tokens around the board. The tension began to ease as we joked and teased one another until I saw something I didn't like.

"Clara," I intoned, my eyes narrowing on her.

"What?" she asked breathlessly.

She'd subtly swiped her hand to move her taxicab token off the railroad space where she'd landed and which I owned. With the card she'd drawn, she'd have to pay me four hundred dollars. Considering who Clara was, I was not the least bit surprised by her conduct. She thought she had to fight dirty to survive and stay on top as a woman in a world dominated exclusively by rough men, but it didn't mean I was going to let her get away with it. When she was with me, I was in control.

She batted her long lashes at me.

"Put it back," I warned, raising myself to a sitting position.

She threw her hands up, waving them to show me they were empty. Too late, I'd already caught her cheating. Although it was an innocent board game, I couldn't let her behavior pass. First, because there was no way I'd set a precedent where I'd let her get one over on me. Second, I might hold secrets close to my chest, but I was no cheat.

Another man might have ignored it or blown it off as cute, but the perfectionist, the rule-abider, the domineering mofo in me couldn't let it go. Especially in front of my sister. What kind of lesson would that teach her? Yeah, I got that I was obsessed with raising her right, but it was my responsibility, and I wasn't about to fall down on the job.

"I saw you edge your taxicab off the train station. The one I own. Put it back, cheater."

Her eyes flashed with anger, but the flush on her face didn't lie. Instead of admitting to her wrongdoing, she dug in. It was adorable. Really, it was. Not that it would stop me from disciplining her appropriately. I leaned back on my elbow and watched the show. This was going to be fun.

Clara didn't let me down, either.

Clutching her chest in outrage, she let out a gasp. "I am not a *cheater*."

I glared across the Monopoly board at her in mock anger. Inside I was elated. My heart rate ticked up, but I played it cool and simply lounged back nonchalantly.

She scrambled to a sitting position from where she'd been laid out, like a sacrifice for me to devour, and thrust a finger in my chest. "I. Did. Not. Cheat."

I swatted her finger away from me.

"You did. Put it back," I ordered.

We glared at each other, fixed in a staring contest. Star's gaze swung back and forth between us. You could cut the friction with a knife with the tension between us. My inner demon was wide awake and salivating as he surveyed our edgy interaction.

I'd called her out, which pricked her pride, and Clara was all about pride. I didn't need to win the stupid game, but I did need to win our battle of wills. Problem was, how was I going to make my point while finding a way for her to save face?

"I don't want to play this stupid game anymore," she snapped. "I'm done."

She slapped her palm on the wooden floor, the tokens and dice shuddering from the impact of her hand. She made to stand, but I grasped her wrist and kept her in place. Star let out a little wheeze of surprise at my purposeful touch.

My attention solely on Clara, I said, "Oh, we're not finished playing."

She gritted out between clenched teeth. "I don't like to lose."

It didn't take much to figure that out about my woman.

Not breaking our stare for an instant, I demanded, "What do you need? Money? Properties? Utilities?"

"I need five hundred dollars," she bit out.

I grabbed a fake bill from the piles on my side, because obviously I was winning, and slapped it down beside her knee.

"Done. You need anything, you come to me. Now sit back down and roll the dice again."

"I just had my turn," she replied testily.

I glowered until her eyes shifted to the side. I was not mad in the least, but this was purely about imposing my will.

"Again," I challenged.

"Fine," she muttered, eyes cast to the board.

She settled back in, threw the dice, and plunked her taxicab token down on each space before releasing it and crossing her arms peevishly over her chest. "Happy?"

"Infinitely," I confirmed smoothly.

Star cleared her throat and took the dice to throw, the strain throbbing between Clara and me. I planned to force this game to continue for another hour, just to prove my point, but I was relieved of my duty by a light rap on the door.

It opened with a creak, and Gabriela, Star's best friend, stood in the doorway.

Her eyes popped out of her head, probably from seeing the Lupu *consilier* on the floor playing a board game. "Your mom told me you were in your room."

Star jumped to her feet in relief and hugged Gabriela. "I'm so happy you're here. Oh my God! Are you okay? Clara and Alex's mom and grandma had the worst time of it. They're sheltering here, and there's no internet, so we're passing the time playing Monopoly."

"That explains why you didn't answer your Snap," Gabriela said, her shoulders slumping forward in relief. "I was worried."

I got to my feet, smoothing the creases of my pressed shirt and adjusting my cuffs. Clara's eyes greedily ate up each of my movements, and I wouldn't deny that my ego puffed up with pride under her scrutiny.

"I'll leave you ladies to it, then," I said.

Gabriela gave me what she thought was a sultry look under her lashes.

"Don't leave because of me," she murmured.

I caught a side glance of Clara rolling her eyes and suppressed a smirk. Clara had nothing to worry about with Gabby. She was a young girl flexing her newly honed flirting skills, nothing more. It was a running joke among the Lupu brothers that the young girls crushed on me, but I was pleased to see Clara's jealousy flare-up. Good sign.

"Internet might be down, but I can still make calls. Which is what I'm going to do."

Turning to Clara, I paused for a moment, drinking her in. Her pouty lips parted slightly. I loved their natural color and the glimpse of her pink tongue that poked out just a tad. Her tits pressed against the fabric of my sister's shirt and her peaked nipples poked through. Damn, it took a strong man to tear his eyes away from that sight.

"Alex will be coming as soon as he can to go over the house and check out the damage. Do you need me to get anything from their house?" I asked, struggling to tear my eyes away from her lovely face.

She gave a slight shudder that made me want to grab her and pet her long, silky hair, maybe bite those tight nipples through the cotton shirt.

Pressing her lips together, she thought for a moment. "I brought my laptop the night of the storm. That's the most important thing."

My brows lifted in surprise. It had been a deluge the night of the hurricane, but she'd made sure to bring her laptop. That was some work ethic she had.

Clara gave an embarrassed little shrug. "I'm in the middle of learning a new accounting program, but it's been days since I've been able to do anything. There's only so many days I can go without working. Anything you can do about that, Tatum?"

Clara was the only woman I knew who worked. Matter of fact, besides Luca's wife, she was the only woman I knew who'd gone to college. She recently graduated with a business degree, I recalled.

"I'll figure out something," I promised. "But for now, do you need anything from the house, like clothing?"

"No," she replied instantly, her lashes fluttering nervously.

Hmmm, what did she have in her drawers she didn't want me to see. Naughty panties? A vibrator or two?

"You can borrow any of mine until you buy new ones," Star said in a rushed voice.

"Very well," I replied. With a nod, I said, "Thanks for the game, ladies. It was a pleasure, despite the little mishap."

My voice dropped to a rasp, remembering the wrath in her eyes when I called her out. God, I liked her angry. She was just so sexy when she got riled up.

Clara's cheeks bloomed a pretty shade of pink.

It was bad form to refer to her cheating, but if she only knew the kind of punishment I itched to give her. In the privacy of my own bedroom, I'd swat that beautiful ass of hers until it was a pink that rivaled her cheeks.

Even in mixed company, the idea of laying my hands on her would be glaringly obvious to anyone who so much as glanced down at my trousers, so I slipped past and closed the door behind me. Thrusting my fists into my pockets, I stalked down the hallway before I did a turnaround and found myself back in Clara's room.

10

CLARA

"Hey girl," Gabriela greeted me as she moved deeper into the room. Plopping down on the carpet, she dropped her Hammitt handbag beside her, a sunset pink color in snakeskin that made me salivate it was so luxurious. I might have mostly grown up around men who were heathens, but it didn't mean I couldn't appreciate an exquisitely feminine fashion statement.

"Hey," I replied, suddenly feeling a little timid. I was comfortable around rough *mafie* men but get me in a pink bedroom with two young girls and I felt like a fish out of water. Especially around Gabby, as she insisted I call her after the way we first met in the bathroom following the Tatum kiss rejection, as I'd come to call it. A girl's first kiss should be special but mine only proved my father's claim that I was never meant for love.

"What have you guys been doing without internet?" Gabby asked, her hazel eyes wide with horror. "I don't even know how I'd survive that for, like, one day."

Star let out a soft chuckle.

While I carried a tortured mix of emotions for her brother, there was no doubt I'd never met a person as sweet, kind, and authentic as Star. I gave Tatum and his mother credit for bringing her up right. She'd been reared with so much unconditional love she didn't know how to be anything other than what she was. The only criticism was that she didn't realize just how badass she was. There were holes in her self-esteem, and I couldn't imagine where they'd come from growing up as she did.

Touching the Monopoly board, Star explained, "We found a way to while away the time—videos, makeup tutorials, thanks to my new big sister here. And Monopoly. Tatum even took time out of his busy day to play with us, if you can believe it."

"I like the eyes, girl," Gabby praised Star's makeup. Star blushed, actually blushed, for wearing sexy eyeshadow. "As for Tatum, you know he'll do anything for you. After what he went through as a kid, he's super protective of you."

My ears pricked up, the tips burning with curiosity. I shouldn't want to know more about him, shouldn't feed my growing obsession with him, but I was dying to hear about his life.

Casually, I asked, "What happened?"

Gabby's eyes darted to Star for permission to answer my question. Star nodded her acquiescence.

"Well ... you might not know this, but Tatum and Star's father was Rudari, and you know how Romanians can be about the Roma. It didn't matter that their mother was *mafie* nobility. Tatum got the worst bullying. Kids called him awful names, like *țigani* and *corcitură*."

Țigani and *corcitură*. Gypsy and half-breed. I cringed at the words, imagining how they'd been used to hurt him. *Ouch.*

"Yeah," Star confirmed. "He didn't look like he does now, all big and strong. He was scrawny and small, with a shock of thick blond hair. When kids found out the pale, blond kid with the Anglo looks had a father who was Roma, they had a field day. I was just a baby, but my mother told me how he would come back from school every day beaten and bruised." She swallowed. "My father insisted he not back down from any fight."

My throat convulsed as I stifled a cry of outrage. A surge of rage shot through me, fury clanging in my heart at the thought of his callous father throwing him to the wolves day after day. Toxic masculinity at its best. Like a superhero, I wanted to fling myself into the past and stand up to those bullies on behalf of the skinny boy with wild blond hair.

Star's eyes glistened and she sniffed. "It went on for almost a year. My mother begged him to let Tatum switch schools, but he refused."

She cut herself off with a fist to her mouth.

My own lips pursed in a disapproving scowl.

Gabby picked up the narrative. "Her father wasn't going to pull his son out of the one and only elite academy where all the *mafie* kids were sent, no matter how much they tortured his son. It didn't stop until Alex came to Tatum's rescue."

"Alex?" I asked.

"Yup," confirmed Gabby. "He took Tatum under his wing, and they've been thick as thieves ever since. Of course, everyone fell in line after that and kept their vile opinions to themselves."

"When it came time to decide who would be his *consilier* after his father was killed alongside Gabby's father, who was Mihail's *consilier*," explained Star, giving Gabby's hand a squeeze, "there was no doubt it would be Tatum."

"That year of hell stuck with him," Star rattled on. "He's not married, and I think it's because he doesn't trust the other families. He trusts Alex and his brothers. Especially Luca. But that's it. He knows that, at some point, he has to marry a *mafie* girl, but whoever he marries will be the sister or cousin of one of his past tormentors, and that vexes him."

Oh, wow. I did not expect to hear such a heartrending backstory. It explained why a man as handsome and powerful as Tatum remained unmarried, why he laughed off the many girls who tried to catch his attention and flirt with him. He knew the underbelly of every one of those girls' families.

My phone rang. I flipped it over and saw my father calling. He only contacted me during the day if it had to do with family business. I took the call out in the hallway and came back in when I was finished.

When I returned, Gabby resumed our conversation by motioning to Star. "Tatum gets uptight when I mention his sister's future marriage. I mean, with turning eighteen soon, it's just around the corner, but whenever I bring it up, his face screws up really tight like he's sucked on a lemon."

My stomach swooped low as a realization dawned on me. Shame burned my cheeks.

"I taunted and attacked him like those bullies did," I confessed.

Gabby's eyes grew wide. "No—"

"No," exclaimed Star vehemently. "You're nothing like those bullies. It was different then. They took advantage of a sweet, kind, and helpless child. He's a man now. He can handle it. I'm not exaggerating when I tell you he can handle anything."

"You couldn't hurt him," Gabby chimed in.

My world stuttered to a stop as my past words reared

their ugly heads in my mind. Swallowing the burning guilt rising in my throat, my fingers blindly found the fake money and started fiddling with it. "You don't know how I treated him when he was in Los Angeles with Sebastian and Nicu. I was awful."

I felt the need to explain myself because it suddenly mattered what Star and Gabby thought of me. I liked them and I wanted them to like me back. I didn't want them to think that I'd been as bad as those childhood bullies.

"You have to understand," I pleaded. "My clan viewed the Lupu as a threat. Back in LA, I saw them as an invading force, a group of *mafie* men who came to take over what my father and clan had built with blood, sweat, and tears."

I blew out a breath, winded from explaining myself. It certainly wasn't a position I was used to being in, but I was trying my best. For these girls, I was willing to try.

"Do you trust them a little bit more now?" Gabby inquired.

Star interjected, "More to the point, do you trust Tatum more?"

"I do trust him more ... It's strange, I won't lie. I'm not used to being around strangers or trusting anyone outside of my clan. You know how it is," I responded with a shrug of my shoulders.

They grew up *mafie*, just like me. They'd been raised to fear strangers as much as I had. Growing up as we did, we knew the rest of the world hated us. If it wasn't another mafia or syndicate trying to take a piece of what was ours, it was the police and FBI trying to infiltrate our clans from ten different entry points. Despite it all, I had begun to trust Tatum and the Lupu women I'd met.

"We understand, believe us," Gabby said with a pat of my hand. "It was brave of you to come to New York by yourself, live with another family, and open yourself up to another clan. That's impressive."

I nodded solemnly. Of course, they didn't know I'd fought my father tooth and nail. I had only done it because it had been a direct order, and until recently, I'd been as close-minded as ever.

Honestly, getting to know the Lupu women is what did me in. Alex's mother and grandmother took me in as if I were their own flesh and blood, constantly fussing over me, giving me a taste of something I'd never had—female companionship. After my brother was born, my mother had stuck around for a few years, but she was a broken woman before she disappeared for good. After she left, I took up the mantle of woman of the house. I'd never had the kind of unconditional love Alex's and Tatum's relatives showed me. These women treated me like a daughter, and Star treated me like an older sister. I might be tough, but I wasn't a monster. I couldn't fight against the overwhelming feminine love they'd enveloped me in.

"You know ...," started Star. "I've never seen Tatum look at another woman the way he looks at you." She widened her eyes and pursed her lips together as if to say, "Do you know how significant that is?"

"I'm serious," she went on. "I'd never seen him look at another woman, period. And then the way he looks at you ... Whew. I wish a guy looked at me that way."

"Bitch, stop it. You're beautiful. One day, a man will look at you that way, believe me. It's going to happen," Gabby pronounced with determination.

Star waved her hand dismissively. "This isn't about me. This is about Clara and Tatum. Something's happening between them, even if they like to pretend it's nothing."

"Naughty of you to bring this up," I teased, gnawing on

my bottom lip. I'd been doing my utmost to resist Tatum, but it was getting increasingly harder. Hearing about his childhood split my chest into a chasm of compassion for him. The poor, struggling, browbeaten little boy who was clever enough to befriend the boss's kid and work his way to the top, pulling his family up with him.

"I'm serious," Star said. "There's no reason you and my brother shouldn't be together. People get trapped in arranged marriages with strangers, or worse, with people who are awful." Star's eyes darted to Gabby, whose face pinched. There was a story behind that.

"What I'm saying is that the two of you have more intimacy than most *mafie* couples have going into a marriage."

What I loved about Star was how she wore her emotions on her sleeve. I had to remind myself she was a young girlish romantic with stars in her eyes. Her beautiful, loving childhood allowed her to conjure up Disney-like fantasies about love and marriage.

I had the opposite. I'd seen my father work himself into the ground, seen it destroy his marriage, seen my mother bring treachery into our family. I'd been brought up knowing my place was at the head of my clan. In the world my father had forged for me, there was no place for anything beyond love of clan. Certainly not marriage. But I couldn't tell her that, could I? On the other hand, it was my duty to show her life for a *mafie* woman didn't automatically have to center around hearth and home.

"Do you know what my clan calls me?" I asked them, holding first Star's gaze and then Gabby's.

They shook their heads. Of course, they didn't know. Nothing existed beyond New York City for them.

"The Virgin Queen," I replied.

Their eyes grew wide.

"Want to know why?"

Oh, they were about to get the shock of their young lives.

I leaned in close and whispered as if I was about to tell them a coveted secret about life. In turn, they leaned in toward me.

"Because I am to become their *şef*."

Both their bodies reared back as if I'd slapped them.

"What?" they gasped in unison.

I lifted my gaze and stared at them smugly. Pride thrummed through every cell in my body. Although negligent in many ways, it was the one thing my father had done right. After taking care of the clan, what love and energy he had left for me as a little girl, he'd poured into forging me for this role. The neglect, the suffering of my mother's betrayal—all of it had culminated in the knowledge that I would one day rule. It would all be worth it once I became queen. It gave me a rush of power like nothing else in the world.

Nodding sagely, I confirmed, "That's right, I will be the first female *şef*. Once my father retires, I will lead my clan."

"But what will your husband do?" Gabby asked with an adorable, confused look on her face.

"I won't have a husband," I responded matter-of-factly.

"No husband," Star murmured in shock. "Like a vow of chastity?"

"Yes ... well, no. I didn't make a *vow*, but it's the one condition for holding the world in the palm of my hands, for having the honor of taking care of my family and my clan, and for earning the right to take over my father's kingdom. He came from a small city in Romania with nothing but the clothes on his back and a fire in his belly to become something in this country. He succeeded where so many have failed, and even now, people want to take what's his.

One day he will retire, and I will take over. Do you see why I have no time for things like love and marriage?"

"No, Tatum?" breathed Star.

"No, Tatum," I replied firmly. "No husband. No family."

For the first time in my life, saying those things soured my stomach. For the first time in my life, I wasn't proud. I wasn't anticipating that moment like I had for most of my life. I spoke with every intention of showing these girls how incredible and powerful my life would be, how I would change the world and leave a lasting impact. But I abruptly felt deflated, empty.

Star's nose wrinkled. "I don't understand. Why can't you be the boss and have a husband?"

I blinked at her. *Wasn't it obvious?*

"Because business and pleasure don't mix," I said, repeating the phrase my father had echoed throughout my life.

"Marriage is more than just pleasure. Pfft, from what I've seen, I'm not sure marriage has much pleasure in it," confessed Gabby. "Marriage is about ... Oh, I don't know, but if you're lucky, it's about companionship, partnership, children." She canted her head to the side. "Don't you want children?"

I swallowed hard. Of course, I wanted children. I loved little kids. I loved babies. I loved cuddling them, I loved the way they smelled, I loved their innocence and the way they turned to you with so much hope and conviction in their eyes. Conviction that you would take care of them, protect them, give them anything and everything they needed or wanted. But I knew I couldn't have everything. I couldn't have my clan and have babies, too.

"I have my brother," I blurted out. "That should be enough."

It wouldn't be enough, but it was the extent of what I was getting.

Star's mouth gaped open. "I love my brother, but he definitely wouldn't be enough for me."

I smiled. "Your brother isn't like my brother. My brother's on the spectrum. He will always need me, and I will always be there to take care of him."

"I get that," Gabby said reluctantly. "But do you really think you'll be satisfied? *Mafie* women are meant to have children. Don't you want to get pregnant and have a fun baby shower *and* also have a job? Your brother will always be part of your life, obviously, but can he take the place of an entire family? I don't know, but it seems like you'll be missing out. I'm only a silly teenager, so what do I know?"

Star snorted. "Don't underrate yourself like that, Gabby. You've never been silly and know more than the average teenager."

"Shush," Gabby said, sterner than I'd ever thought she could sound.

Yeah, there was definitely something going on there. I remembered when she'd confided in me about her hare-brained scheme to run away and escape the *mafie*. I didn't dwell on it because their lives were so circumscribed their chances of pulling off a Houdini escape were close to zero.

"I said it before, and I'll say it again. I've never seen Tatum look at other women the way he looks at you. I honestly don't see why you can't have everything, rule your clan, and have your own family. I mean, it would tear my heart apart to have my big brother move to Los Angeles, but I guess I could visit."

She stretched out her pale, bare arms and inspected them. "I could do with a nice tan."

I burst out in laughter. "What are you talking about? You're so ridiculous."

"I'm just saying if it makes him happy to be with you, then I'm willing to let him go so he can rule by your side in Los Angeles. He obviously can't stay here if you're going to be the queen of LA. Maybe there are some cute *mafie* boys out there. Let's face it, the boys in my school are stupid and full of themselves. I might do better looking in another gene pool, one that happens to be in sunny California."

Another peal of laughter escaped, and I clapped my hand over my mouth. "Sunny California is the best, but you're hilarious. I just said I was called the *Virgin* Queen. I'm pretty sure that means I have to stay a virgin."

Star scrunched up her cute nose in disgust. "Why? Simply because your father says so? You're supposed to be your own boss, Clara. You're going to represent a new kind of woman. You're going to be the role model of what women can be in our world. Why must you follow rules dictated by someone else? Don't simply follow your stodgy father and whatever stupid rules he's imposed on you. You're already breaking the mold. Why stop there? Create your own rules. Otherwise, you're no better than we are, allowing these old people to arrange our marriages and our lives for us."

I licked my suddenly parched lips. How was it possible for these two young, seemingly unworldly girls to tear down the scaffolding of my life with their innocently posed, yet deadly, questions? How? I thought with frustration because there was a throbbing, pounding unease building inside me.

"Yeah," interjected Gabby. "I don't quite understand the rationale behind you staying a virgin. First off, that doesn't fit with the values of our culture. *Mafie* women are *supposed* to get married and have families. If you're going to be a badass boss, then go all the way. Why hold yourself back over something that doesn't even make sense."

"Hear, hear! I second Gabby's suggestion. I say you do what you want. Rule your clan and get married to Tatum. See!" Star clapped her hands excitedly. "Problem solved!"

My mouth dropped open. Okay, now they were taking things a bit too far. I appreciated their enthusiasm over me becoming the first woman şef, but they were going off the rails with ideas about me having everything.

My family's history was a prime example of how you couldn't have everything.

"I can't have everything I want."

Star's eyebrows slashed down low.

"Why not?" she asked somewhat hostilely.

"Umm, because the world doesn't work that way," I replied in a somewhat defensive, high-pitched tone.

Suddenly, I saw the tide turning. I sensed my answer wasn't going to go down well.

I wasn't wrong.

Gabby jumped to her feet, fists slamming down on her hips, and asked irritably, "Why not?"

I licked my dry lips. When she asked in that challenging way, the question tumbled around in my head like tennis balls in a dryer. *Why not? Why not? Why not?*

Hedging, I said, "Because … it's … not expected of me?"

Okay, that was not the most convincing answer.

"Woman, you need to broaden the way you think," Star said in the tone of a woman with far more experience than her seventeen years. Perhaps she was mimicking her mom's tone or something.

"No, I'm serious, Clara. You blow our minds with the idea that a woman can become the şef of her own clan. You tell us that, oh, you can be the boss, but then you pull back and say, no, you can't have a husband. *Puh-lease.* That's scrambled logic. You can't stuff it back into the Pandora's box you've opened."

My expression shifted to a grimace as I contemplated her words. When she said it like that, it did sound illogical. This young, overprotected teenager, who'd seen nothing of life, called me out, and I had no good response. But they had a point. If I could become the leader of my clan, then I could get married and have a family. Sure, it wouldn't be easy, but with the right man, it was doable.

My father had imposed this rule out of fear, out of the desire to protect me, out of a drive for me to succeed. He'd been wounded by my mother. We'd both been burned. Besides giving me my brother, I loathed my mother for her weakness and duplicity. He also feared that if I got married to a *mafie* man, from either my clan or another clan— because several clans were vying to usurp our position—I would lose my power to my husband.

But there was nothing to fear from Tatum. He was *consilier* of the most powerful *mafie* family in the world, but he wasn't greedy. Part of my training as a boss was to learn how to read people. Yes, Tatum could be ambitious, but his ambitions were personal. He was ambitious for the safety of his family. He was ambitious for the happiness of his sister. But he was not ambitious to overthrow Alex or abandon him to start his own clan. No, I would've instantly recognized those kinds of ambitions.

Truth be told, if I were ever brave enough to have a man, Tatum would be perfect.

My heart sank.

My father's dictum wasn't only about protecting me from a grubby, greedy man.

Regardless of how tempting it was to buy into their argument, I had to be realistic. My mother's betrayal was living proof you couldn't have everything. If my father couldn't, and he was a man, how could I? If it was only a question of my father's stubbornness, I would figure out a way to have what I wanted once I became boss, but there was a greater existential question at stake.

I'd seen my family destroyed by my father's neglect, by my mother's subsequent infidelity. Their combined sins ripped our family to shreds, still reverberating through us years later.

No, there was no getting around it. I could become the Virgin Queen, but Tatum and me?

We'd never be together.

11

TATUM

Every powerful family had a *pied-de-terre* in Sunnyside, Queens, the hub of our *mafie* world. Everyone had a family member living in what was originally a small brownstone that had been expanded upon. In the most ostentatious cases, a family bought the buildings on either side of theirs and built a monstrosity of a McMansion.

The Lupu boys and I grew up in the houses where our women still remained, so we kept things humble. However, that didn't mean we didn't bling out in other ways.

Clara planned to shop for new clothes, and I had my heart set on lavishing her with everything under the sun. It took a bit of doing to convince Clara that I would not only be accompanying her but that I would be paying for every single item her dainty fingers touched. With Star's help, we eventually wore her down, and she ceded to my will.

We were on our way to our first stop, the Louis Vuitton store in Soho. It would be one of many stops today because I had every intention of draping my woman in the finest of everything, including lingerie.

I was biding my time, giving her the chance to get to know me, and myself the time to figure out my next move, but if sitting beside her in the Range Rover was any indication, I didn't think I'd be able to restrain myself for long. It had been hell sitting in front of Clara when I was trying to avoid her. Sitting beside her in the back was infinitely worse.

She was dressed in my sister's casual clothing again, and no lie, I enjoyed her looking so carefree and youthful. I knew where her tastes ran, and I wanted to encourage her toward softer and more feminine clothing. Ever since she left California, she toned down her structured suits, even though one would think they would fit better in the city than on the West Coast. It was as if she didn't feel the need to wear them here, away from her clan. After the hurricane, she didn't want to retrieve her clothing. Fair enough, but the dominant in me wanted to test her, to see if I could lead her toward clothing I chose.

I'd appointed a personal shopper to meet us at the store for backup. Sheyna was the go-to stylist everyone in the *mafie* world used because she could do everything from modern and cutting edge to classic and elegant. Or so my mother told me.

Clara was unusually quiet on the ride to Lower Manhattan, but she needed time to adjust and transition from hating me to accepting me and ultimately wanting me. The passion was always there between us, and hopefully, her suspicions of the Lupu clan, or at least of me, would dissipate over time.

The yellow taxi driver beside our car leaned on his horn as he cut us off and raced ahead, crossing a red light. Glancing over at Clara, I couldn't help but admire her. My gaze took in her smooth, creamy skin, her high cheekbones, and the elegant nose from which she liked to look down on me. I craved to lean over and bite her bee-stung lips.

Her crisp, summery scent drifted over me, and I had to fist my hands to stop myself from reaching across and mauling her. I was a man of control and restraint. Or so I thought until Clara came into my life. Even when we were at each other's throats, sexual tension was thrumming between us and upended my self-possession in ways I never thought possible.

The car stopped, and I ducked out to go around and open her door myself. Extending a hand, I waited to see how she would react. She paused, threw me a suspicious look, and ever so warily placed her hand in mine. Her delicate fingers wrapped around my grip, and damn, did it feel good. Her willingness to let me touch her, to guide her out of the car, was a silent opening, and I'd make sure to repeat it every chance I got.

We reached the storefront and she immediately dropped my hand, but those extra moments when her hand was protectively wrapped in mine had my chest puffing with pride.

I opened the door for her, but her head swung to the side. Her eyes narrowed slightly as she spotted something halfway down Greene Street, a row of ornate cast-iron façades from an assorted mix of neo-Grec, Italianate, Renaissance Revival buildings. Pivoting to the side, she strode away from me.

"Hey," I shouted, but she dismissed me and streaked across the cobblestone street, dashing between cars.

I cursed as I shot after her.

Leave it to Clara to abandon whatever plans I had for her and go off on her own.

She skipped up a few stairs, ducked under a fire escape,

and slipped through a large door of a funky Soho clothing boutique. I didn't recognize the name.

Huffing in irritation, I followed her inside. It was a huge sleek space with a few island displays and one wall lined up with racks holding a minimal amount of clothes. Crossing the glossy, black flooring, I stalked up to Clara, who was already sifting through one rack.

Grabbing her arm, I said, "Don't run away from me without even letting me know where you're going. Follow instructions. Why are you so difficult?"

Over her shoulder, she tossed out, "I wasn't running from you."

I shook my head. "You literally ran across the street."

She gave a little shrug and muttered a half-assed apology before tacking on, "You're so controlling."

"This isn't a top-of-the-line fashion house and I had a personal shopper meeting us at the Louis Vuitton store."

She made a scoffing sound, taking a dress off the rack. "You're such a snob. Anyway, I'm a grown woman. I don't need help shopping. I have my suits handmade for me from Savile Row in London. If I go shopping in New York, the whole point is to wander around and find interesting treasures on my own, not go to the same old boring designers I can find in Los Angeles and Paris. Chanel, Dior, Louis, Hermes. Boring, boring, and boring."

I grimaced. "What the hell are you talking about? That's what every *mafie* woman wants to wear."

"Maybe I don't want what *every mafie* woman wears. Have you seen what I wear? Do I look like I dress like them?"

"No," I said with a snort. "Only woman I know who wears suits."

She stopped rifling through the clothing, turned to face me, and cocked a hip. "Exactly. I want something different."

Huh, that sounded promising. She seemed to be doing exactly what I wanted her to do. Of course, she ran away from me and didn't go about it the way I'd planned, but Clara was nothing if not spirited and single-minded. Hopefully, the day would come when she'd give me permission to dictate what she wore. I glanced down at the dress she'd picked. It was a slinky, silky-looking number. I'd appreciate seeing her in something like that, and if she was naturally inclined to switch it up, then I'd take it as a win.

"So, you're looking for different things to wear," I confirmed.

She gave me a look as if I was an idiot, tapped her foot, and said, "Uh, yeah. Is that a problem for you, Daddy?"

I bit back a groan and took a step away from her before I grabbed her in public. Lifting my hands up, I said, "Nope. Carry on."

"Oh goodie, I really needed your approval on this," she said, sarcasm lacing her tone.

Pointing to an armless lime-green chair, I said, "Just ... don't run off. I'm in charge of your safety."

"Sure, Daddy," she said. I didn't know if she was innocently using the phrase or messing with me, but one day soon, I swore I'd have her calling me Daddy for all the right reasons.

A salesperson approached Clara and, after a brief discussion, went into action, swooping items into her arm for Clara to try.

I took a seat in the ugly, yet surprisingly comfortable, seat and an employee approached me to ask if I wanted anything to drink. Lounging back in the chair, I couldn't tear my gaze off Clara as I absently ordered a cappuccino. I didn't expect them to know how to prepare Turkish coffee.

We made no sense together. Our lives didn't fit, either with our respective clans or with her future plans. Then there was the pesky little problem of my life-defying secret. I had no business taking on a wife, but I couldn't deny how good it felt to have her living under my roof.

Her nightmares had faded away, but I still spent a couple hours in her room each night, watching over her as she slept. I should be concerned about my mental health because I'd never done something like that before, but I didn't care. Now that I had her near me, I didn't know how I would live without her.

The woman returned with my drink and tried pulling my attention off Clara to flirt with me. Was it not obvious I was here with a woman? Annoyed, I was about to put her in her place when I saw Clara glare in our direction.

Ahh, now this was an interesting development. Deciding to test her, I initiated a conversation with the salesgirl.

"What's your name, angel?" I asked.

Inwardly, I rolled my eyes while maintaining the ruse of being vaguely interested in her.

"Samantha," she quickly replied.

"How long have you worked here, Samantha?" I asked.

Seriously, I couldn't care less, but I was quite enjoying Clara's attention, who'd stopped in the middle of sifting through a row of hanging shirts to toss us a ferocious scowl.

"Going on three years," she answered breathlessly.

Clara's face got pinched, lips pressed into a flat line. Watching from my side-eye, I noticed she was distracted, ignoring the salesperson, and grabbing random items of clothing, absently piling them in her arms. Another employee walked up to her and tried to unburden her of her clothing, but too absorbed in following me, Clara hugged them to her chest protectively. Realizing I caught her distress, she spun on her heel and stalked off to the dressing rooms at the back of the store.

I stifled a laugh. Shaking my head, I took off after my woman. It was a cruel joke on my part, especially since things were not yet settled between us. I shouldn't have done it, but it was hard to break the habit of taunting her, especially when I was aching for her so damn badly.

Reaching the dressing room, I called out, "Clara, let me see what you've chosen."

The curtain was jerked open roughly, material swirling in the air. Her elegant fingers clutched it in a death grip. She glowered up at me and jeered, "I'm surprised you even noticed I was gone. What do you want?"

As always, she was glorious in her fury, and my cock stirred in response. I mean, how could I not respond to this woman with her blazing eyes and flaming cheeks?

I stepped right up to her, toe to toe, and backed her into the small room. I snapped the curtain shut, enclosing us in the tight space of the dressing room. Her spine hit the mirror. Caging her in, I slapped a hand beside her head and leaned in until her short puffs of breaths fanned over my cheek.

"I'm aware of every move you make, sweetheart. You think it's a good idea to challenge me in public when you know how hard it makes me?" I asked rhetorically.

"I know nothing of the kind," she retorted. She lifted her chin at a haughty angle, but her chest rose and fell rapidly, giving her away. Yeah, she was as aroused as I was.

"Stop pretending, Clara. It's beneath someone as strong as you. I thought I made my position clear, but let me reiterate it, just in case you missed it the first time. Any day. Any time. You name it, and I'll do whatever you want to your tight little body."

Before she could reply with a comeback that would make me lose all semblance of control, I ran my thumb over her pouty bottom lip. Since the hurricane, she didn't wear any makeup. Nothing more than a swipe from a tube of lip gloss.

Her mouth popped open in shock. I didn't know why she seemed so surprised. Wasn't I clear enough? Maybe words weren't enough. Maybe she needed me to demonstrate my intentions. If it was solid proof she needed, I was up for the task.

Groaning deep in my chest, I felt the demon thrashing inside me, fighting me to get out. For a brief moment, he escaped his bars, jumped on my shoulders, and lashed my sides like a bull, spurring me on. Only with her did I lose control so thoroughly.

I sealed my lips over hers. Clara tasted clear and clean, just like her name. Kissing her was like sunning on a beach: sun, heat, sand, and wind combined to create the perfect summer day.

In my world of darkness, violence, sin, and secrets, she tasted like light, peace, purity, and truth.

She tasted like everything I wasn't.

A low moan vibrated from the base of her throat, getting louder by the second. I pressed closer, her curves melding against the ridges of my hard muscles. Clara was taller than average, but I dwarfed her. My hands touched every inch I could. Her tits, her hips, her ass, her pussy. I was a fucking octopus, all eight tentacles on the loose. Jesus. Any other *mafie* woman her age would've freaked out by now. But not my Clara.

Our mouths dueled, and she gave as good as she got. Her

own hands got busy, shoving my jacket off my shoulders, raking down the fine weave of my shirt, sharp nails leaving tracks. She yanked at my tie.

She raked her teeth over my lower lip, broke off our kiss, and murmured, "I hate this tie. Such an ugly color on you."

I laughed, a hearty, full sound that shook my entire chest. This. Woman. So demanding. So strong. So vocal. I loved everything about her. Even in the middle of a passionate kiss, our second one, she cut it off to express her disapproval. She'd be so much fun to play with in the special ways I liked to play.

I sank my fingers into the thick mane of her hair and hauled her head back. "Shut up and let me kiss you."

Her eyes flickered closed for an instant. A shiver coursed through her body.

Her lashes batted open, and she halted me with her hand on my chest. "What about that bitch outside?"

I almost broke into a smile but pulled it back in the last second. "What about her?"

"You were flirting with her," she spat out.

"Only to test you," I admitted.

"That's not a nice thing to do," she said with a pout.

"I'm not a nice guy. Don't mistake me for one. Once you're mine, I'll treat you like gold. Submit to me and I'll worship you like a queen. But beautiful, don't foolishly think I won't play dirty to get what I want. If I hadn't made it clear before, what I want is you."

I moved to take her mouth again, but her palms on my chest kept me at bay. "Why, Tatum?"

She gestured outside the dressing room. "You could have any woman you want, including the one outside. Why me?"

Her eyes were suddenly bleak. What the hell happened?

One second, I was fucking her mouth with my tongue, and the next, she was pulling away from me.

My gaze bored into hers.

I realized this was a serious moment. This was important. While it was obvious to me that I'd fallen into a full-blown obsession, she needed to hear the words, and I wasn't about to screw it up.

"Because you're gorgeous," I declared. "Because a smart, stubborn woman with a sharp tongue turns me on. But most importantly, because you're strong. Only a strong woman can handle a man like me. You're too strong for your own good, and I like that even more. To be a power player, you'll need a strong man at your back. Turns out, we're a perfect fit because I need to be needed. When it gets to be too much for you, that's where I come in. I'll take care of you, baby girl, in ways you'll learn to crave. I *see* exactly what you need, and I *know* I'm the only man who can give it to you."

Her brows gathered. "You're talking in riddles." She shook her head. "You're not making any sense."

I sighed. I didn't want to get into this conversation here, in a semi-public space. I'd already come to terms with the fact that I was going to be the man to take her virginity. After months of foreplay founded on hate, I was done fighting, but I'd hoped to ease her into such a serious conversation. My plan was to make her come on my cock, and when she was limp in my arms, easing off her high and reveling in her afterglow, I'd approach this discussion.

Leave it to Clara to jump the timeline and go straight for the jugular. However, there was no throwing her off once she caught the scent of something. I'd have to get used to thinking on my feet around this woman. Conveniently, it was one of the things I loved about her.

I touched my forehead to hers and elucidated, "I'm talking about kink."

Her eyes flared wide. I could see the splinters of jade green receding from the blue. I hoped she had a big dick kink because she was going to have to manage that as well once I had her stripped bare and underneath me, ready to take me fully.

"I'm talking about the fact that I see you as you are in your truest form. You need a man who will walk one step behind you in public, but in private? In private, you need the exact opposite. Behind closed doors, you'll thrive under the rule of a man who takes control, makes the decisions, gives the commands. You need a man who will take care of things and one who knows how to wallop your ass when you're acting like a brat because you're overwhelmed by your responsibilities. I've ruled alongside Alex for over a decade, Clara. I know what your life will become once your father steps down. You need a special environment to relax and recoup, and I'm the man who can provide it for you."

She gasped. "H-how do you know about my father's plans for me?"

I huffed out a soft laugh. It wasn't the talk of kink or dominance that disturbed her, but what I knew about her father.

"I'm the Lupu *consilier*. I know everything there is to know about any clan from here to China and back."

Her eyes narrowed in suspicion. "Is that why you were so determined to have me come to New York, to butter me up because you knew that my father intends to hand the clan over to me?"

My face hardened. I gave her a forbidding look. I was insulted by her suggestion that my motivations weren't pure, but I saw her accusation for what it was. An excuse to pull away from me. I felt the irritation rising, but I locked it down. Clara would always be a handful. It was what I loved about her, and it only gave me an opportunity to hone my skills when it came to her. A challenge? With my little quee-nie, I was more than up for it. Time to give her a taste of the control I'd referred to earlier.

My hand wrapped around her throat, tightening, and pressed her into the mirror. A big man like me, making a move like that, would scare the average woman, but Clara's expression didn't change. If anything, the fact that she sunk her teeth into her bottom lip was a sign of lust.

"Listen, I'm not going to talk about business with you right now. This conversation is about you and me. Us. About how I'm going to fuck you hard when you need it and smack your ass harder when you need that. I'm also going to lavish my attention on you and this sweet pussy. Baby doll, I'm going to spoil you rotten, and you're going to love it," I promised darkly.

Her gaze shifted away from mine. "H-how do you know what I need?"

"Because it's my job to know. A man with my specific tastes, in the world we live in, has to be careful. You know how nosy and judgmental the *mafie* are. What we have between us, stays between us. If the vanilla world can barely understand, do you think the *mafie* world can? Nah-ah. They're even more traditional and conservative."

"Is that why you're not married?"

I gently tightened my grip around her throat. "One of many reasons. I'm a complicated man, Clara. I see your brilliant mind clicking away, trying to figure me out. I promise you, there's no way you can comprehend the extent of who I am in a few minutes or even a few days. You need to commit to me. Submit to me first. Then, I'll open myself up to you," I counseled her.

"I don't trust you enough to submit," she whispered over my lips.

My jaw muscle ticked at her admission. I wanted her heart instantly, but I, better than anyone, knew how to work hard to get want I wanted. On the positive side, she hadn't dismissed the idea out of hand, which meant that she was aware of that side of her, even if she'd never had a chance to act on it until now. I liked the idea that I'd pop her cherry in every way imaginable, from her first kiss to fucking her ass.

"I'm sorry. I'm only being honest," she murmured, her eyes downcast.

"Hey." I lifted her chin until her gaze was back on me. "I appreciate the honesty. Not used to it, but I appreciate it."

I moved my hand to clasp her nape while the other slipped down her torso, under her shirt, and over her bra-clad breast.

Thrumming her nipple, I said, "I'm going to show you that you can trust me. You just have to start by giving in a little bit."

"But I can't get married," she exclaimed.

I stifled a groan. Leave it to a *mafie* girl to go from point A straight to marriage.

"Let me worry about that, sweetness. We'll cross that bridge when we get to it. Let's take things one step at a time."

"But it can't happen—"

I squeezed her nape, cutting her off. Good girl, she was a natural at responding to my unspoken demands.

"Listen to me," I said again to get her attention. "I know it's not how you were raised to think, but let's put that aside for now. Why don't we try things like normal couples and get to know each other first?"

Her eyes blew wide with trepidation, but she slowly nodded her acquiescence. A wave of triumph cascaded over me. It was a huge win, considering the culture she'd been brought up in.

I had no idea how this was going to work. Between her father's demands, her future responsibilities, my allegiance to Alex, and the secrets that bound me to him, Clara and I were a failure waiting to happen. For once, I didn't care. I didn't give a fuck. For once, I wanted something, and I was going to take it. Just like a Lupu would.

I was done talking. It was time to show her what I was made of, and more importantly, it was time I leave my mark on her. There was no way I was introducing her to my cock immediately, and especially not here. It was a moment to build up to, but at least I could implement step one of my plan to get her addicted to me: fuck her with my tongue.

12

CLARA

He was done talking. I could tell by the look on his face. Tatum had turned all growly, pressing into me until there wasn't a shred of space between us. He was aroused, that much was clear by the feel of his cock against my abdomen. It felt thick and hard, and my belly fluttered in response. I'd never been this close to a man's cock before. I'd seen it, big and long, pressing against the zipper of his slacks, but I never knew for sure whether I was the reason for his arousal.

His heat and strength enveloped me, his thick fingers scraped along the skin of my throat, exciting me. Arching my back, I rubbed my hard nipples against the fine cotton of his shirt, luxuriating in feeling his chiseled muscles beneath. His jacket was already off, laying abandoned somewhere on the floor of the dressing room.

I clawed at his tie until it joined his discarded jacket.

I took a deep breath of his scent, reveling in his unique fragrance of sin, darkness, and violence. As in the wild, the lizard brain instantly recognized his scent, blaring out *danger, danger, incoming predator*. There was a seething monster roiling beneath the tailored, refined mask he wore, and it called to me. A part of me wanted to run so he could catch me. Run me to ground, get his claws in me, drag me to his lair, and do wicked things to me.

He proved me right because the first thing he did was twist my locks around his fist, yank my hair back, and sink his teeth into the juncture between my throat and shoulder.

Like a mating alpha beast, he claimed me.

Ouch, it stung! I bit my bottom lip to stifle my cry, but then his tongue was out, laving and soothing it better.

"Get used to my marks on you, little girl. Not one day will pass when you're not sporting black and blues from my mouth and hands," he warned.

Fuck, that was hot. My panties stuck to the cleft of my pussy. All from his words and a little love bite.

"I already know no one's touched this pussy," he mused.

"You don't know that," I taunted between pants because, yes, I was outright panting by now. It was a little dig to get him back for flirting in front of me earlier.

His head snapped back, black eyes slitted like a snake's.

"The fuck you say?"

He'd cursed.

Good, his control was slipping.

I strained against him, but his fingers repositioned over my throat and tightened.

I squirmed to get away, knowing he'd like my little game. God knew I liked it.

A snarl rumbled from his chest.

"You heard me," I rasped.

He pressed his hips into me, pinning me in place, and pressed threats against my mouth—quiet assaults against my lips. "Anyone touches you, and I will sever his hand from his body. Anyone kisses you, and I will surgically remove his lips from his face."

I was truly sick because his words made me groan, made me grind my wet pussy against the underside of his cock. His hand slipped between us. His fingers pressed deep into my entrance, the heel of his hand abrading my clit.

"This pussy is as pure as the day you were born," he intoned. "When I burst through the final barrier and stamp the imprint of my cock inside you, you will be mine in every way that counts. I suggest you don't tempt me to stretch your cunt open and smear your cherry on my cock right here and now. Even if they tear this curtain open while I'm balls deep inside you, I won't stop. Don't doubt it, I'm a fucking savage."

"I dare you," I hissed back at him.

Losing my virginity to a man like Tatum in a dressing room sounded like a fine idea to me. I wasn't sentimental. I didn't need flowers and candlelight to fuck, even for the first time.

But I couldn't lose my virginity. Remember the stakes. My father, my clan, my crown—*fuck it all*—I wanted this, I wanted *him*. I wanted to feel what it was like to have Tatum take me, use me, treat me like his precious princess and his dirty little slut at the same time. It would be worth defying my father this one time. Then I'd hide it and pretend it never happened.

He threw his head back and laughed. "Damn, you're precious. But I'm not going to be manipulated by a little girl like you. I'll fuck you when I'm damn well ready, and I can assure you it won't be in the back of a Soho store."

Releasing my throat, he dropped to his knees. "But I will give you something to remember me by."

Startled by his sudden change in position, I grabbed hold of his shoulder to steady myself. I was confused. What was he doing? No, he couldn't be—

Leaning forward, he took a strong whiff of me as if catching the scent of my pussy. Oh my God. My face flushed hot. Images of internet porn flashed in my mind. Assuming I'd never experience this for myself, I was salivating at the bit to have it happen. Even so, it was unnerving because I never imagined a *mafie* man doing it. It seemed unthinkable that these conservative, old-fashioned, macho men would. Then again, Tatum was different.

"Pull your pants down, gorgeous. Let me get to that pussy. I'll love it and lick it until I have you creaming around my tongue," he promised.

I blinked down at him. Strands of hair were sticking up here and there from when I'd mussed it up earlier, ruining his perfect hairstyle.

He lifted his face to me, eyes a shiny jet black, glowing with animalistic lust.

His lips twisted to the side, and he promised hotly, "Brace yourself because you're about to get the tongue lashing of your life."

Without giving me a chance to reply, he ripped the capri pants down my legs. Then he tore my panties right off me, the sound of rending silk reverberating through the air.

My hands landed on his head, twisting his short locks between my fingers. His hair felt so soft, such a contrast to the man kneeling before me.

His fingers touched my dripping sex and I jolted against them. Undeterred, he pressed inside. I was soaking wet, and he had just two of them inside me, but I already felt the burn.

"Christ, you're tight." He chuckled. "Baby, no cock has

been inside this snug channel. I was right, you're as pure as the day you were born."

"Shut up," I muttered.

"Oh, I'm not shutting up for anything. Can't wait to have you on my cock, wiggling and trying to take me whole. Baby, I'm big. It's going to be a struggle to take my entire cock in this tight hole. Even if it hurts, take it you will, because my woman is going to learn to take my cock."

"I'm not your woman," I countered, the thrill of defying him keeping me on the edge.

Oh, he didn't like that one bit. Searing me with a look that could kill, he was about to fire back a retort when I squirmed around his two thick digits, spearing me, invading me, and he got distracted. Resting his cheek against my thigh, he shut his eyes and inhaled deeply, savoring the moment.

Turning his head slightly, he nuzzled my wet pussy.

Oh God, oh God, oh God.

The tip of his nose played with my clit, his lips dropping light kisses on the seam of my pussy. His tongue snaked out to lick the length of me. My knees buckled, and I let out a little scream.

"That's right. Scream my name, Clara. When you come, I want to hear my name dropping from those pouty lips," he demanded.

I shuddered as he leaned in and licked again. He hooked one of my legs over his broad shoulder, spread me open, and went in for the kill. Licking, sucking, and lapping away, he ate me out. And the slurping. My belly flexed, my thighs trembled, my pussy shuddered and clenched, and I started riding his mouth. But undeterred, he kept going with single-minded determination.

Humming into my pussy, he clipped my clit between his

front teeth and sucked it. I stiffened, at the same time as tremors convulsed through my body and I broke apart. My pussy fluttered around his fingers and tongue. I yanked his hair as I fought the wave of sensations pounding through my body. I heard nothing, saw nothing, swept away in the rapids of an exquisite climax.

Delirious in the throes of pleasure, I screamed his name so loud, there was no doubt everyone in the shop heard.

He chuckled against my clit.

"Nah, that wasn't God. That was me."

Oh, no. I said that out loud?

"Yup, you did."

I did it again.

"Yes, you did."

I slapped a hand over my mouth.

He laid his head on my inner thigh and took a bite. His second mark.

"Don't silence yourself. I like to hear you scream my name when you come."

He licked one last time, causing more tremors and goose bumps to burst over my skin.

"That was delicious," he mused, licking the wetness smeared around his mouth. "You taste so fucking *good*."

I stared at him, wide-eyed, as stunned as a deer in oncoming traffic, breathing as if I'd run a marathon.

And then my phone rang.

I jolted in place. Stumbling, I pulled my leg off Tatum's shoulder and tumbled to the floor. On my knees, I scrambled for my purse. Naked from the torso down, my ass was up in the air as I dug around for my phone. He gave my pussy a few smart pats and squeezed one buttock. I stuttered out a breath of surprise.

I shot a look over my shoulder but froze when I again saw his wet, smirking mouth. Jesus, nothing was sexier than when a man's face was coated with your juices.

Wiping his mouth with the back of his hand, he said, "Better get that," and stepped outside to give me privacy as I tugged my capris on with one hand and swiped my phone open with the other.

"Clara," came the male voice.

My heart jangled in my chest. I wheezed. Damn, I should've checked the number before picking up.

"Grigore?" I croaked out, my throat suddenly parched.

"How are those motherfuckers treating you?" he asked.

I cleared my throat and rasped out, "Fine."

"Can you talk?" he demanded.

"Yeah. How are things at home?"

"Good, good. Listen, I have some interesting news. I've been digging around for info on the Lupu bastards. It's the least I can do since they're doing the same to us. It's a fucking vault with every single one of those fuckers in New York."

My mind was reeling, but I winced at his coarseness. Tatum rarely cursed, and only when he lost control, which only made it sexy as hell.

"One thing I did learn about that insufferable, stuck-up prick, Tatum, was that he's a fucking *corcitură*, a gypsy half-breed," he spat out.

"Grigore," I chided, my heart tearing in two at hearing him insult the man who had been on his knees, tongue in my pussy, only a few moments before. "That's way out of line."

I imagined his face when he realized what he'd said to me, a woman. For obvious reasons, I rarely brought attention to that fact, and he often let loose with his colorful language, but every once in a while, I called him out on his coarseness. This wasn't simply vulgar, it was outright wrong.

There couldn't be a greater contrast than between Grigore and Tatum. He had his uses, but I was nothing more than a means to an end to Grigore. He knew of my father's plans, of course, and wanted me to take over so he could rule on my behalf. His motives were transparent.

In contrast to Grigore, Tatum seemed entirely disinterested in my position. I never saw the glint of greed in his eyes like I did with Grigore. Or rather, I did, but it was a greed of an entirely different type. Tatum watched me like he wanted to fuck me into oblivion, like he wanted to devour me whole. The hunger emanated from him in waves. In one way, Tatum was a scarier prospect because he didn't want my power or future position. He wanted to own *me*. The temptation, of course, would be that he had the power to make submission taste oh so delicious.

"Couldn't get much out of them," continued Grigore. "So I moved on to the other mafias in New York. I've been fucking with the Bratva—"

"You shouldn't do that, Grigore," I interceded, shimmying my hips as I yanked at the waistband of the capris. "If Alex ever finds out—"

"Don't worry about me. I'm not afraid of those fucking assholes. I'm not blood bonded to them, like the Popescus. Turns out they're no better than mongrels, either."

Grigore was furious that the Popescu *şef* went into partnership with the Lupu clan after the death of his nephew, Simu. Simu wasn't just any old clan member, either. He was the Popescu *consilier*, but he died at the hands of Luca, and we later found out, Nicu. Before New York, I saw them as brutes who killed another clan's *consilier* in cold blood. Now, I knew there had to be more to the story. The Lupu men respected power; they were not impulsive, trigger-happy thugs. They wouldn't have killed a *consilier* without provocation. Something happened to make Simu's death an absolute necessity.

"I'm going to find out every dirty little secret this pit of vipers they call a clan has, and once I do, we'll have every reason to turn our backs on them permanently. They will learn to fear the name Hagi, but you must stay strong, Clara. I'm sure they're doing everything in their power to dupe you into thinking they're civilized. Believe me, they're anything but. Don't get conned by these fuckers. You have your clan to rule here. They are the only ones who deserve your loyalty. Your *undying* loyalty."

"Okay," I breathed out because what could I do? I couldn't tell my father's *consilier*, *my* soon-to-be *consilier*, that I'd just hooked up with the enemy. Grigore talked a big game, and he wasn't just talk. He was a cunning, shrewd man, and his digging made me nervous.

Glancing around the dressing room, I spotted my panties and stuffed them in my handbag as the ghost of Tatum's tongue lingered on my clit.

It was only much later, while lying in bed at Tatum's house late at night, that I realized Tatum hadn't batted an eyelash at the notion of a woman taking over a *mafie* clan. His remark about walking a step behind me in public but taking care of my needs in private, looped over and over in my head. He'd put into words a life I hadn't dared hope for and then added fuel to the fire with his claim that he'd take care of needs I didn't even know I had.

I'd never met a *mafie* man like Tatum before—one who

so easily accepted every aspect of me, and there were many. His wholehearted acceptance was almost frightening. Hope was scary for someone like me. I might be young, but I'd seen how the world worked, and in my experience, if it seemed too good to be true, it usually was.

13

TATUM

Clara fiddled with the hem of a slinky new shirt showcasing her breasts in a way that left me salivating.

Glancing up at me briefly, apprehension lined her forehead as she cautiously suggested, "You can leave, you know. Go back to your penthouse in Manhattan. We'll be fine. We lived here alone before the hurricane, without a man to protect us, and we survived. The threat is over."

Eyes darting to mine, she trailed off at the scowl on my face, not daring to finish her thought.

Smart girl.

She might be brave, but she wasn't stupid, and she promptly realized her comment was a provocation. I heard the caution in her tone, and she was right to be wary because she had to know that I would hate what she was doing. She was retreating, backtracking, running away.

A snarl vibrated in the base of my throat, and I made no attempt to suppress it for her benefit. The sooner she accepted who I was, who we were together, the better off we would be.

After I went down on her and ate her cunt to my heart's content yesterday, I heard her talking to Grigore in the dressing room.

Ever since, she'd been distant, avoiding me to the point where I had to deliberately stop by her bedroom at the end of the day.

I leveled a glare at her that had her eyes slipping away from mine. She took a step back, putting more distance between us.

Good, my ego was slightly appeased by her fear. It was strong enough I could scent it in the air.

"Over my dead body," I jeered, softly closing the door of her bedroom behind me. The place was a wreck with clothes strewn over every surface imaginable. There was a pile of silky lingerie piled high on top of her nightstand that distracted me for a moment.

She wasn't intentionally taunting me, I knew, even though bringing up the hurricane ripped the fresh wound wide open again, reminding me how close she'd been to getting hurt. If I'd been doing my job as *consilier* instead of letting my emotions get in the way, Clara would've already been living with Mama. Instead, I'd been more than happy to fob her off to Alex's mother. Once the hurricane warnings sounded, I should've immediately gone to my mother's house. At least then, I would've been close by to retrieve Alex's relatives and Clara.

After the fear and terror I'd lived through, nothing on God's green earth could drag me away from her or my family.

Getting into her space, I bent my head and growled into her ear, "You should've been in my house, sleeping naked in my bed, not in Alex's mother's house being rattled around like a rag doll by a tornado."

"I hated you," she shot back. "I wouldn't have stayed at your place, much less in your bed."

"You think I would've given you a choice?" I admonished. By now, the tension was hot like a live wire, snapping and hissing between us. I was close to the edge of snapping myself.

"I wouldn't have slept with you, Tatum, so I most certainly would not have been 'in your bed,'" she finished with air quotes, twitching her shoulders for good measure.

Dear God, this woman tested my patience.

And I loved it.

I gave her my most arrogant smirk. "Who said there would've been any sleeping, sweetness?"

"Oh my God. You're incorrigible," she said, her voice tight with fury.

I took a step back and leaned against the door of her room.

"You'd be in my bed," I said matter-of-factly, crossing my arms over my chest. Her gaze shot to my biceps stretching the fine Egyptian cotton of my dress shirt. "Even if I slept in the guest bedroom, you would've been writhing that tight, hot little body between *my* sheets. Touching your sweet puss in *my* bed."

"I doubt it. I didn't like you," she persisted.

I heard the past tense. I *didn't* like you, not I *don't* like you. I grinned down at her scowling face. Yup, definitely past tense. Even in the middle of fighting me, she couldn't deny the change in her feelings toward me.

Pushing myself off the door jamb, I twisted the lock. It resounded loudly in the silence lying heavy between us.

Approaching her, I said, "Is this how you want to play it? Want me to show you what I would've done to ensure your place in my bed, legs spread-eagle for me, my tongue *deep* into your sugarcoated pussy?"

She threw her palm up to ward me off. I barreled down on her. Forcing her to fall back on her bed, I leaned in and caged her in my arms.

"You think it's a good idea to test me when I'm on the edge like this?"

"I-I don't know what you're talking about," she stammered. "The hurricane was days ago. You're not on edge."

"It's as raw as if it were yesterday," I bit out.

"I'm not your charge," she protested.

"Like hell you're not. You're perfect and you're mine, Clara. Mine from the hair on the top of your head to the tip of your painted toenails. *Fucking* mine."

She shook her head in denial, her chest rising and falling like an overactive bellows.

I gnashed my teeth at her. "Do you understand?"

Her wet, pink lips parted. Her eyes dilated with excitement and a bite of fear.

"No," she denied.

Her teeth pressed down on the plump flesh of her bottom lip. She was testing me.

And I snapped.

Her palm made contact with my chest, but I pushed it down, crushing it between our bodies.

I slanted lips over hers. I curled my fingers around her jaw, forcing her mouth open. My tongue swept in like a marauding crusader and conquered her candy-tasting mouth.

Groaning, I inhaled her like she was my next breath.

Her crushed hand pressed into my solar plexus.

"Don't," she pleaded, breaking our third kiss.

I ignored her and swept in again. My tongue

unearthed places unknown, like a discoverer staking a flag on new land. She tasted like pure sugar melting in the sunshine.

Our fourth kiss.

I was keeping count.

Moaning into my mouth, Clara went pliant beneath me. Her tongue tentatively sought mine. She was hesitant, and I hated that after the passionate kiss we'd shared yesterday. At the same time, her timid innocence was seductive. I restrained myself, giving her the space she needed to come back to me. With time, she grew bolder, becoming more daring with each swipe of her tongue.

A needy little mewl came out as she strained to get closer to me. Her breasts pressed into my chest, her hand was still caught between us. Her hips twitched against mine, rubbing against my cock. Her taste engulfed my brain, leaving me light-headed.

Suddenly, she ripped her mouth from mine.

Wiggling underneath me, she begged, "I'm a virgin."

Of course, she was, but the fact that she felt the need to state it was equivalent to a confession. She knew where this was going as much as I did.

"Not for long," I promised, dropping kisses along her jaw and down her throat. It wasn't happening now, especially when I hadn't even introduced her to my cock, but it was happening.

She stiffened underneath me and shoved hard. "No, it can never happen."

Maintaining our closeness, I murmured against her lips, "What the hell are you talking about? You'll get married one day." *To me.* "You'll have children." *Again, mine.* "You'll grow old with grandchildren." *Alongside me.*

"You don't understand," she said, twisting her face away

from mine. "I can never lose my virginity. Never marry. Never have children."

I brought my head up. My brows furrowed. "You're not making sense."

Our society was based on family, if only to breed men for killing and women for bearing children. The idea of a princess like Clara never marrying was preposterous.

Pressing her lips together in a tight line, she shook her head in denial.

Showing great restraint, I moved off her. Taking a seat beside her, I pulled her up and into my lap. Her plump ass nestled against my hard cock, giving me the worst case of blue balls, but this was important. Luckily, restraint was my thing.

"Explain yourself," I demanded.

She didn't push me away or try to scramble off my lap, which pleased me, but a dark flush crept up her neck. A neck I wanted to leave a hundred marks on, to prove to her and the world she was mine. Only mine. All mine.

She swallowed. "I can't lead the Hagi clan unless I remain a virgin. It's why my people call me the Virgin Queen."

My mouth parted in shock. This was outright madness. Sure, I'd heard the nickname, but I'd assumed it was because, at twenty-one, she was still unmarried. I didn't think it was a condition to her becoming their queen.

"That's crazy. You're *mafie*. You're a woman. You're meant to marry. To have children. It's your duty," I declared exasperated. I couldn't fathom why I had to state the basics. She knew them. Everyone, man, woman, and child, knew them.

"Not *my* duty. Not if I want to lead. It's not a nickname because I'm not yet married if that's what you think." *That was exactly what I'd thought.* "It's what I will always be." *Hell, no.* "It's a reminder and a warning. My father will make me *şef* on the condition I dedicate my life to my clan, and that's what I will do. I *will* become the first woman *şef* in the history of the Romanian *mafie*, whether here or in Romania, Italy, France ... anywhere in the world."

I looked at her in horror. Not have this gorgeous, strong woman by my side? Not feel her tight channel strangle my cock until I spray my come into her womb and breed her? Not watch her grow fat in the middle with our child? Not possible.

I leveled her a hard look, then shook my head in denial of this new development. It wasn't her fault. This was 100 percent her father's fault, and I'd gut him for it if she didn't care for him so much. He'd done a crazy number on his one and only daughter, supposed apple of his eye, coveted princess, and privileged successor.

Inhaling deeply, my nostrils flared.

Fuck her father.

I'd made her mine, period. Let her try to fight off my seduction 'cause I wasn't going to take this lying down. There was a niggling fear in the back of my mind, fear of hurting her because she'd never taken a cock before. If she was attached to me, she'd be ready to take on the challenge when she saw me for the big ugly brute I was.

"None of this changes the fact that you're mine," I asserted. If anyone—her father, her clan, *anyone*—thought they could take her from me, they had another think coming. I didn't need to fuck her to claim her. I was claiming her now. End of story.

A sad, resigned smile spread on her lips. "God, you're such a man. Such a Lupu. Saying I'm yours doesn't make it so, Tatum."

I caressed her soft cheek with the back of my hand.

"Baby, you're mine, regardless of what we do or don't do." Skittering my fingertips down the side of her throat, I continued, "I'm here for you to fuck or not to fuck. There's no reason you can't be *şef* and get married and have children."

I carefully formulated what I was about to say because Clara hero-worshipped her father, but it needed saying. "Your father can go to hell with his twisted ideas of what power looks like. You should be given leave to decide what's right for you, not *him*. It's wrong and unfair, but hey, it's your choice. If this is how you want to play it, then you do you, but I'm not backing down. On that, you have my oath."

Her eyes flared with fear. She knew what an oath from me meant. It meant she'd never be rid of me. "Why can't you understand? I can't have it all."

I directed a look of derision at her. "You're mine. You can have anything you damn well want. Me and *şef*hood included." I flicked my fingers offhandedly and tsked. "If you think you can restrain yourself, go at it."

I unfastened the top button of my dress shirt.

"W-what are you doing?"

"Undressing," I replied lazily.

"For the love of God, why?"

"Because we're sleeping in the same bed," I pronounced.

"We are *not*," she retorted with horror. "Your mother will know."

"She won't say a word," I replied blithely.

I moved her off my lap, stood up, and shed my shirt. My fingers landed on my belt.

"Get out," she cried, pointing at the door.

I undid my belt and slipped it from my pants.

Bending it in two, I slapped it against my palm.

"Listen carefully, Clara. I'm sleeping in your bed. No

one will talk. Not my mother. Not Star. You can be a good girl and follow orders, or you can fight me, that's up to you, but whichever way you decide to play this, I will still end up in your bed. To sleep or more, that depends on you."

She shifted to her knees, looking disheveled and gorgeous, her lips bruised, red, and puffy from my mouth.

"What do you even mean?" she exclaimed, throwing up her hands. "I don't even know what you mean!"

I grabbed hold of her tresses, fisted them, and brought her close to me. Caressing the side of her arm with the edge of my belt, I said, "It means I do whatever I want with you."

She yanked her head away, but I only tightened my hold on her. Her nails came out to play, scoring down my chest.

Aww, my little kitty wanted to play.

"Have it your way," I warned. Pulling her head back, I pressed her into the bed, grabbed her wrists, and brought them together above her head. Dragging her up the bed, I tied them to the bars of the headboard with my belt. She thrashed beneath me, but it took very little effort to get her under control. She might be strong, but I was huge. She was no physical match for me.

"Dammit, Tatum. You're such an asshole. You can't just tie me up like a fucking hog."

"Language, Clara. This vocabulary is beneath you," I warned with a clucking of my tongue.

"Fuck you," she hissed with a glare.

I easily parted her legs and settled between them. Her skirt rode up her thighs, giving me a good look at the wet spot in the gusset of her panties. I didn't need more proof she was mine, but I appreciated it, nonetheless.

"Mmm. I'm going to taste you," I warned her with a smack of my lips.

"You are not," she raised her voice in alarm. "Anyway, I said I'm to remain a virgin."

My gaze snapped to hers. "Are you hard of hearing, girl? I said I'm going to *taste* you. There's a lot I can do to this hot sexy body of yours without busting through your cherry. But outside of that, nothing is off the table."

"No, please don't," she whispered, surprise filtering through her voice. She was used to her word being automatically obeyed, but I wasn't one of her Hagi lackeys, I was her man. Time for her to learn what that meant.

In any case, her hips were making circles on the bed, her body instinctively seeking relief. Her skin was flushed. Her eyes were dilated. Her pussy was wet. Oh, my queen wanted it.

Without further ado, I ripped her shirt straight off her. Her chest heaved, breasts practically spilling out of the black satin bra I'd bought her. The knowledge that she was dressed in clothing I'd provided made my heart sing.

Unhooking her bra from the front, I kissed her hard on the mouth before tonguing my way down her throat, playing with both nipples before continuing my journey along the slope of her belly to the lace edging of her matching panties.

Eyes wide with shock, her mouth gaped open. Breathing hard, she just stared at me as I angled my gaze to hers when my mouth made contact with her satin-covered mound.

A sharp gasp. I had to remember she was an innocent, even if I'd already fucked her cunt with my mouth, but I had to bind her to me.

A moan escaped as I exhaled warm air on her needy pussy.

I fondled her tits, thumbing at pink nipples as tight as screws under my tongue.

"Oh, fuck."

Throwing her a glare, I took my mouth off her and warned, "Language."

A flicker of worry crossed her face. Afraid I would punish her for her indiscretion, she apologized. Clara was a quick learner, even if I sensed that she'd test me soon enough. It was in her nature, and I was more than ready to withhold her pleasure as punishment. But first, I had to get her cunt addicted to my tongue.

Shoving her panties down her legs, I made myself comfortable between her splayed thighs. All that pink, glistening flesh laid out for me like a feast. And feast I would. Feast and gorge.

I gave her a few laps of my tongue, each one eliciting a gasp or moan, before delving into the heart of the matter. I suckled her clit and lapped at her lips, repeating the motion wherever her body jolted in response. Soon, I had her writhing beneath me, lifting her hips to grind her pussy against my face.

I pressed two fingers deep inside her. I didn't doubt her when she told me she was a virgin, but man, she was as tight as ever.

Her smooth, milk-white skin was marked red where my fingers had dug in too deep or where her skin heated up in excitement. There was a high flush on her cheeks and sweat glistened on her hairline.

I liked seeing my fingerprints on her skin and pressed harder to leave a more lasting imprint. I loved how strong Clara was. She moaned each time I tightened my grip on her, manhandled her, or yanked her hair. I turned my head and sucked a hickey into her inner thigh, biting down for good measure. She gave a little scream.

Ahh, my baby girl liked a bite of pain.

That would come in handy for her in the future.

I returned to her gorgeous, soaked pussy and smeared her honey across my face before thrusting my tongue back into her sweet juices. Thank God, my mother and Star were out shopping. I didn't need any interruptions when this beauty broke apart on my tongue.

Soon, she was screaming my name in a looping chant.

Her thighs clamped around my head, and I had to pry them open to have enough room to maneuver and continue until she fell down the rabbit hole of her second tongue-fucking.

As she was coming down, I loosened my belt and massaged the red slashes marking her wrists and hands. My gaze surveyed the chaos of her room.

Clara must have read my expression because she said pertly, "I'm a *mafie* princess." Swallowing gulps of air until her breathing returned to normal, she continued, "In LA, we have maids who take care of everything."

She reached over to her nightstand and hooked a pair of dainty white lace panties with her index finger and smirked at me. "Considering you bought these, I'd imagine you'd like to see them."

"See them on you," I corrected. "Not all over your room. My mother cleans and takes care of everything. She doesn't trust people snooping in her house, as she puts it."

"That makes sense," she replied with somber eyes. She knew, as well as I did, the many dangers of our lifestyle. The FBI made regular attempts to infiltrate families like ours.

"I'm a princess, so I'm allowed to be spoiled," she said, sticking her tongue out at me.

"Darling, you're not a princess. Star's a princess. Gabby's a princess. You're a queen, and don't you forget it," I scolded.

Her breath caught. Her eyes glistened.

Dammit, what did I say?

She sniffed back a little cry.

Tipping my head to the side, I cupped her cheek and asked gently, "What is it, baby girl?"

She shook her head, indicating that nothing was wrong.

Realization dawned on me. "You like when I call you queen," I noted.

"To hear someone outside my family say it makes it feel all the more real. Considering I'm sacrificing my life to become queen, it means a lot to hear it."

"Baby, you don't have to sacrifice anything to be my queen," I assured her.

"I'd have to renounce my clan," she replied, her lips drooping on the sides into a frown.

I snorted. "You most definitely would not. You choose to follow your father's scheme, no one else. I've seen the way your clan members treat you. They love you. Put your foot down with your father, and if he doesn't accept it, then go for it anyway. They'll support you."

"Not all of them," she murmured.

I clucked her chin. "Listen, gorgeous, it's the *mafie*. You know you'll inevitably have to fight someone to claim or maintain your throne. It's part of our culture. What does it matter if it's sooner or later?"

"Hmmm," she said, clearly wanting to move past our conversation. Her fingers reached for my zipper as I rose to my knees, on either side of her hips.

My hand landed on hers, stilling her movement, and I asked, "What are you doing?"

"Something I've been fantasizing about for a while," she replied coquettishly.

My grip tightened on her. My throat constricted, my Adam's apple bobbing up and down as I swallowed.

"I'm ugly," I rasped out. Hadn't the boys taunted me with those same words when they stripped me naked in the school bathroom before Alex stormed in and ran them out?

Her eyelashes batted furiously and her breath stuttered out. "W-what?"

I shook my head, licked my parched lips, and said, "You don't have to do this."

In the clubs, I did the touching. I rarely allowed women to touch me. When it came to fucking, I took them from behind and zipped up once I was done. These were experienced women, while Clara had never seen a dick in the flesh before.

She scrambled up and pushed her face in mine fiercely. Voice shaking with anger, she demanded, "What did you just say?"

"You heard me," I retorted.

She curled her hand around my nape and pulled my head down until we shared the same air.

Her mouth pouted in an unhappy downturn, her bottom lip trembling a little. "Why would you say something so awful? First of all, that's patently untrue. Have you not looked in the mirror lately? Every *mafie* girl crushes on you."

I huffed out a little self-deprecating laugh.

"Only because I'm now *consilier*. Before that, the brothers of those same girls would forbid them to look at me. I'm a half-breed." And half-breeds were ugly, I finished silently.

She had to already know, and if she didn't, then it was best she found out now. Of course, I'd been with women before, but they didn't know me, know who I was. *What* I was. The harrowing truth of it hadn't hit me until this moment. Honestly, I didn't know if I could survive her turning away from me in disgust.

She drew in a harsh breath. "Don't you ever, I mean ever, call yourself that again."

Frustrated, I pulled away and waved at my hardened cock. "I am ugly. I'm huge everywhere."

She made a pained sound at the back of her throat. "Granted, this will be my first real penis, but I've done 'research,' and I promise you, I'm prepared. You're not going to shock me, and anyway, I don't scare easily."

"But—"

"But *nothing*," she cut in, tugging me closer.

Lifting her pleading gaze to me, she said, "I never thought I'd get a chance to do this, and I'm not about to let anything get in my way. Not even you." She licked her lips. "So can we get back to it because I can't wait to put my mouth on your cock. I feel like I've been waiting forever."

The tight band around my chest loosened, and I did as my queen ordered. Slowly and deliberately, I peeled off my pants and boxer briefs, laying them carefully over the back of one of the chairs, heaped high with discarded clothing, tags still hanging off them.

I stalked back over to her, my thick cock bobbing in the air. I'd been hard as a rock since walking into her bedroom. One of the reasons I'd licked her cunt twice, with the intention of doing it many more times, was to get her hooked on my tongue work before she got an eyeful of my cock.

Stopping right in front of her, by her bed, I waited for her reaction.

Gaze riveted on my shaft, she drew me onto her bed and laid me down. I propped myself up on pillows because I wanted a ringside view of this event. Pushing my legs apart, she settled in, and with a final look in my direction, she bent down, ass up in the air, which was a beautiful sight in itself, and licked her way up my shaft.

I hissed out a harsh breath. Goddamn, watching her pink tongue lick up the length of my shaft was a sight to behold. This wasn't going to take long. My thighs quivered slightly just from one long lap.

"You like it?"

"Who wouldn't like your tongue on their cock, baby girl," I grunted out. Seriously, how could she doubt it? But this was her first time tasting dick, so everything was new to her. She wanted to learn how it made me feel, she wanted to see how I would react and hear what sounds I made.

Damn, I felt like a king, with my queen between my legs, lovin' on my cock.

Wrapping a hand around my shaft, she swirled her tongue around the crown, dipping her tongue over and over again into the slit, lapping at the pre-come like it was an ice cream cone. Christ. This was going to kill me. Then, she dipped down a little and angled her head to access the underside, lapping at the sensitive area like the little cock-tease she was.

"Take me all the way in your mouth, little girl," I warned. "You made it this hard, now you must take care of it. It's going to get messy, but you're going to swallow every last drop of it, you hear?"

Instantly, she engulfed my shaft with her mouth, taking as much as she could.

I wheezed out a harsh breath of surprise.

"So eager," I murmured.

"God, you have no idea," she replied before returning to her mission of driving me insane.

She couldn't take more than half, but the image of her lips stretched so wide over my girth was priceless. It was almost garish, the stretch of her lips, but to watch her struggle to take more of my cock was the hottest sight I'd ever seen.

My hand glided over her silky hair, taking hold of it to move it out of my way and to guide her. The slick wet slide of her hot mouth on my cock was earth-shattering. A shiver racked my whole body, and I was a big guy.

"You'll learn to take the whole thing, but, for now, jack it with your hand," I directed.

She did as I said, but stubborn girl that she was, she pushed herself further down on my cock. Fuck, only a woman like Clara could go further the first time than most women did in general. Eyes watering, she stared straight at me and took a long, hard suck. My hips punched up in an automatic response. I'd accidentally choked her and she came up with a ragged breath.

"Touch my balls gently. Toggle them like a pair of dice in your hands," I guided her as her mouth came back down.

She did as I said, and I moaned at the incredible feeling of it. My hand fisted her hair tightly. With the suction of her moist, hot mouth on me, her gentle touch on my balls, I gritted my teeth in my inner battle for control. She hummed, and the sound ricocheted down my shaft, *ching chinging* in my balls like a pinball machine.

"Christ, you're a natural."

She popped off to say, "You haven't seen anything yet. I'm just getting started." Then she went back down, pushing down harder, and I hit the back of her throat again as she gave it an extra rough suck. She choked a little, but my brave girl pulled up just enough to breathe before returning to her position, lips stretched taut around the width of my shaft.

"Take a breath before you do it again," I ordered, breathing shallowly. "And swallow deep."

Acting like such a good little slut, she pushed back down. She was an overachiever, and it showed.

My eyes rolled to the back of my head, I snapped my head forward in attention before I lost it completely and commanded, "Play with your clit. I'd do it myself, but I can't focus with your mouth fucking."

She moaned around my shaft again, her fingers rushing to do my bidding. And then I had the view of her fingers working furiously on her hot little cunt. Add her jacking hand and her sunken cheeks sucking me hard, and I blew. Thank Christ, I'd already told her to drink my come down because the look on her face when she choked and sputtered as she swallowed for the first time ever was more precious than gold.

Ears ringing, I was distantly aware she was climaxing, too. The moaning on my sensitive tip was making me twitch.

"Slurp it all down," I stumbled out, the edges of my vision edging black as the orgasm shuddered through me.

I collapsed back on her bed, my cock still in her mouth. Catching my breath, I got the joy of watching her pull back and give my crown one final lick before straightening up, her high, young tits bouncing in the air.

I was wrecked, but I needed to see one last thing.

"Show me your tongue," I croaked out.

Palms flat on the bed, between her splayed thighs, Clara opened her mouth wide, stuck out her tongue, and proudly displayed traces of my come.

"Damn," I breathed out. "I knew it before, but now it's official. I'm never letting you go."

14

TATUM

With internet access on the blink, Clara, Star, and I were getting desperate. I had to return to my penthouse to get any work done, sometimes with Clara, sometimes without. The days I went alone, spending hours apart from her, frayed my nerves. The nights I spent tangled with her in bed were both exhilarating and frustrating. Exhilarating because for a newbie, she was both curious and adventurous. Frustrating because nothing was resolved between us, and the little possessive demon inside me was chomping at the bit. I barked at Luca the other day, and the look of surprise on his face was almost comical.

With my sanity on the line, I made the unilateral decision to move Clara and Star to my penthouse in Manhattan until the internet was restored on a permanent basis. Mama stayed to host Alex's mother and grandmother, who were overlooking the repair of their townhouse.

Installing Clara in my terrain, even if we were not alone, hugely improved my mood. After a couple of days, Star complained about the commute to and from school and asked if she could stay with Gabriela until the internet was back on at our family home.

I dropped her off at Gabby's house with a warning to be a good girl. It was unnecessary because Star was always good, but I had to make certain to communicate my high expectations of her.

Mafie families were uber protective. Even sleepovers were frowned upon, and here I was allowing my little sister to live with another family for days. Edgy, I glanced at Clara in the back seat through the rearview mirror, and a smug grin spread over my face. I couldn't have planned this better if I'd tried.

"Move up front," I ordered as soon as Star was out of the car. Clara slipped out of the backseat and settled beside me, her refreshing beach scent wrapping around me. I would forever associate her fragrance with California, and if I had my way, one day I'd have both. I put the car in drive and whipped out into the street, desperate to get back to my penthouse.

My jaws clamped together as I dragged my gaze up and down her luscious figure. She was like a dainty little present begging to be unwrapped. I needed her. I mean, I *needed* her. I needed to mark her. Fuck her. Take that cherry and thrust my cock right through it, pull out, and see the smear of her crimson blood on my shaft. The demon settled when I had my tongue in her tasty pussy or when she had her mouth on my cock but was otherwise restless. Whereas, before I hated being touched, now I hated every moment she wasn't touching me.

I needed another hit of her, and soon.

Taking her hand, I drove one-handed toward the

Queensboro bridge to take us back to Manhattan as the sun began to set. The silence settled between us comfortably.

Yes, I knew she wanted to stay a virgin, I knew things between us were complicated, but God forbid if things didn't work out and she ended up flying back to LA alone. I couldn't stomach the idea.

I'd finally found a woman strong enough to take me as I was, who wasn't scared of the things I'd proposed to her, and who was a virgin in every way. Yes, I was the dirty possessive bastard who wanted to be her first everything.

Assuming we could get her father's bullshit virginity condition out of the way, I'd have to move to Los Angeles. Before her, I'd never considered leaving my mother and sister. Never considered living outside of the Lupu clan or New York. I sure as hell had no idea if I could sever the twisted, guilt-ridden bond that shackled me to Alex. Then there was Grigore, who'd had years to dig his sharp claws into her. My grip tightened around the steering wheel, knuckles turning white. No way any sane man would let her go without a fight, and that man was far from sane.

I was going to take her virginity, knowing that worst-case scenario, she could leave me and carry the burden of being deflowered back to LA.

As for my secret ... Why not throw it on top of the bonfire of secrets I held and light the match? I was already burning in hell. What was one more secret?

"I can finally relax," I confessed. "We're finally alone with all the time in the world. No one to intrude. No one to walk in on us."

We had done everything but fuck. I'd respected her boundaries, and she'd held strong, but she was close to cracking, and with my kid sister gone, she was all mine.

She glanced at me from underneath her lashes, suddenly bashful, and hell if that didn't rouse the little demon in me.

"Are you sure that's for the best?" she asked shyly.

She was intimidated, I got that.

"We couldn't go on without consistent internet. I have work. You have your work to do for your father."

Clara was intricately involved in the Hagi clan's distribution of drugs in southern California. They did things differently over there. We looked toward Europe, Russia, and Afghanistan as sources and routes for our drugs. The California clans looked to Mexico and South America. From what I'd gathered, they had more competition with the Mexican drug syndicates. I didn't see how the Hagi clan would expand in a sustainable manner. Part of it was the infighting between the western clans, but even if they unified, they'd struggle to spread out beyond their current territory.

"I would've managed," she mumbled.

"Why manage when I have a perfectly good apartment ready for you to live and work in. Plus, you can't deny the amenities. It's much more in line with how you're used to living in LA."

"I like your mother's house. It's cozy."

"It's small," I countered. "And you deserve something better than to live like that."

"Your mom's and Alex's mom's houses remind me of Romania. I mean, come on. The ceramic stove in the middle of the living room in Alex's house definitely reminds me of the old country, but even your mother's house has the old-style Romanian decorative embroidery scattered around the place."

"Hey, I have that, too. I'll have you know that people

envy the embroidery on my walls," I informed her, referring to my living room, which displayed abstract woven pieces by a renowned Romanian artist.

"Those are modern renditions, not the real thing," she said.

"Same thing," I argued.

"Oh my God, so not the same thing," she retorted. "Yours are huge, tall pieces of embroidery. Sure, they're geometric, but not in any of the old styles, and I should know. I'm from the mountains. Never saw any patterns like that before."

"Semantics. Anyway, the artist in question was riffing off those styles. It's like freestyling on a hip-hop track," I explained as we drove down toward Manhattan, the East River spanned underneath us. The bright winter sunlight hit off the spread of geometric skyscrapers in front of us. There was the dignified United Nations on the waterfront, it's turquoise-tinted windows reflecting the water below. I could pick out the long oblong structure of the Citicorp building in Midtown with its slanted diagonal roof, shining a brilliant silver color.

We were ten minutes away from my place in this traffic and already our little tiff was getting me antsy to get her underneath me.

"Okay, I don't know what you just said," she replied with a laugh. "But I can tell you that the woman who embroidered those ... those ... thingies—"

"I prefer the term art pieces," I interjected. "But go on, don't want to interrupt your flow."

"Fine. Art pieces, whatever. She's trying to be conceptual or something, but they don't make your place feel homey or comfy like your mom's house or my home in LA."

"Your home in LA is filled to the gills with stuff. It looks like the leftovers from a Dracula-slash-haunted house

movie set got dumped in your house. Every piece of furniture is antique-y and made from heavy, dark wood. On top
of that, not one surface is free from clutter and tchotchkes,"
I elaborated.

"Your place looks empty," she fired back. "Like one of
those modern art galleries in Chelsea. It doesn't feel lived in.
It could be an avant-garde dance studio in Bushwick, it has
so much space in it."

"Then change it," I challenged her.

Pretty blue eyes widened like bursts of sky and her
brows shot up.

"I'm serious. Change it. Change anything you want," I
clarified. "I want you to be comfortable in my space."

"But I'll be going back to Cali in a couple of months. It
doesn't make sense for me to change anything in your apartment," she argued.

"It does to me," I grumbled, despising the reminder that
there was a risk of her returning to Cali before I could claim
her as mine. Unease rippled down my spine. My shoulders
tensed, my hand spasmed around hers. "I want you to feel at
home."

"I'll be going back to your mom's house once the
internet is back on," she said, by way of an excuse.

I didn't want to hear excuses, I just wanted her to fix my
apartment—make it feel like home to her. As for what she
said, I didn't respond because we hadn't talked about what
would happen after the internet was back on at my mother's
house. I'd just gotten her alone, and I wasn't about to let her
go. Even if I had to explain to Alex why Clara remained
with me.

Clara was someone who could move back and forth on
things with surprising ease, but I only moved forward. I
didn't backtrack. Ever. It was what kept the sinking feeling

that my life was stagnant at bay. Stagnant because my secret always held me back. I didn't dare conceive what my life would've been like if I'd had the freedom to forge my own path from the beginning.

We'd arrived at my building, so I didn't bother arguing with her. If my intended seduction went according to plan, any dispute on the matter would be moot.

I WAS ON EDGE.

After Grigore's phone call and his reminder to stay vigilant around the Lupu clan, I tried to pull back from Tatum. Instead, he ended up sleeping in my bed that very evening. Our bedroom activities were fun and sexy and satisfying, but it was no longer enough.

I ached to be filled by him. Even sitting beside him in the car, my pussy was wet, clenching and releasing, yearning to be stretched wide by his shaft the way he stretched my mouth when I gave him oral. I knew how thick his cock was, so my imagination ran rampant with fantasies of him finally *finally* taking me.

If, as I suspected, his plan was to get me addicted to his touch and make me yearn for more, then it was a resounding success. To be fair, it was in my nature to want more, and I was driving straight into obsession. Last night, while we were messing around in bed, I sneakily shifted around so that the crown of his shaft slid into the slippery cove between my thighs. It was a test. Would he circle around my opening, maybe push in a little bit? I was hoping he'd pretend to not know how his cock had ended up there, take advantage of the situation, and thrust into me.

But not Tatum, dammit. The man's leash on his own self-control was twisted.

He only made a sexy grunt and pulled away just as my clenching pussy was weeping to be filled, apologizing as if it'd been accidental. *That was no accident, buddy!*

Fuck, simply thinking about last night got me even more hot and bothered. He pulled into his parking space beneath his building, and the instant he stopped, I swung the door of his Mercedes G Wagon open roughly and hopped out. Shutting off the engine, he got out and followed me with his gaze, eyebrows gathered in confusion at my aggressive handling of his car.

Ugh. I didn't know how much longer I'd last.

Even walking alongside him, his size made me feel small, and that drove me crazy, too. I just wanted him to take me, *ravish* me.

Ever solicitous, he took hold of my nape and squeezed. "You okay, baby? You look tense."

I huffed. *What an understatement.*

He massaged the back of my neck and I softened against his hard body with a moan. Oh, God. This was only making it infinitely worse. I was like molten fire. My muscles, sinews, and joints ... all melted under his magical fingers. Things got exponentially worse when he pulled me into his chest because then I was enveloped in a haze of his woodsy scent. Faint smoky notes reminded me of bonfires on the beach. The scent was achingly evocative of my life back home. Adrian liked bonfires. Many nights my father and I found a secluded strip of beach, lit one for him, and enjoyed an evening by the ocean.

We got into the elevator and he didn't miss an opportunity to kiss me, leaving me breathless when the doors opened on his floor. I'd been living in his apartment for a few days now, but it always struck me as cold and clinical, so unwelcoming. I couldn't believe a man as passionate as Tatum actually appreciated the laboratory-white walls and the cavernous space that felt, well ... empty. From the furniture in his living room to his dining room table and chairs, everything was modern, sharp-angled, and bland. The view was gorgeous, and the bones of the place were good, but the decoration was as appealing as a hospital ward.

No wonder he thought that abstract Romanian embroidered artwork was interesting. The pieces were colorful, I'd give him that. Certainly in comparison to the drab whiteness of his apartment.

Eyeing me, his lips twitched. "Now that I know you don't like it, you know I won't stop until you've changed it to your liking."

"It's not important whether I like it or not," I replied blithely.

The expression on his face changed from serene to stormy. Uh-oh. Wrong thing to say.

He was on me in an instant. Pushing me up against the wall, he penned me in with his forearms braced on either side of my head. He wasn't touching me, but that only made the tension in my body thrum harder. He leaned forward so that his face swamped my vision. His wolfish, jet-black eyes were impenetrable. So much emotion there, that much I knew, but it was inaccessible to me or any human. Even I couldn't pierce his walls. He wrapped his hand around my throat, a habit of his. Encircling my throat seemed to calm him down like it was a talisman or something.

"Swear to God, don't make me repeat myself. I want you to be comfortable here. No expense will be spared. I don't care if you have to tear down the fucking walls to do it."

I blinked. He'd slipped into profanity.

"I want you here," he continued. "I want you at ease, relaxed, happy, *snuggly*. Am I making myself clear enough?"

The column of my throat moved up and down under his grasp, his demands giving voice to what I'd always wanted. To be accepted, to be wanted wholeheartedly, without conditions, stipulations, or prerequisites. He wanted to change everything to fit *me* and my needs. Not the other way around. Not like my father.

"Crystal," I replied irreverently. What could I say, I was a brat.

He leaned in closer, rubbing his nose with mine. "Cheeky."

Then he pressed against me, engulfing me in the frame of his larger body, his chiseled muscles firm and solid.

"I like it," he finished, releasing my throat.

"I can tell," I sassed.

"Hmmm."

Oh, that sound of male satisfaction was too scrumptious to resist tasting him. Dipping my chin slightly, I started at the base of his throat and licked up to his jaw, which I nipped for good measure.

A rumbly growl vibrated up his throat. Abruptly, he swung me into his arms before he stalked down the corridor to his bedroom.

It was the most welcoming room in his apartment. There, he'd seemed to let go a little. The furniture was made of pale wood, but at least the bed was large, comfortable, and piled high with pillows that matched the cobalt-blue pattern of his duvet. A pair of overstuffed chairs, in a darker blue hue, faced each other and overlooked a wall of windows. Besides the bookshelf, there was a small wooden table that had a neat pile of books on it, just waiting for his attention. The very top book was a biography of Constantin

Brancusi, a modern sculptor. It certainly fit with his taste in art.

This cozy little corner, I knew, was where he relaxed at the end of the day. Either he read a book, scrolled through his phone, or picked up The New York Times, because, yes, he was the only man under fifty who got the paper delivered to his front door every morning.

He swung me down to my feet and, once I was stable, placed a hand on my chest and pushed me onto his bed. Sprawled out, I watched him raptly as he undid his cufflinks and pulled off the pin-striped dress shirt.

The man wasn't only controlled, he was a neat freak. I'd gasped when I opened his walk-in closet. Everything in my closet at home was a jumbled mess, cocktail dresses crammed in beside sweatpants. In his closet, there was a half-inch of space between each hanger. The shirts were color-coordinated, and the pants—hell, I couldn't begin to fathom how he organized those, but I knew there was a system behind it.

Dragging his shirt off his wide shoulders, he exposed his ripped chest. Some *mafie* men covered their skin in tattoos down to their knuckles, but Tatum only displayed one tat, the Lupu wolf, which every Lupu man received after induction. Not only did it fit his clean-cut look, but the lone tat demonstrated the importance of his clan in his life. Having seen enough men without their shirts on at pool parties and on the beach in California, his scarless skin was instantly noticeable. Tatum was either a phenomenal fighter or scuffles were above his paygrade.

My pussy fluttered as I remembered how his rough chest hair felt against my nipples. I loved his abs, stacked like perfect boxes, one on top of the other. There was a carved arc on either side of his sculptured belly, and his thick cock bulged against the zipper of his suit pants.

I reached for the ribbon holding my wraparound dress together, which he'd made no bones about letting me know was one of his favorites.

"Stop," he commanded.

My fingers froze.

He unzipped his pants and slipped out of them. "I'll do that. It's like unwrapping a gift, a gift for my eyes only."

I laid my hands on the bed, spreading my fingers wide in expectation.

"I love when you look at me like that," he commented. "Your eyes wide with eagerness, watching my every move like the little rabbit you are." He leaned over me, his arms braced on either side of my shoulders. "I'm going to *devour* you, little rabbit."

A shiver staggered down my spine. "I want you to fuck me," I blurted out.

His dark, inscrutable eyes blew out to a black the shade of the universe. He liked when I straight talked him. Staring deep into my eyes, he scrutinized me as if he could delve into my soul and explore the hidden crannies that no one else knew existed.

His breath drifted over my mouth as he said, "I need your submission first."

We'd talked about this. About submission and domination, about how it wasn't just about inflicting pain or following a man's commands for the hell of it. He explained how I had needs and how he had needs and how our needs complemented each other, fit together like two pieces to make a unified whole.

If any other person had requested this of me, I would've spit in his face. Being a strong woman was the basis of my identity; it was me at my essence. But I'd been doing research since he'd first brought it up, and I knew my submission wouldn't intrude on my sense of self. On the contrary, my submission would elevate it.

We'd played a little bit with a few smacks here and there, with me following his edicts, with him treating me like I was an object for his pleasure alone. I had an inkling of the depth of his fixation for me, and if I had to choose a word to describe it, I would choose worship.

As if making a vow to me, he said, "If you agree, then today, I make you mine. I swear to you, I take care of what's mine. I'll never abuse your trust."

He cupped my pussy reverently, an expression of awe on his face, and said, "And don't think I don't know what a gift this pussy is. I'm going to use this sweet cunt and make it sing."

"I promise to be your good girl," I replied.

His eyes flashed, two burning pits of black fire.

We'd fought each other for so long, but the hurricane forced him to give up fighting his desire for me. In turn, that desire blazed through us like a wildfire, scorching both his hatred and mine.

The burnt-out crust of our past relationship gave way to earth primed for new growth. He began tilling the fresh, fertile earth and it was upon this land we now stood. Land covered with delicate tree shoots, teeming with insects and birds and *life*. We were at a point of rebirth, and Tatum was asking me to jump into this new world alongside him.

"That's right," he concurred. "You be a good girl in my bed, give me the privilege of taking care of you outside our bed, and be a badass boss lady to everyone else."

I never spoke of this, but a part of my heart had gone missing when my mother cheated on my father and exploded the illusion of our family. Even though Adrian was a gift, her adultery was a violation in every other way. Tatum filled the hole, stuffing it with love and care, and making my heart whole once again.

I was ready to join him in this new adventure, come what may.

"Yes," I said.

An instant later, his mouth sealed over mine, his silken tongue moving slowly, reverently. His teeth found my bottom lip and bit down just enough to remind me of what a bite of pain could do. I moaned around his upper lip as his teeth bore down. Meanwhile, his fingers found my pussy, spreading my juices around my clit.

Moving his fingers inside me, he pressed deeper, testing my hymen, and said, "There it is. Still unbroken after everything I've done to you."

"Well, you didn't put your cock inside, so I'm not exactly surprised."

"Oh, I could've popped this precious seal with my fingers, but I kept it intact for this moment. I want you to *know* the moment I burst through your cherry, the moment I make you mine forever."

My heart thumped against my ribcage. We'd preserved my virginity, and today I was giving myself to this man. Like a wedding vow, breaking through my hymen was symbolic of the day he took possession of me.

Stripping off his boxer shorts, he returned to me. His long, hard cock bobbed like an arrogant baton, tempting me to reach out for it.

He gripped it hard and said, "If you want this cock, I want to hear the words."

"You know I do," I croaked out, pushing his hand out of the way to glide up and down his thick shaft. "I want it."

"More."

If he wanted more words, I'd give them to him.

"I want your big cock. I don't care if it hurts, I want you to burst through my cherry and fill me."

He let out a low hiss.

Planting his hands on my breasts, he gave my nipples a little twist and then slid his big hands down my torso as if caressing a religious relic. Awe and splendor sparked in his dark eyes as they tracked the path of his hands. Brows slashed down in concentration, he played with my wet folds, teasing me. His gaze shot to mine, holding my gaze with such seriousness, I had a jolt of panic.

"You're going to watch me fuck this pussy for the first time," he said, and I melted like sugar and butter in a saucepan. "I've never had a virgin before, but I'm going to make sure you come on my cock. Even the first time, I swear it."

With his oath made, he pulled me up the bed and covered my body with his much larger one. I felt treasured, like the bunny he'd nicknamed me. My mind emptied of everything but this man, this moment.

I was going to lose my virginity. I didn't care if it hurt. I didn't care if I didn't come. I'd been torturing us for weeks, and I couldn't hold out any longer.

Spreading my legs to invite him into my body, I slipped my hands over the short, rough hair of his chest and braced them on his wide shoulders. He could've been a linebacker in a past life, his shoulders were so naturally broad. Broad enough to carry the weight of ravishing me, of my father's fury, of my future as head of my clan.

Tatum might be broad on top, but he had trim hips, yet he spread me wide, nonetheless. Settling into the cradle of my hips, he gave me a distracting kiss as he pushed forward, barely inside me. The tip of his cock spread my lower lips open while the rest of his long, thick shaft pressed against my clit. Arching my back, I shifted my hips, rocking into him.

There was no pain, not yet, but I felt his hard throbbing shaft piercing me, stretching me open to fit him. He pushed in another inch and then another, spreading my wet lips apart, but then he stopped, meeting resistance at the same time as I felt the burn. Lord, he felt huge inside me, like an invading, penetrating force.

"Huge, you're huge," I said, the snug walls of my vagina locking up, keeping him out.

A rumbly growl of frustration vibrated in his chest.

"Tight. Tighter than I thought. Going to get inside," he swore, pressing in harder.

"It's stuck," I accused, glaring down to where we were joined, where he'd only managed to push himself halfway - in.

His hand swept over my hair in a soothing caress.

"Shhh, I'll fix it," he promised before blowing out a long breath. Lowering himself on his elbows, he distributed his weight evenly and rocked into me with slow, winding swivels of his hips. Each time, he moved in deeper and deeper. In this position, the burn had an undercurrent of something else, something good. I let out a brief sigh of relief.

We moved together, in counterpoint to each other, until he hit a specific spot and I gasped, as a burst of white flashed in my vision.

"Fuck," I moaned, not knowing if he'd broken through, if he was fully sheathed in me yet, and no longer caring.

He did it again, hitting that same spectacular spot, and I

was captivated with him, with his heaving body above mine, his breath whispering over my temple, his cock pressing up against that magical place. It was still tight, still a fiery burn, but I met him thrust for thrust, chasing that elusive jolt until I was slamming up onto his cock, wedged so deeply inside of me.

"Don't think I didn't see the way you tested me, rubbing this fine, silky pussy up on me last night, seeing if I'd break. Well, I *fucking broke*. This is where your smart mouth gets you, Clara. Along with that tight, round ass and those wide hips. All of it gets you here, getting your tight cunt pounded into."

He thrust hard, branding me with his monster cock. Twisting his face inward, he sank his teeth into the side of my throat. I cried out and bucked beneath him. His filthy words and his bite riled me up, making my body hum with pleasure. The remnants of pain only added to the friction as his cock found that diabolical spot again.

Each hit built on the other until I spun out.

In blinding light, a climax crashed through me. I flew high, broke around his cock on a scream, and he surged forward, burying himself completely into the soft vessel I'd become to receive him. My fingernails clawed down his back. My limbs jerked and twitched as I became remotely aware that he was coming. His sculptured lips spread wide for a lion's roar. Bearing down around his cock, I milked him. His pistoning hips became disjointed, and then the moment I'd been waiting for, the proof of all proof, his warm come shooting deep inside me, marking me as his.

I collapsed on the bed, limp with pleasure. Tatum surrounded me, his forearms planted on either side of my head, his forehead kissing mine, his cock buried inside me. I'd never felt as whole and complete as in that moment. He rolled onto his back and dragged me to him, perspiration glistening on his skin and chest hair.

I never thought I'd have sex with a man, much less have it feel so incredible. There was no turning back now.

"I'm yours," I said in awe.

15

TATUM

Raw ownership pounded through me. I didn't expect much out of life. Nothing had been handed to me on a silver platter, and being dogged with secrets my entire life, I knew that my world could implode at any time. But the moment I'd taken Clara's virginity would be etched in my memory, in my fucking body and soul, forever. If I didn't have to stay alive to protect her and the women in my family, I could've died a happy man right then and there.

I'd battled her and won her surrender. Broke her apart and put her back together. Her utter and total abandon was the most beautiful thing I'd ever seen. Ever seen a queen surrender? Well, I had, and I was an addict after the first hit. I yearned to see her break, time and again. And I would. There was no way she was getting away from me now.

Cuddling her into me, I draped myself around her like a wrapper around a sweet piece of candy. Her honeyed hair, with streaks of sunlight and gold, spread over my chest like streamers. Her fragrance, the beach scent of the hot sand

and salty seawater of California enveloped me. She smelled like the warm, sunny future.

Eventually, she stirred in my arms, saying she had to use the bathroom, and I reluctantly loosened my hold on her.

She slid to the edge of the mattress, slipped down, and landed on her feet. Her knees wobbled like a newborn foal. Abruptly, she crumpled to the floor, her naked thigh hitting the carpet with a harsh thud. She let out a cry, a tear tracking down her cheek. Horrified, I jumped from the bed to help her.

The dominant and perfectionist inside me railed against what had happened. Her adrenaline spiked and now her body was crashing. I knew I'd broken her wide open, but this confirmed it. I should've known it'd been too soon for her to get up on her own. Scooping her up, I seated her gently on the bed, positioned myself with my back to the headboard, and dragged her over my lap. Securing her to my chest, I snagged a blanket and covered her naked, trembling body.

Then I breathed evenly, shushing her gently, praising her as beautiful, as my good girl. The last compliment did the most to settle her shivering body.

Softly, I brushed off the strands of her hair stuck to her wet cheek. She covered her eyes in embarrassment.

Firmly removing her hands, I warned her, "Don't hide from me, beautiful queen."

"I'm not a queen anymore," she sniffed.

I huffed. "You may not be the Virgin Queen, but you're undoubtedly the Hagi queen. Only a queen has the inner strength to give herself to me the way you did. You're as regal as ever, and you'll *always* be my queen."

She pouted.

"Plus, your pussy's worth more than your weight in gold."

She let out a little giggle and slapped my chest lightly.

My heart sang.

"Exaggerate much?"

"Hell no," I rejoined. "I rarely joke, and certainly never about the power of pussy."

She cuddled into my arms.

"Are you regretting it?" I asked tentatively, my body tensing as I waited for her response.

"No," she retorted, a little too quickly.

"Because you can, you know," I proposed. "You can't take it back, obviously, but you can feel regret. You can have more than one reaction. You've disobeyed your father, violated his rule—"

"A rule I'm beginning to question," she clipped out. "I don't even understand where the rule that women have to be virgins when they get married comes from. It's positively medieval."

"That it is," I said, then softened my tone. "But it doesn't take away the fact that you broke a fundamental rule, regardless of how absurd it may be, and you defied your father's wishes. Neither are easy things to do."

She pressed her pouty lips together in a firm line. She drew her brows together, a notch etched between them. She looked downright adorable.

"I wanted to lose it to you," she said vehemently. "I *chose* you. I could've stayed strong—"

Cutting in, I waggled my eyebrows and said, "You're sure about that?"

She grasped an errant lock of hair and tugged on it. "Hush. Yes, I could have. At least, for a little while longer."

"You're like Alex in that you're resilient. Tough. Maybe it

goes hand in hand with the drive to be a leader, but you know, you're allowed to be a human. It's something I remind him of all the time."

"I can't, though, can I?" she argued.

"You can be human with me. That's what I'm here for," I asserted.

"It feels dangerous, Tatum," she whispered.

There was a shift in the air. Suddenly, we were talking about something else, something far more serious.

Clara squeezed her eyes shut tightly and licked her lips. "It's dangerous to want too much. I'm being greedy, and you know what happens to greedy people." Her eyes snapped open and bored into me. "You know what happens, right?" she insisted.

My heart seized. She was confiding in me about her monsters. Was this gorgeous, formidable woman pursued by monsters and ghosts the way I was?

"What happens?" I asked back, my voice soft, yielding.

"They're cut down," she murmured back, so low I barely made out what she said. It was as if she was afraid to speak out loud for fear she'd call up the monsters that would tear her away from me.

"If you get too greedy, if you ask too much of life, everything will get ripped away. I learned that from my parents. You can't have everything you want; it's risky to even wish for it."

Her eyes turned as bleak and cold as a birch forest covered in brittle snow.

She spoke as if she was an oracle, "You can't have love and power."

I gripped her chin and turned her to face me. Her gorgeous blue eyes fled from mine.

"Eyes on me, woman," I demanded.

I gave her a forbidding look, pouring out the ironclad determination that had made me who I was, that had saved me from the sins of my father and wrestled me and my family out of the cesspool of his legacy. I poured everything into that look so she could see that I was prepared to burn down the world for her.

"Listen to me, Clara, and listen well. I will make it happen. I keep telling you, that's why I'm here. To do for you what you can't do for yourself. You're smart to know your limitations. A *şef* shouldn't be so arrogant to think they can do everything, but you're not alone anymore. You have me, just as I have you. We complement each other, and together —not individually, but *together*—I swear to you, we *will* have it all."

"But my father ... my clan...."

She trailed off, pushing against my hold.

I slid my hand to her throat, lifting her chin so she had no freedom of movement. I felt the fluttering of her pulse like butterfly wings beneath my thumb and fingertips.

She swallowed hard.

"Stay still," I commanded. I delved deep into her gaze and confronted her reticence, her lack of belief in my vow.

"What is it?" I demanded.

"We don't speak about it," she began. "It happened, but we don't speak about it in my family. My brother was born from it, and yet, we've never spoken about it once."

Secrets.

Her family had secrets. If only she knew that was my element; I lived in the shadowy world ruled by secrets.

"I know all about dirty secrets," I assured her. "I know how they fester and eat at your soul like a growing cancer. You can tell me, baby. I will keep your secret as if it were my own."

She gave a cute little snort. "What could you know about secrets?"

"More than you could possibly know," I blurted out. A part of me ached to confide in her, to confess and be cleansed, but it was never to be. I wouldn't foist my secret on her. Seeking to cover my impulsive admission, I quickly followed by saying, "I'm *consilier* to the Lupu clan."

Air got caught in my throat, strangling me, but I forced the lump down. It was the closest I'd gotten to admitting my own secret. Inside me, the little demon cringed, cowered, and scurried away, covering his head as if it'd somehow make him invisible, as if it'd somehow extinguish the secret, *poof*, like the delicate flame of a candle in a windshaft.

"Oh, good point," she said with a knowing nod as if that explained everything. *Far from it, sweetness.*

"But that's neither here nor there. We're talking about you. Come on, tell me," I pressed.

"It's not like I'm the only one who knows the secret," she hedged. "For all I know, it might be an open secret among a few select clan members. Grigore might even be privy to it. But it's shameful, and if my father ever found out I'd told anyone, especially a stranger, he'd kill me."

I softly caressed the pulse point battering away on her throat and pressed a soft kiss on the side of her mouth to give her courage. Her comment about me being a stranger rankled a little, but I knew she hadn't meant it hurtfully. Clans were very protective; we constantly spied on one another for the very purpose of digging up damaging information to use as bargaining chips.

"I swear on my mother and sister, the two people who mean the most to me in this world, that your secret is safe with me," I vowed.

My promise seemed to appease her.

Going limp in my embrace, she began, "Adrian, my brother, is technically my half brother. My mother had an affair with my father's *consilier* and best friend. Of course, he was disposed of immediately for his treachery. She was spared because she was pregnant. My father was humiliated, but he also blamed himself because he'd neglected her. Since he came to America, he's spent every waking moment making sure our clan survived and prospered."

Her eyes pleaded with me for understanding.

Please, as if I'd judge her. If she only knew of my father's crimes.

"He accepted Adrian as his own to hide the fact that he'd been cuckolded. Of course, Adrian, being Adrian, was too good not to love. We both fell in love with him, and I know my father regrets having resented him when he was first born."

"He loves Adrian as his own," she said vehemently.

This was a significant confession, and the very last point was crucial. Adrian meant the world to her, to her father, and her clan. She was making sure I comprehended the full extent of her love and loyalty toward her brother.

"He loves Adrian as his own son," I confirmed, proving I grasped her explanation. "As do you."

She nodded her head, the spiral of her eyes wide with relief.

"Yes, I would protect him with my life," she concurred.

"It's not my place to condemn your father. I know something about betrayal, and in my experience, it's an insidious snake that leaks poison into every crevice of your life. You start to question everything. It breeds fear, and fear is a powerful force. But, let me be clear, it's *his* fear. He was wrong to infect you with it."

Her eyebrows arched.

"I'll say it again because you need to understand me, to believe me. With me, you can have it all," I promised.

Hope slipped into her eyes, tilting the color toward the moss green I loved so much. My chest puffed up in pride seeing the effect I had on her. I'd do anything to keep that strain of hope alive. I'd have to prove my sincerity, my willingness to do anything for her, including trying to convince her father or fight him, if it came to that. The point was, I was willing to do whatever was necessary to bring my pledge to fruition. I didn't know the details yet, but I'd have to start with facing my guilt-based relationship with Alex.

Her pearly white teeth pressed down into her luscious bottom lip. "You think so?"

I tightened my hold around her throat, feeling the *thump, thump* of her calmer pulse beneath my hand.

"I know so," I replied solemnly.

16

CLARA

I woke up to the sound of light snores. *Tatum?* I shifted my head on the warm plane of his broad chest where I'd conked out the night before and looked up. Yup, it was him. Wait, the most perfect man I knew snored? This was the first time I'd ever woken up before him. Usually, he'd showered by the time I opened my eyes. Real sex must have worn him out in a way fooling around didn't.

How very human of him, considering he otherwise acted like a relentless machine. I don't think the man slept more than five hours a night. He certainly fucked like a machine, all that strength, those muscles and sinews shifting above me as he worked his hard cock inside me. A shiver swept through me at the memory.

Now that I knew what it felt like getting fucked by him, I was almost angry with myself for depriving myself these past few weeks. I could've been having this kind of out-of-body experience sex this whole time. What had I been thinking?

Not wanting to wake him, I carefully lifted my head and found myself curled up on top of him like a cat on its owner's lap. Only this owner had his hand possessively stamped on my ass.

Long, tawny eyelashes shadowed the perfect shelf of his sharply edged cheekbones. He had a strong straight nose, which was unusual in our world. Most men have had their noses broken once or twice. It spoke to the fact that he was either wise to get out of senseless scuffles, or he was such a dirty—I mean good—fighter he rarely got his ass whipped.

Lightly scraping my nails over the bristles of his square jaw reminded me of the abrasion he'd left on my inner thighs only hours before. His golden mane was a riot of messy curls, no remnants of the hair product he used to bring them under control.

He took my breath away.

His heavy-lidded bedroom eyes dragged open. Dark pools of shiny onyx stared back at me.

Busted.

I was caught checking him out.

One side of his sculpted, lush lips ticked up.

A cocky smirk.

"My queen," he murmured, his voice gravelly and unused.

My tummy dipped at his greeting. His queen. God, did I want that label to be true.

He bent down and slanted his mouth over mine for a kiss. I felt his hard shaft near my hip and pressed down, my way of signaling I wanted more.

He broke off our kiss and said, "Uh-uh, we missed dinner last night, and I'm certain you're sore this morning. Plus, we need to shower since you fell asleep with my come painted on you."

My pussy clenched. Who spoke that way? I mean, seriously. It was impossible to not melt over words like those.

"Oooo ... a shower," I said, perking up as I rubbed myself against him again. I was shameless, but I didn't much care if it got him between my thighs again.

"Not together," he growled. "I just finished saying you're sore. If we take a shower together, there's not a chance in hell I won't fuck you again. Getting inside you after weeks of restraint, I'm not going to be able to hold back, so off you go ... *alone.*"

I gave him a forlorn look.

"Don't pout at me, girl, not unless you want to be taught a lesson. I assumed it was a little early for that, but I can accommodate you."

"Ugh, you're such a taskmaster," I said as I rolled over to the end of the bed and jumped down.

I winced and he was on me in an instant.

"See, that's what I'm talking about," he scolded.

"Well, it didn't hurt until I stood up," I argued.

His face turned to stone. "It hurts?" he asked, in a low dangerous tone.

"No, it twinges. It was a twinge," I insisted. "Just a twinge."

"Uh-huh," he replied in a disbelieving tone, sweeping me up into his arms and striding into a huge bathroom decorated in elegant white and gray tones.

Placing me gently on the marble counter, he bent over and twisted open the knob of a sleek, vintage clawfoot soaking tub, set against an accent wall of white marble with gray veining.

My brows raised in surprise.

"You didn't seem like a soaking bathtub kind of guy," I quipped.

He gave a shrug of one shoulder. "Alex's father installed them when he bought out the four penthouse apartments in this building. Not gonna lie, I've enjoyed using it occasionally."

"Occasionally? That's it?" I scoffed. "With how cold it gets in the winter in this city, I'd be using it all the time."

He glanced up at me with a smoldering look. "I'm starting to see the real advantage to having one now," he said, giving me a slow perusal that left a blaze flickering over every inch he touched with his gaze.

"If he bought all four penthouse apartments, then he'd planned to install you here, along with his three sons. He must have loved you very much," I mused.

"Not to the extent he loved Alex and Nicu, but he certainly treated me better than Luca." His eyes turned pitch black, like a starless sky during a thunderous night.

"Now, every penthouse has a fiancée or wife installed inside," he noted, heavy with intention. Was he suggesting he wanted to install me in here as his fiancée? The thought had my tummy flip-flopping.

He pulled open a drawer beneath the sink and took out a small pair of scissors. Catching a lock of my hair, he asked, "May I?"

I gave him a smug smile and teased, "You want a lock of my hair?"

He nodded solemnly.

I gave a little one-shouldered shrug, even if heat suffused my chest, and I swooned at the gesture. Tatum, so steady and stoic, surprised me with the intimacy of his request.

"Sure."

He tugged one wavy lock, clipped it, and left the bathroom. From the counter, I leaned over slightly to watch him pull an antique locket out of his nightstand drawer, carefully curl the lock of hair inside, snap it shut, and return it to its place.

My heart pitter-pattered with unexpected delight, but feeling suddenly bashful in his presence, I resumed the thread of our conversation as if the hair-clipping had never happened. "Every penthouse but this one. How is it you've avoided marriage at your age?"

He gave my inner thigh a light pinch. "Hey, I'm not old."

"You're over thirty," I noted. "An unmarried *consilier* in his thirties is a unicorn."

He gave a little self-deprecating shrug. "One of the advantages of being in my position. I have enough power to carve out my own life ... for the most part. My mother would never impose on me, and Alex treats me like a partner. A run-of-the-mill *mafie* virgin couldn't handle my brand of fucking. I may have clout, but not enough to marry an outsider like Alex and Nicu did, so I waited until a gorgeous, strong *mafie* woman bulldozed her way into my life and swept me off my feet. After torturing me for months, that is," he finished with a wink.

I placed a hand on his upper arm and squeezed. "I'm sorry about that."

His eyes flashed. "Don't be. How would I know you were so strong if I didn't test you?"

I snorted. "I don't know how much testing you were doing. I attacked you from the get-go."

He caressed my cheek. "It happened the way it was meant to happen. I'm not like other *mafie* men. We've been socialized to seek out a meek, virginal woman, but my soul would've shriveled up if I'd been forced into marriage with an immature girl like that. I'd rather be alone and not fuck—"

"You didn't fuck?"

He sat on the edge of the tub and explained, "Except for the occasional breaks when I dropped in at an exclusive sex club to get it out of my system, I refrained. What was the point? I was focused on my job, and I didn't want complications. I wasn't opposed to relationships, but I wasn't about to be saddled with a woman who wasn't better than I am. 'Cause I don't need my equal, baby. I need a woman who's above me, who drives me to be better, stronger, sharper."

"I don't know if I'm anything like that …," I hedged.

He made a little harumph sound. "Modesty isn't a good look on you, Queenie. You're ten times stronger than I am. Quicker. Smarter. Finding you was like finding a diamond in the Sahara Desert. One in a billion. I know a gem when I see one. My pride got in my way for a stretch of time there, but now that I've had a taste of this," he said as he cupped my pussy, "I'm never letting you go."

His hand skimmed down and curled around my thigh, thick olive-skinned fingers completely encompassing my leg. He slid down until he shackled my ankle and brought it up to rest on the edge of the marble sink, exposing me to him.

"And oh, so sweet-tasting and pink. I couldn't have asked for a better bitch if I'd conjured her up myself. You've surpassed all my expectations of the woman I thought I wanted."

He dropped down to his knees.

My breath stuttered in my chest.

"My apologies in advance, baby girl," he murmured against my inflamed, wet flesh. "I know you're sore, but you brought this on yourself by tempting me. I'm going to get you nice and ready with my tongue. Then, I'm going to fuck my cock into you so hard, you're going to scream until I go deaf." His blackened eyes bored into me. "Hear me?"

I gulped and gave him a nod as his tongue flicked

against my clit a moment before he buried his golden head between my thighs.

After making me come, Tatum sponged me down in the tub, meticulously cleaning every inch of me. Of course, as he'd warned, he wasn't able to stop from taking me again. Bending me over the sink, I took every one of his delicious thrusts as he pounded into me, just as he'd promised.

He might be right, I thought to myself. This man could succeed in giving me everything. We might be able to have it all.

Later, the same thought bounced around in my head while I sat in the little nook in Tatum's kitchen. I was willing to cook, but he insisted on preparing breakfast.

Not only was he purposely tormenting me by walking around shirtless, but the sweats he wore rode low on his trim hips, showcasing that delicious V of his abs. I was wrapped in one of his robes with my arms around my knees, watching raptly as he bent down to pull food out of the refrigerator. I couldn't tear my eyes off the two perfect globes of his buttocks. Jesus, his ass. Seriously, the man was beyond fit. It was sick.

He pulled out a pot and started boiling water. My toes wiggled as I watched, instinctually knowing what he was about to prepare, *mămăligă cu lapte*, porridge made from polenta or cornmeal. I hadn't had it for ages, but it was perfect for a cold December morning. Unlike lumpy oatmeal, this was cooked, allowed to cool down, and then cut into pie-shaped pieces. Once done, it was served with milk poured over it.

Out the window in the nook, I glanced through the lingering fog at the cars and buses circling the statue in Columbus Circle, so many floors down below. The city didn't look so bad from up here, I could begrudgingly admit. Even for a winter day.

Not used to staying still, I asked, "Do you want me to make coffee or something?"

Tatum shook his head. "I want you to stay just as you are, wearing my clothes and relaxing in my kitchen. Seems to be one of the few rooms in my apartment that doesn't make you wilt. Will the *mămăligă* be enough for you, or should I make a spread of ham, cheese, bread, and other stuff for you?"

"Like your mother and Alex's *bunică* prepare every morning? No, I don't need that," I replied. Those two women whipped up a feast every day with cold cuts, various spreads, and cut tomatoes, cucumbers, and green onions. And that was without including any made-to-order options I requested, like eggs. Romanians liked eggs in the morning. My father ate a soft-boiled egg every morning, without fail.

Dropping a kiss on my nose, he took out the *ibric* and began preparing Turkish coffee for us.

"How did you learn to cook, or is *mămăligă* and coffee the extent of your abilities? Not that I wouldn't be impressed by those two things alone," I added quickly.

"I've been on my own for a while. As you were so quick to mention earlier, I'm old, being over thirty," he joked. "I can cook a few more dishes, some of them are even intricate. Alex's mom made sure her boys knew how to cook, and since I was always over at their house, I benefited from her cooking lessons."

My mouth dropped. "All of them can cook?"

What an anomaly. Romanian men were not known for their culinary abilities. Hell, I doubted my father knew how to boil the egg he ate every morning. I'm certain he never tried.

"Not only do they have skills, but they enjoy it." Stopping in the middle of pouring the polenta in the boiling water, he promised, "I can do anything you want, baby. I can fuck you, feed you, take care of you so you're healthy and fit to rule. I'll be whatever you need. Cook. Bodyguard. Advisor. Husband. Whatever it is, I'm there for it."

The last one made my lungs seize up. Some men talked for the sake of talking, but not Tatum. It wasn't his simple words but the pledge behind them. If he promised something, he'd deliver. It was almost too good to be true, but my heart burst with hope. Perhaps he could be the one to support me, perhaps my dreams could come true, and we could rule together.

Perhaps.

Tatum's phone vibrated on the counter. He picked it up, and whatever he heard made his jaw go hard. His eyes narrowed and then turned on me, softening for a moment. With a few clipped orders, he hung up and said, "One of our trucks got ambushed. Product stolen out the back in Jersey. It was right in front of a gas station, and the footage suggests it was Bratva, the bastards. Back to their old tricks now that the Lupu and the Popescus have joined forces. The unity makes them nervous."

A surge of pride shot through me at the ease he had with me, divulging something surely only meant for clan members.

"You have to go now," I replied firmly, pounding my fist to the table to emphasize my point. "You can't let them get away with this. They've been a thorn in the sides of the Romanians for long enough. It's only going to escalate if you don't shut them down now."

He stalked up to me and gave me a forceful, demanding kiss, thrusting his tongue into my mouth, giving no quarter.

My hand curled around his nape, pulling him in deeper for a few moments before dragging it down and pushing at his chest.

Breaking the kiss, I said, "Go and take care of it."

"You're a precious treasure, you know that?" he mused reverently.

I winked and smacked him on the butt. "Oh, I know."

17

TATUM

I took a seat on one of the couches in Alex's living room, leaning forward to take the Turkish coffee he offered. Nerves thrummed through me. Alex and I shared the penthouse floor, so it was only a matter of time before he realized Clara and I were living together. Not three days after taking Clara's virginity, I already found myself in his apartment for what would likely be an inquisition.

What I intended to be a blissful bubble of nonstop sex with Clara was rudely interrupted by the Bratva hit. It was quite a new sensation to come back from work and have someone to discuss it with, to bounce ideas off each other on how to best handle the situation. Clara might be young, but her father had done an impeccable job teaching her the ropes of the business. Her acumen was sharp, and she'd come up with suggestions that helped me track down the missing shipment of drugs in Jersey.

"No cookies or cake?" I asked innocently.

Normally, he'd have something to nibble on, but since *Bunică* was spending her time in the kitchen of my family house, and not his, she hadn't been baking as much for the boys. Star was back home. Between her high metabolism and being a fussy eater, Star had become startingly thin, so it was no surprise when Bunică took on the mission of fattening up my sister. It must be working because she was starting to show slight curves.

"You know damn well *Bunică's* obsession with feeding Star like her life depended on it," Alex replied in an indulgent tone, falling into the seat beside me.

"It's going to be a while longer. The construction on the house doesn't sound like it's going to be completed anytime soon," I commented.

He groaned. "Christ, don't remind me. The house sustained structural damage. At this point, we might as well tear the thing down and throw up a new one."

I chuckled, "I don't think your mother would approve. She's attached to the house Mihail bought and renovated for her."

"Tell me about it," he grumbled. "There's no way she's going to change anything in the 'house my husband bought me.' As if that house is worth as much as the land it stands on. But nothing I say seems to be working to change her mind." He eyed me. "How's your mother holding up with the both of them in the house? *Bunică* can be a challenge."

"Oh, please, she loves it. And it's not like my mother doesn't know your grandmother inside and out. They've been neighbors and friends going on thirty years now. You know how she is, she's glad to have the house full of people. I know it was tough on her when I pulled Star and Clara out to live with me."

I'd purposely brought up Clara, knowing this was the reason I'd been summoned.

"Speaking of Clara ...," he started. "I'm guessing you're fucking her. Think that's a good idea overall, Tatum?"

I huffed out a self-deprecating laugh. "Have you seen her? Think I could stop myself?"

He clapped a hand over my shoulder. "Hey, I'm not criticizing."

I was defensive, but I couldn't help myself when it came to her.

He shook his head. "I'm not, believe me. Who am I to judge when I ended up falling for an outsider?"

His voice was tight on that last word. He didn't like to think of Nina as having once been an outsider. Considering she was his little sister's best friend and our neighbor since forever, she'd always been part of our world. But she wasn't born Romanian, and quite a few clan members were put out by the fact that the most eligible and powerful Lupu man didn't pick a woman from a prestigious family. Marriages were generally arranged, even when they weren't used to forge or fortify alliances.

"Then what are you saying?" I asked him, somewhat tersely, considering I was conversing with my *șef*, not my friend. I was *consilier,* and I never fucked *mafie* women, so being with Clara, and Clara being the power broker she was for her clan, was no laughing matter.

This was business.

Only it didn't feel like business to me.

"Don't get your hackles up," he warned. "You grew up in this world, you know it like the back of your hand. Don't act like your conduct doesn't impact the clan because you can't fuck a princess like her, even if she comes from a lackadaisical clan from out west, and not expect consequences."

Staring straight ahead, I clenched my hands, unclenched them, and then balled them into fists.

He watched and let out a long sigh. "You know we're

brothers. You know I've got your back, but what you did complicates things."

"I don't care," I said, low and hard.

His eyes narrowed. "You don't have the luxury to not care. Just as I don't."

He paused, and then asked carefully, "Was she a virgin?"

It was a double-edged sword of a question, a damned if you did, damned if you didn't sort of question. If I said she wasn't, then I'd be lying and disrespecting her. If I said she was, then the significance of what I'd done was graver.

Although I hated revealing anything personal, I decided to go with the truth.

"She was," I replied simply.

"I'd assumed as much, but I had to ask. It's hard to tell what customs they still abide by out West. At least, we know they follow this one."

"For her, at least. I can't speak for the rest of them. She's a special case. Her father gave her an ultimatum. She has to remain a virgin to rule."

"So the rumor about her ruling is real, huh? I wasn't sure what to believe, it's so off the wall. But she's certain, eh?"

"She is," I answered.

"And her recent deflowering? Will that affect her position?"

Now he was digging. For the clan, of course.

"I'm not sure he's committed to the literal reading of the word *virgin*. From what she says, his main motive is to keep power-hungry men away by taking marriage off the table. He also believes she should focus solely on ruling. No family," I clarified.

His eyebrows hit his hairline. "My, my, my ... no family. No family whatsoever? He's a brutal bastard to put a condition like that on his one and only daughter. That would mean the end of his line."

"She has a brother. He's on the spectrum, but I believe the plan is for him to have the family. The father basically flipped roles for them."

"Savage move. Clever, but savage," Alex ruminated. "I admire him, but he's also fucking insane. And cruel. I understand the desire to pass on the mantle to your kin, but it's heartless of him to take the opportunity to have a family away from his only daughter."

Alex took a sip of his coffee, placed it on the coffee table before us, and leaned back into the cushions of the couch. "What are your plans? I don't know Clara well, but she looks to me like someone who won't easily renounce something she wants, and it's obvious she wants you. She didn't remain a virgin until she was twenty-one, only to relinquish it for a roll in the hay."

I took in a deep breath, released my fists, and met Alex's eyes because what I was about to say was going to be a bombshell for him. "She wants me to return to Los Angeles with her and convince her father to allow me to rule beside her."

Alex's teeth ground down. His body stiffened.

Leaning toward me, he said, "You can't leave me, Tatum. I've never done this without you in my corner. I trust you more than anyone else when it comes to my family, my business. Sure, shit has settled down with the Popescus, but you know better than anyone things can change on a dime. Look at the way the Bratva are coming at us right now."

I expected this reaction. I knew the way he thought. And for him, the clan was his number-one priority, outside of Nina and the baby growing in her belly. But just because I was prepared for it didn't mean it wasn't a sucker punch to the gut. I hated that he had a final say, that he could twist my life's path with a flick of his little finger, but nothing would come from losing my cool.

Fingering the cufflinks of one sleeve—a nervous tick—I replied carefully, "True, but I took care of it."

"For now," he countered. "The potential for more mischief from them is present. What happened a few days ago wasn't the end of it."

I didn't care. I didn't care about the Popescus, the Bratva, or whatever other potential problems would inevitably come up in our rancid world. I wanted Clara. It had taken me thirty-two years to find a woman I wanted to fuck more than once, much less spend the rest of my life with, and I wasn't about to let her go.

I remained silent, thinking it was better to stay mute than to speak my mind. I'd dedicated my life to Alex and the Lupu clan. A part of me was honored, proud I'd succeeded in making myself essential. But there were darker motivations as well. There was the desire to protect my family, fear, and finally, guilt. It lay in my belly like a coiled snake, ready to strike at any moment.

This clan had occupied every moment of my life, but I was ready to pivot in another direction, to seek out more. Suddenly, I understood Clara's fear of wanting too much because it felt terrifying to reach for more. As she'd so eloquently put it, it felt greedy.

The heart wanted what it wanted, and mine wanted Clara. As long as my family was safe, I was ready to step away from the strictures that defined my life since the day my father's secret wrapped itself around my neck like a noose.

"Neither of my brothers can replace you," Alex continued. "Luca and I have come a long way, but there's no way we would get along well and work as closely as you and I do. As for Nicu, his strengths lie elsewhere."

"What about Sebastian?" I asked, although I already knew his answer.

"He's not ready. I'm not saying he can't grow into the role, but you and I have ruled together since the beginning. Honestly, it never occurred to me you'd marry outside the clan, that you'd want to move out of New York." There was an accusatory lilt to his tone.

"I've finally met a woman who's my match. I'm not attracted to the sweet, innocent women like you and Luca are. Clara is unlike any woman I know, but especially *mafie* women. She's like me but on steroids. She can take me as I am," I stated, not wanting to explicitly state my predilections.

"I understand," he replied simply, knowing where my predilections lay.

"Then you know she's a gem, one in a million," I shot back.

He shook his head. "Nevertheless, I can't let you go."

I flinched. Disappointment, tinged with an unfamiliar rage, flared through me. I needed this, I needed her. I couldn't let her go, yet I couldn't ask her to give up her ambitions for me. She was made to be a leader.

"Fuck," I cursed.

His face went slack for a moment before he caught himself and smoothed over his expression.

Wiping my hand over my face, I rubbed my chin. "Do you think you could ever? What about if I personally train Sebastian until I can guarantee that he can take over for me?"

I was grasping at straws, but claws of desperation squeezed around my throat. Grinding down on my back teeth, I said, "Come on, Alex. I've never known you to be selfish."

It was a risk, daring to criticize a man like him. It was untrue and unfair; he was one of the most selfless men I knew. I'd played him a dirty hand, but I had to make him see how much this meant to me.

His green eyes glittered. He didn't like what I'd said.

After a long period of dead silence, he leaned back against the couch again, mimicking relaxation, although, having known this man most of my life, I wasn't fooled by his posture.

"I don't make any promises, but I'll consider your suggestion. Sebastian is loyal. Eager to learn. But he has a long way to go, and even if he improves, he can never be you. You understand what I'm saying, don't you?"

"Yes," I replied instantly. "You'd be making a sacrifice. For me."

"You're irreplaceable," he said softly.

My heart ached and sank at the same time. Of course, who didn't want to hear such praise? It felt good to be wanted, but not if it kept me away from what was mine.

I huffed out a little derisive laugh. "You know better than I, Alex, that no one is irreplaceable. Your father was the most ruthless and successful *şef* to live, and yet he died and you took his place. I am, most definitely, replaceable. I will mold Sebastian to take my place. Don't worry, I will prepare him," I promised.

"Does he have what it takes?" Alex asked dubiously.

"Definitely. He wants to prove himself as a Romanian and a *mafie*-made man. Your father gave him an out. He could've easily left well enough alone and never contacted you. If he wanted a relationship with you and your brothers, he could have left it at that without getting into the business, like Emma has. But no, he committed himself immediately. I sense he has something to prove," I concluded.

"With my father, there was always something to prove," he said with a sigh. "It was part and parcel of being his son."

"I wouldn't leave you high and dry, Alex, but I won't lie to you, I'm committed to Clara. I'm committed to making this work for both of us."

Alex hadn't said yes, but he hadn't categorically said no, either. I'd hang on to that. I'd get Sebastian in shape.

"Talk to Sebastian," I persisted. "Give him a heads-up because starting tomorrow, Sebastian will be my shadow. Unless I'm in bed with my woman, I'll be putting him through his paces."

I wasn't going to waste a moment. Tomorrow, he'd start on the accelerated track.

"Don't get your hopes up," Alex warned me, as if hearing my thoughts. "The decision ultimately lies with me."

How could I forget? I didn't need a reminder that my happiness, my life with Clara, hung in the balance. But I was no stranger to hard work. I'd work on this harder than anything else I'd ever done. Pray to God, it worked out.

18

CLARA

I was in Tatum's penthouse, wrangling with the new accounting software I couldn't seem to figure out. Numbers were not my forte, but I was determined to get a handle on a program supposedly made for civilians like me. After pouring hours into trying to figure it out, my frustration was at a boiling point. I wanted to slam the cover of my laptop shut and hurl it across the room.

Realizing I wasn't getting anywhere, I wrapped up in a cashmere coat, took the penthouse elevator down, and went for a walk. Skirting around the busy traffic of Columbus Circle, I passed a huge silver globe sculpture on my way to Broadway. It was a bright sunny day, despite the cold, so I strolled north toward Lincoln Center. The crisp fresh air helped dispel my frustration, which I realized wasn't only about the software.

I was falling for Tatum. It wasn't hard to see why, with his rigid sense of honor, his love and tenderness for his family, his way of taking care of me. But this was uncharted territory for me. I'd never trusted or depended on anyone outside my family or clan before.

Oh, and did I forget to mention I was also addicted to Tatum's brand of fucking?

Dear God, the way he fucked ... like a man stranded in a desert, clutching his last flask of water. If it had simply been a good fuck, I could've handled it. If I'd simply lost my virginity, I could've handled it. If I was no longer the Virgin Queen, I could've handled that, too. But what I couldn't cope with was how well he handled me. He used every weapon at his disposal—tongue, fingers, cock, and *words*—with deadly precision and went for the kill. The kill being capturing my heart.

I reached Lincoln Center, with its Christmas tree decorated in blue-white snowflake-shaped lights in the plaza surrounded by three stately buildings. As cold and miserable as I thought the city would be, I couldn't help but admire the backdrop of the open-air pop-up Christmas market surrounding the tree. The white limestone façade of the Metropolitan Opera House was beautiful in the bright sun, with its five tall arches, large glass windows encased in bronze. The crisp blue sky soared above it, like a block of color in a geometrical abstract painting.

Like this city, Tatum had disarmed me. Broken me. And the worst, the absolute worst part, was that he'd scraped the pieces of me off the floor and put me back together again. In his image. Yes, his image ... of me. And that image was bad. Truly bad. It was the image of a woman who sought his approval, who sought out the best way to serve him, to surrender, to *submit*.

I wandered around the stalls, stopping to get a cup of hot cocoa with whipped cream, and then made my way back to the penthouse.

Until last night, I didn't realize the depth of this desire. Sure, I'd ached for a man's touch, but I'd assumed it was because I'd been a twenty-one-year-old, sex-starved virgin. Turned out, the yearning went much deeper.

What was the big deal about feeling this way? Wasn't this just swapping out one man for another?

No, no it was not. I loved my father, respected him, and yes, I'd been brought up to defer to him, but I wasn't driven to do his bidding. If I thought something he'd asked of me was wrong, I stood up to him. I already planned to confront him about this Virgin Queen business.

But with Tatum, I yearned, I ached to please him. The drive was like a spike of cocaine in my system. I got high off him and on letting him do whatever he wanted to me. What if it made me weak? What if I wasn't able to stand up to him? Worst, what if those were unfounded fears and he was perfect?

I naively thought once I'd had sex, I could pick myself up and go on with my life just as before. But he'd demanded so much more than my virginity. He'd demanded my very soul. And I gave it to him, lock, stock, and barrel. I was so confused. Was this good? Was it bad? My body and soul wanted to turn themselves over to him, but my inner bossy bitch told me it was wrong. It was the antithesis of what I should be. I should be the queen everywhere, as much inside the bedroom as out.

I was in the middle of this inner battle as I opened the door of the penthouse. Tatum took one look at me from the couch where he was sitting, stood up, and stalked over to me.

The blast of his forceful personality shot out, enveloping me in the blistering heat of his intensity. Tatum came off as quiet, but it only added to the aura of danger. He was the stealthy type, the kind you had to be careful around. I thrived on knowing I was his Achilles' heel, as he was mine, but I also resented how a man I used to hate had unexpect-edly invaded my life, made me question my values, and turned my world upside down.

"What is it?" he demanded, as he distracted me by strip-ping my jacket off and dumping it directly on the floor. His broad shoulders and wide chest loomed over me.

"Nothing," I replied mulishly, glaring up at him. I was acting bratty but couldn't help myself.

He rocked back on his heels. "You're lying." He paused. "Is it your father? Grigore?"

"No," I snapped. My gaze fell away, and I covered my face, embarrassed by my conduct. "Nothing like that."

He took my hand and led me to the couch. Sparks exploded on my skin at our point of contact. I withdrew it, or at least tried to, but he tightened his clasp on me. I jerked my hand out of his and fell back, accidently shoving my laptop off the couch. It crashed to the ground, but I couldn't bother to check if it was still intact.

"I'm not letting you go," he informed me in a clipped tone that was more growl than gravel. "I'm warning you, that's *never* going to happen."

My spine straightened. "Is that a threat?"

His brows slammed down, his eyes morphing into two black pits.

His hand dove between my thighs, seizing my pussy. "Sweetness, I don't require threats. I have better methods in my arsenal to subdue you back into the tame little rabbit I own."

To my embarrassment, I let out a moan.

Oh, God, that felt so good. I needed his touch and his bossy words to anchor me. It was so wrong, but it felt so right.

Fingers tapping my clit, he chuckled darkly. "Baby girl, if

you wanted a fight, all you had to do was ask. I'll match you any day."

A rush of desire dampened my panties from that one sentence, dammit, which only made me madder. I gritted my teeth. How did he read me so well? He knew my compulsions before I knew them myself.

"You're ready for your first lesson, I see." Releasing me, he took a seat beside me, spread his legs open, and pointed to the ground. "On your knees."

Pushing into his space, I spat out, "Hell fucking no."

I swore he almost laughed, but at the last instant, he wiped the amusement clear from his face.

I flipped my hair and crossed my arms over my chest. "Now, what are you going to do about *that*?" I taunted.

Quick as lightning, he shot his hand out, grasped my hair, and dragged me to the floor until he had me exactly where he wanted me. I squirmed, not stupid enough to jerk my head considering the tight grip he had on my hair. Fuck, that was good. Exactly what I wanted.

"This is what it means to be mine," he instructed coolly. "And you're going to find yourself in this position and many, many naughtier ones until you learn to behave as a queen should."

"A queen should bow to no one," I snarled, eyes prickling with the threat of tears. *Where was this coming from?*

"Ahh, I see the issue. You think bowing to me is weak. You doubt this is a position of strength. Don't let the outside world dictate the dynamics of *our* relationship," he warned. "Our road to happiness is not paved with the intentions and judgments of others. You like to play the brat, and I like to let you play, but I'm dead serious right now. Giving me control doesn't make you weak, in this or any other position."

He paused. "And believe me, sweet girl, your body and mind are mine. I *own* every single part of you."

I trembled under his hand. I wanted to believe him, to believe that he was my rock, the harbor I could turn to regardless of what happened elsewhere in my life. If I was out of sorts over a stupid accounting program, how would I manage the future trials and tribulations that would come at me once my father gave me his position? I wanted Tatum to be the solid-gold core that kept me stable and balanced, but I was scared. My mother was the only example I had and look how epically she'd failed my father.

"A queen bows to no one," I reiterated stubbornly, my voice shaking.

"This queen does," he replied, as if that somehow explained everything. "Your power gets rejuvenated at my feet. They will take and take from you until you have nothing left to give, suck you dry until you're an empty core. I've seen it happen to Alex. And just as he goes to Nina to restore him, you need to be on your knees in front of me for it to happen. I don't make the rules, Clara, I just implement them."

I pulled back a little to test him. His grip stayed strong, which was answer enough. He wasn't going to budge. Our battle of wills dragged on for some time, me glaring at him, him staring back at me passively. Passive, my ass. There was nothing passive about this man. I wiggled and shuffled this way and that, but he corrected me until I ended up back in the exact spot where he wanted me.

Finally, I rolled my eyes, let out a frustrated sigh, and mumbled, "Fine."

"Good girl," he crooned, and the sound of his deep voice, hushed and tinged in softness, melted my core. My core might be gooey chocolate, but my pussy clenched in anticipation. She knew what she was doing, treacherous whore. To me, this had been a battle. To her, it'd been fore-play. Unfortunately, I was near out of energy to fight him. There was a natural eroticism in being caged between the thick, solid muscles of his thighs, gazing up his long torso to his sleek jet-black eyes. At this point, I simply wanted to roll onto my back and beg him to fuck me.

I licked my lips, biting down on the bottom one in eagerness for what he'd do next. The expectation on my face must have convinced him that I was done fighting. I was. For now.

Releasing my hair, he leaned back.

"It's time for your correction," he intoned.

"Oh, and what is that?" I asked with a coquettish bat of my lashes.

"A spanking."

"A what?" I gasped out.

"Yes."

"No," I said, shaking my head with rejuvenated energy. Heat dipped in fear bloomed over me. I wanted to be coveted, treasured, not punished. I wanted to be a spoiled brat and get away with it. I wanted to stamp my feet, pound his chest, and have my little tantrum.

I crouched in readiness for a sprint, but his hand snapped forward and caught my thick, golden-brown tresses again.

"A spanking," he echoed.

"I don't want one," I whined obstinately.

"You've had one before," he cajoled.

Sure, when we were in bed, he smacked my butt a little.

"Yes, but that was different. This is a punishment."

"That it is," he agreed, as he drew me up to my feet and pressed on my lower back until I tipped over his thighs. My vision spun as I followed his lead, and then I was draped across his hard legs, on my belly. How I ended up there, I barely understood. It was as if he'd cast a spell over me.

His tone tightened, "This will be much different."

Lifting my skirt, he rubbed lazy circles over my buttocks. Heat crackled over my skin from his large hands smoothing over my panties. At least I had them for protection. As if hearing my thoughts, he slid his finger under the band and slowly peeled them off me. A flash of cool air brushed over my warmed skin.

"You need this," he murmured and then dropped his open palm on my ass with a hard clap.

"Ouch!" I cried. "Fuck."

"Not the right thing to say, baby girl, but I'll let that one pass."

I threw him a glare over my shoulder only to find him smirking. Oh, he was enjoying this much too much, the bastard.

He caressed my lower back and buttocks with a warning. "Settle down."

Just as I relaxed, another stinging smack had me puffing out my cheeks.

Through gritted teeth, I demanded, "Not so hard, dammit."

"What would be the fun in that?" he teased, giving me another wallop that brought the pain up a few notches.

"Jesus, Tatum."

His response was a series of swats that left an itchy burn. And heightened arousal. It hurt, but at the same time, the pain was doing something else. I rubbed my throbbing clit discreetly against his solid thigh, my pussy clenching desperately to be filled. Damn the man for what he did to me.

"I do with you as I see fit. You're not the one in the driver's seat, Clara. Not with me. The sooner you realize that—

"Yes, yes, the happier we'll be," I said sourly. "I've heard it before."

My obstinance provoked him because he grasped one of my hot pink ass cheeks and said, "That's right, but I don't like your tone when you say it. You're not taking it seriously."

"Oh, believe me, I'm taking it seriously enough," I retorted. "I'm lying over your thighs, letting you spank me, aren't I?"

His grip on my flesh intensified, hitting my pain threshold. One would think it would shut down the pounding arousal coursing through me. Wrong, so wrong. If anything, I had to bite back a moan of pleasure. I clasped my thighs and buttocks together to ward off the somersault of warring sensations. He was speaking, saying something to me, but it was hard to concentrate on his words.

"—and listen well, little girl. Right now, you need to know I'm tough enough to take anything you throw my way. That is the lesson this spanking is meant to teach." He gave me a hard swat. "And you'll learn to give me control, if it's the last thing I do."

Earlier, he'd said he owned me. He wasn't wrong because only someone who owned me could touch me in this way. How else could I explain being laid over his knees, with his hand swatting my buttocks?

To make matters worse, he knew I was soaked and on the edge of coming. His fingertips caressed the curve of one cheek and parted my thighs. I pressed them tightly together.

"Open them before I yank your legs apart and smack that filthy little pussy."

I threw them open.

He made a humming sound of approval as his fingertips languidly stroked down to my pussy and flicked my clit.

But instead of kindly continuing until I peaked, his nimble fingers slipped away. He began to torturously alternate between playing between my thighs and smacking my ass, keeping me off balance until I swung like a pendulum from pain to pleasure, all at his discretion. The only things keeping me tethered to reality were the scratchy material of his trousers, the hard muscles beneath them, and his familiar musky scent.

Incrementally, my mind shut down the flutter of constant thoughts and worries. My accounting woes flew out of my head. My fears about my father evaporated. And my body melted underneath Tatum's skilled hands.

Soon, my hips were writhing of their own accord. His smacks grew in intensity, and I tilted my hips to strike my clit against his thigh, causing it to spark each time. The pain melded with the pleasure until they were entwined as one. The heat and brand of his palm against my sizzling flesh had reached a zone that was beyond pain, amplifying my arousal in a way that was worlds apart from what we had done before.

Thrashing my head from side to side, I moaned and panted without reprieve. He kept me on the verge of orgasm, refusing to release me in order to teach me the lesson that he was in control.

"You want to come?" he finally demanded.

"Yes, yes, yes," I repeated as a mantra. "Please, please, please, Tatum, please."

"Don't worry, baby, you'll come." He flipped me upright and dropped my searing bottom on his lap, scraping it against the material of his pants. I yelped.

"On my cock," he finished.

I wheezed in shock and pain. He carefully slid me onto the cool leather couch, which was a huge relief against my burning skin.

Ripping at his tie, he tore it off, undid his cuff links, which flew and clattered on the wooden floor, and quickly undressed. Then, he stomped toward me, showing off muscles upon muscles on his chest and abs. His proud, arrogant cock swayed as he stepped in front of me. I licked my lips, remembering how delicious he tasted.

"Nah-ah, none of that," he rebuked as he parted my thighs with his own, stepping into the space as if he owned it. I scooted back, hissing at the rush of pain on my butt. He glided his hands up my torso to my chest. Seconds later, he pushed his tongue into my mouth. After giving me a hard kiss, he licked his way down, twirled around one nipple, and sucked it into his mouth.

"Oh, God," I breathed out, grabbing hold of his hair, and arching to thrust my breast deeper into his hot mouth.

He settled into me, and his powerful cock parted my slick inner walls.

I gripped his firm ass cheeks and yanked him toward me, screaming, "Deeper."

He plunged to the hilt, and I moaned in relief.

He gave me a searing look and pulled out, saying, "You don't call the shots."

Damn him.

"You don't own me," I fired back, goading him on with the fire in my belly.

"Oh, I think I do. If you want my cock, you know what to do."

"Fuck you, Tatum," I hissed.

His somber gaze on me, he replied smoothly, "I have every intention of fucking you, VQ. As soon as you comply."

I narrowed my eyes at him. I was used to being in charge, to having my word followed, but with him, I lived in another dimension.

"Why do I always have to listen to you?" I huffed. "When do we get to switch it around? When do you get to be *my* fuckboy?"

His eyes flashed.

Oh, shit, he liked the idea.

I'd been whining and the words had inadvertently popped out of my mouth. I hadn't meant it. He had such a dominant personality I didn't think he'd even consider such an idea. I certainly hadn't, but the look on his face told me otherwise.

"You want a piece of this," he said, tugging his long, thick shaft. My gaze immediately zoomed down to his wide fingers slipping up and down, a thick vein curled around his cock, snaking in and out of sight.

Leaning forward, he murmured against my lips, "You want to take it? Use it? Use *me*?"

My head canted to one side. "Uhm ... yeah."

"Come here," he ordered as he leaned back into the couch.

I swung myself over him. His cock pulsated beneath me, magnificent and hard.

"Down," he ordered.

"How is it that I'm the one using you, but you're the one still giving the orders?"

Not bothering to reply, he grasped my hips and pressed me down. Swallowing his bulbous crown, I dropped, inch by inch, his wide girth stretching me wide. The walls of my pussy conformed and compressed around his shaft. God, nothing, but nothing, felt like this man.

I was supposed to be the one using him, but how would I ever be in control on his huge cock?

I was only halfway down when it got to be too much. From my position, it was more difficult than it seemed. Granted, he was thick, but I didn't have a problem taking him last night. I wiggled my hips, trying to force myself down, but I struggled to take all of him.

I huffed and puffed until he arched a brow at me and asked, "Is there an issue?"

Stricken, I looked at him and nodded. Dammit, even when he gave me control, I seemed to fail. I gulped, feeling suddenly awkward, like a stupid, inexperienced girl. Tears pricked my eyes and my bottom lip trembled.

He came up and cupped my cheek. "Hey, what's wrong?"

Shaking my head, I said, "I don't know."

"We both know you have a greedy pussy, so that's not the problem. You think you should be in control, but it's not what you want. Stop overthinking things, Clara. It's not what gets you off. Let me take over, okay?" he suggested in a soothing voice.

I nodded in relief, feeling a weight slide off my shoulders.

"It's a process, baby. Acceptance of your nature takes time," he said tenderly. "Just follow what feels good, without judgment, alright."

I nodded at him reflexively again.

He patted my hip and I pulled off him.

He was back in the driver's seat, and everything felt right. Nervous expectation thrummed through me. Standing in front of him, I asked expectantly, "What are you going to do?"

"Mmm, I'm going to put you on your hands and knees for starters," he revealed, doing just that. Nudging my legs wider, he stepped up to me and rubbed his cock up and down my opening.

"Good girl, see how much better this feels?"

My heart fluttered at his praise. Relaxing under his guidance, I arched my spine and threw my head back. "God, that feels so good."

He stabilized one hand on my hip, the other on my lower back. He pressed his mouth to my ear, and said, "Your cunt is still so tight, you can't take me on your own yet. I do love that you're so greedy you can't help but try and force your snug little hole down my big, thick cock. I love watching you get frustrated trying to take it whole, but this is how it's done, baby."

With that warning, he buried himself in one demanding stroke.

I let out a screech, my skin flashing white-hot as he pounded into me, driving out every doubt or thought from my head. I reveled in the way he filled me, not a millimeter to spare. I swore I could feel the veins of his shaft rubbing against my inner walls.

"Look how your wet cunt stretches around my cock. I own this pussy. Say it, Clara," he ordered darkly.

I pushed back onto his cock; the path made smooth by my juices. "Tatum. Tatum owns this pussy," I shouted.

"That's right, and I'm going to fill this tight, slutty pussy with my come. You'll be so full, you'll be spurting and squelching out come for days. I'm going to breed you, and there's nothing you can do to stop me."

His teeth marked me again, clenching down on the same spot where my neck met my shoulder. Teeth hanging onto me, fingers clenched around my hips, he tunneled in and out of me. I didn't think I'd ever get over the feeling of being impaled by him. Claimed. Taken. Possessed. And with that final thought, as he plowed into me with ruthless thrusts, I exploded.

I scrambled for purchase and scratched deep gouges in the pristine white leather of his couch. Flashes of light hit my retinas. Words may have spilled out, maybe even a shriek, but I couldn't hear them over the roar in my ears. My cheek landed on leather. I twitched as my orgasm quaked through my limp muscles.

This was what I'd needed. Vestiges of reality came drifting back into my consciousness. I was pinioned by his huge cock, my knees and palms pressing into the fibers of the carpet. His face was buried in my shoulder, his fingers clamped around my flesh, his rough hair rubbed against my pussy, and his come flooded me. He heaved a shudder behind me.

Right or wrong no longer mattered. Tatum spanked me to dislodge the fears and worries tied around my throat like a noose. He gave me the freedom to test my boundaries, and once I fell on my face, he was right there to pick me up and fuck me into oblivion. I was like one of Adrian's finicky violins, but he played me like a maestro, indulging in the slight quirks that gave it its unique sound.

Seriously, after being petted and pampered and fucked in this way, I didn't know if I could live without him. Hopefully, that day would never come.

19

TATUM

I'd left Clara with Luca, who was the numbers guy of our enterprise, to help her learn the software she'd been struggling with when I came home yesterday. As for me, today was the beginning of Sebastian's training. I met him at the Dacia Café, which doubles as Alex's office and our home base, to take him along the rounds of our various businesses in the 'hood.' The plan was to let clan members see him with me and to expose him to my duties.

When Alex first brought Sebastian around, I did an extensive background check on him. He was as squeaky clean as they came. After his father, Mihail's death, he had no contact of any kind with a mafia clan or crime syndicate.

Honestly, it was a bit of a surprise to me, considering who Mihail was, but the man had done an excellent job of isolating his second family from the rest of his life. After his murder, they'd been shielded from our world and lived off a trust fund he'd set up for them. Granted, it wasn't easy to search for us, even if we lived in plain sight, but I was astonished by their total lack of contact with the Lupu clan.

As per Mihail's instructions, his mother gave Sebastian a

sealed letter when he turned twenty-five years old. In it, his father explained his reasons for keeping the two families apart and gave Sebastian the blessing to approach Alex. Needless to say, the first meeting had turned into a shitshow for Alex and Nicu, who'd both worshipped the ground Mihail walked on until that point.

But Alex would never pass up the chance of cultivating a loyal foot soldier and possible future officer. So, Sebastian was brought into the fold.

Despite my initial reservations, I got to know him in California while we tried to woo the Hagi and other smaller clans over to the dark side. He was charismatic and handsome, but most importantly, he looked like a Lupu. He was also bright, although apparently, Emma was the genius of the family. Whereas she was notoriously shy, he was a charmer and had already won over half the *mafie* girls, even with being only half Romanian. It was ironic how Alex and I had switched positions. Now he was reticent while I was the one gunning for Sebastian.

"I need you to do well," I stated as we stepped out of the café onto 48th Street. Our first stop was a Romanian bakery, which doubled as a depot for storing illicit merchandise, down the street on the commercial strip of Greenpoint Avenue.

"I won't fail you," he promptly replied as we passed a row of townhouses, which were soon replaced by larger five-story red brick apartment buildings.

"You'd better not. I've already done my due diligence on you, but I'm warning you, I'm going to dig into everything. I'm going to excavate so far back I'll be going through your kindergarten grades. I'm going to dig so deep your bones will ache from how far I'll tunnel under your skin."

We reached the corner and crossed under the Welcome to Sunnyside sign suspended across Greenpoint Avenue.

"Do it," he shot back. "I'm not scared. There are no skeletons in my closet. You've grown up in the *mafie* world, so you don't understand that regular people don't normally get into trouble. They can live their entire lives without taking one step outside the bounds of the law. That was me before I approached Alex. You don't have to worry, Tatum. I'm your man."

I halted in my tracks in front of a small music shop named Pianos, even though the only items in the display window were a music stand and an upright guitar. Scrutinizing him, I asked, "Why, Sebastian? Why won't you fail me?"

My tone was suspicious, harsh even, but I didn't have time to waste. If he couldn't get the job done, I'd have to set my sights on another man.

"Because I have to prove myself," he said as he held my gaze. "I've wanted to be part of this world since I was a kid, but Mihail forbade it. We were his dirty little secret, his backstairs family, and he didn't want to get grief from his mother, his wife, or his clan. My family was an oasis for him, and he made sure not to mix the two worlds. It wasn't for some semi-noble reason, like protecting my mother or Alex's mother from the truth. I honestly don't think he loved either of them enough to care about their feelings."

"Okay, so you've always wanted to be part of the *mafie*. Is that it? Because that's not enough for me. Convince me. Tell me something I don't know," I said, testing him. "Something no one knows."

An old man in a suit that had seen better days hobbled by with a cane, nodding to me in recognition. I called out a greeting in Romanian and waited patiently for him to be out of earshot before returning to Sebastian.

His green eyes, so much like Alex's, turned hard as emeralds. "One person knows my secret, and that's because she's part of it," he said cryptically.

My eyes sharpened, registering every flicker of emotion on his face. A flash of pain crossed over swiftly before he hid it.

"What is it?" I ordered as I resumed walking. "Tell me."

"I want to succeed in the clan and rise up because of Lana."

I jerked back. "Gabby's older sister? That hellion?"

To say I was shocked was an understatement. The fact that he knew her nickname was significant enough on its own. Only her family, and I knew her family well since Gabby was Star's best friend, called her Lana. "What about her? What does she have to do with you?"

"You haven't done enough research on me yet, I see," he joked, his eyes twinkling for a moment. Then it was gone, and he was serious again.

"Explain," I demanded because, fuck me, there was something there and, as *consilier*, I should've known about it. It should've come up in my research like he'd said.

"Relax. You didn't fall down on the job. There's no way you could've known that we spent time together as kids. The only people aside from Emma who knew are dead and buried," he said.

I breathed out in relief.

"As you know, her father was *consilier*. He was the only one in Mihail's inner circle who knew about us. My mother used to complain about how Mihail didn't share any part of his life with her, so he brought Lana's father along. Over the years, he'd come with Lana, who was close to my age. Gabby was an infant, and he wasn't the type of man to change diapers, if you know what I mean, so I didn't meet her until later.

"One day, when we were teens, we were caught kissing." His eyes turned a stormy green, gray and green swirling around each other, fighting for dominance. "Her father yanked her out of my room and dragged her out of the house by her hair." His eyes turned bleak. "I never saw her again."

He broke eye contact, twisted his head away, and stared off down the bustling street. He rubbed his chin for a good moment.

"Later, I learned that her father had arranged for her to be engaged to Razvan, even though she was barely fifteen. I never knew what hate felt like until that day. I confronted Mihail, stared straight into his craggy, old face, and I realized then he was a monster. A narcissistic, manipulative prick who cared about nothing but himself. Humph, as if I needed any further proof after the way he treated my mother and Alex's mother. "

Eyes gleaming with deadly intent, he swore, "*I will* become *consilier, I will* prove myself to her and this clan, and *I will* win her back."

My eyebrows lifted.

"Uhm ... she's married," I reminded him quietly as I silently acknowledged another Romanian, this time the mother of one of my soldiers. It wasn't ideal to have a conversation on the street, and yet here we were.

Once the woman was far out of hearing range, Sebastian turned abruptly toward me, his face set in granite, and said, "Not for long."

"In case you think you can ever kill him, her husband isn't a nobody," I observed.

"And soon, neither will I be, so let the best fucking man win. Regardless of whatever happens between Lana and me, after what he's done to her, he deserves to die."

"Those are fighting words. He's a made man, so I suggest, for your own safety, you don't repeat them out loud," I counseled as I resumed walking.

One might think that I would take those words of treason to heart against a member of my own tribe, but Sebastian wasn't wrong. Razvan was a miserable bastard. He was one of my main playground tormentors when I was a kid. I knew what he was capable of. He was a bully, and I could only imagine how he treated Lana. Of course, Lana was a tough woman and held her own against him. They didn't have an easy life together.

But that was their business. I wasn't about to get my hands dirty over a potential love triangle, and I said potential because I didn't know what to make of Sebastian's declaration. Whatever Sebastian threatened to do, he'd have to be strong before he could step up to a man like Razvan. As much as I wanted him to take over for me, it wasn't a done deal, and assuming Sebastian became *consilier*, Razvan could take care of himself. It was a dicey proposition to go up against a made man on a good day. And Razvan was as tough as they came.

"I have a plan, Tatum, and I won't be deterred," he swore.

"What would you have done if I didn't consider you as a replacement?" I asked curiously.

"There's more than one way to skin a cat. I would've figured out another way. The moment I saw Lana, I knew we were meant to be together. And when I saw him, I knew he needed to be disposed of. This is an opportunity to bypass a lot of shit and get to the top faster," he divulged.

I clapped him on the back. "Well, let's get to it, brother. You have a lot to learn and not much time to do it in."

"How much time?" he asked.

A car passed pounding out a heavy bass. I let it pass before answering. "Ideally, I want to be gone in a couple months. I'll be here for however long it takes, but now that I know you have a goal in mind and are prepared to do whatever's necessary, I can push you hard."

"Why do you want to leave? I mean, you're at the pinnacle of the most powerful *mafie* family in the world. Why give that up?"

"For the same reason you gave up your former life," I answered.

"For a woman."

"To another man, it might not make sense. I've dedicated my life to this family, and I'm honored to be part of it, but I —it isn't everything, you know? At a certain point, it stopped being enough, and when I met Clara, everything fell into place."

He snorted. "Sure it was the moment you met her 'cause you guys were at each other's throats for a good chunk of time? Would've never guessed from the way you two went at it in California you'd end up where you are now."

I chuckled. "That was prolonged foreplay, my friend. Perhaps you'll be so lucky to play the same game of cat and mouse with your woman at some point in the future."

He made a noise in the back of his throat.

"My woman," he said softly, almost a whisper.

His striking clear green eyes lifted to me. "I don't know when the day will come, if ever. There are many barriers in the way."

"Barriers were meant to be broken by men like us. We

never play by the rules. Why would that change with the rules of love?"

"Touché."

We'd reached the Brutărie București, and I paused, hand on the doorknob of the evergreen-painted door. "Let's get started. While I'm glad to know we're both on the same page, we have a long way to go. Alex doesn't want to let me go, and he's far from convinced you're an adequate substitute."

Sebastian's gaze turned hard as granite. "Then it's time we prove him wrong."

"Amen, brother," I murmured. "Amen."

20

CLARA

Grigore called again.

I was taking a break, my laptop abandoned by my side as I stretched out on Tatum's huge bed. My heart rate picked up when I saw his name pop up on my caller ID. The last time he called, things had not gone well.

I picked up the phone.

"Hey, Clara," he began.

Deciding it was best to be civil, I asked, "Hey, Grigore, how are you doing?"

"Well, well. How's the accounting software going?"

I groaned. "Things were not going well until Luca took time out of his busy schedule to work with me on how to use it. It was very kind of him," I said. "Now things are going much better. I know that we want to get rid of the accounting guy we have, and we'd hoped this would help us avoid having to depend on anyone, but it's complicated software. I don't think you can count on me. This is too important to allow for mistakes."

Frustration ricocheted through my chest. I didn't like not being able to complete a task given to me, especially when my clan was counting on me. But our businesses were too intricate for the likes of me to take care of this. A professional was needed.

He let out a sigh. "Not the answer I was looking for, but alright, I'll look for a replacement."

"Okay, sounds like a solid plan. I've gotten much better, but it's going to take some time, and even then, I may never be more than proficient."

"It doesn't hurt to have someone who knows how it works to keep an eye on the data."

There was a pause. It certainly felt awkward from my side, but I decided to wait it out and see where Grigore was going to go from here. He wasn't one to pull his punches.

"So, how are things otherwise? With the Lupu men to be exact," he clarified.

"It's going," I hedged.

Keeping things vague was a good start.

"Tell me more," he demanded.

"Like I said, I've been spending time with Luca. He's been extremely generous with his time, considering how busy he is having recently returned from his honeymoon. Of course, Tatum checks in with me on a daily basis."

I held my breath as I waited to see his response. I had Luca go through my laptop and phone to find and deactivate any location apps, so Grigore wouldn't know where I was living.

"Tatum and you have become friendly then," he probed. "I'm not getting daily calls from you complaining anymore."

Drat, I'd forgotten how I called him every day in the beginning. My heart was in my throat. Before Tatum, I'd never lied to anyone in my clan.

"We're not at each other's throats, no, but I wouldn't go so far as to say we're friends. We've settled into a nonabrasive, working relationship. It helps that I'm living with his mother and sister. We certainly couldn't argue the way we did back home in front of his mother. Both she and his little sister worship the ground he walks on, and it wouldn't do to insult them by arguing with him," I finished, somewhat annoyed that I had to lie. But it would do us no good to have Grigore suspect something before I got a chance to speak to my father.

"I suppose that's a good thing," he conceded. "But remember, they're still the enemy. Do not doubt that for a moment, Clara. One of those brothers, it might've been Luca for all I know, killed Simu in cold blood. Cold. Blood. They're bloodthirsty motherfuckers, each one of them. Don't underestimate them for a second."

Oh, please, Grigore was the most vicious killer I knew. When it came to the Lupu clan, he had no mercy whatsoever. Of course, I understood—Simu was his nephew and best friend. But since I no longer resented the Lupu clan, Grigore's feud no longer held any weight. Nevertheless, I couldn't admit this to Grigore.

"Believe me, Grigore, I understand your position completely."

This was a half-truth, but I had no choice. My relationship with Tatum was on the line, and I needed to get Grigore off my back.

"Good," Grigore said. "I'm glad to hear it. I'm glad to hear that you haven't been swayed by those bastards. I've been digging and I'm getting close to something with my Bratva contact."

He chuckled darkly, "I want to surprise you when the time is right. Until then, I'll keep it to myself."

"Come on, Grigore," I insisted. "Stop messing around."

"It may be nothing."

"I know where my loyalty stands, and it stands with the Hagi clan," I persisted, attempting to sway him. "You can tell me anything."

I heard a grunt of approval through the line.

"I'll look like an idiot if it comes to nothing. When I have something concrete, you'll be the first to know," he said with finality.

I heard the obstinance in his tone and decided to back off.

"Alright then, I'll let you go," he said, probably thinking it was best to get off the phone with me in case I continued to pester him.

On my side, I couldn't get rid of him fast enough. The Lupu were impenetrable for an outsider like Grigore. I had no idea what dirt he could've gotten on them because I'd been around them for months. I'd watched them carefully, and they had things in hand.

Moving the mouthpiece of the phone away from me, I blew out a breath of relief. I was intent on speaking to my father about Tatum and advocating for us, but I certainly wasn't going to give Grigore a chance at a preemptive strike.

We'd never been on opposing sides before, but this was looking to be a showdown. Grigore expected to continue in his position with me, as he had with my father. He'd proved his loyalty, yes, but I had every intention of installing Tatum as *my consilier* when I took the throne. This would be a down and dirty brawl, and I was fighting to win.

I got off the phone with him and was in the middle of congratulating myself for having avoided any traps when my father called.

A smile spread over my face. I quickly picked up and said, "Hey, I miss you! How are you doing, Daddy?"

He chuckled. "Good, good. How's my girl doing?"

I giggled, happy to hear his low baritone. "Things are well. I'm finally getting a handle on that accounting software. Luca spent hours teaching me how to use it. It's not easy stuff, I've got to tell you. It was really kind of him to do that."

"You're a princess and the heir to the Hagi clan. Why wouldn't he go out of his way to be nice to you?" he sniffed.

A pang of longing for my father struck me. I laughed again. "Oh, Daddy, you're always so quick to take offense on my behalf."

Sobering, I said, "I can finally admit that you were right. It was good for me to come to New York. Although I fought it, you were right."

"I'm glad you've found your footing over there. A father always loves to hear he's right. Of course, we miss you terribly, but it's a good learning experience for you."

Wasn't that the truth? If he only knew what a learning experience it'd been for me. It was a steep learning curve, but when it came to sex, Tatum would say I was fast on the uptake.

"I'm not saying we should let the Lupu clan walk all over us, but I am much more comfortable negotiating with them now that I've lived among them and gotten more insight into the way they live and work. Despite what Grigore says, I agree we can't turn them away without starting a large-scale war, which we don't have the capacity to win, even with all the other clans behind us. It's in our best interest to work with them as partners," I concluded.

"As always, your analysis is spot on," he praised me. "I

made the right decision to groom you as our next *şef*. I suspected this from the beginning, but I needed you to see it for yourself. Don't get me wrong, I wasn't completely convinced. I was waiting for you to get to know them and then come to your own conclusion. And you have. I'm proud of you."

A genuine smile broke out on my face, my heart doubling in size. My father wasn't one to give idle compliments, and I was touched by his approval.

"Thank you, *Tata*," I murmured.

"One more thing. The Radu girl got pregnant by one of our soldiers, Marku, even though she's engaged to the Ionescu boy," he said casually. "Her father is infuriated and wants to toss her out of the house or force her to marry her fiancé tomorrow. But she's insisting on Marku. What should we do about this?"

My smile widened, chest burning with fierce pride. He'd already told me he was going to send domestic issues my way if I proved myself in New York, and this was solid proof he trusted my counsel.

"Eh, Marku's a good guy." I nodded as I thought through the possibilities. After a moment, I decided, "Let her go with him. He may only be a solider and not of such a high-ranking family as the Ionescus, but he's loyal. He'll move up the ranks." Thinking about Tatum's childhood of being taunted for who he was, I concluded, "The Ionescus are too prideful to ever accept her child by another man. They would torture the child and the mother. We can't let that happen. I will call her to confirm, of course, but my final judgment will be to sever the engagement and allow her to marry Marku."

There was a pause, and I heard the unspoken thoughts in his head, heard the guilt in those thoughts, about his original resentment toward Adrian. But there lay the huge difference between my father and other *mafie* men. He was tough and rigid, but he had a heart. He could bend.

"The Ionescus won't be happy," he remarked.

"I'll set up another engagement for their boy with an even more powerful family. That way, they won't lose face."

My father nodded his endorsement of my decision. "Good thinking."

With the unspoken subject of Adrian shimmering in the air, I asked, "How's Adrian doing?"

"Doing well," he replied. "As you can imagine, he's improved tremendously in the past two months. He has a concert coming up at the Conservatory. See, you had nothing to worry about."

"Daddy?" I asked, my voice turning serious.

"What's going on?" he instantly asked, picking up the change in my tone.

"Nothing's wrong, there's nothing to worry about," I started. "For the first time in forever, I'm living with women again. It's strange after living with you and Adrian for so many years."

"I'm sorry about your mother, Clara. I should've done better," he said in a dejected tone.

"Oh my God, Dad, it wasn't your fault," I said vehemently. "Don't ever blame yourself for her behavior. She made her choice. You're not responsible for what she did."

He'd been crushed by her disloyalty. Everything afterward had unfolded just as dramatically. Finding out she was pregnant with another man's child, a man he'd loved like a brother, and a man he'd had to kill in retribution. Having to keep my mother near, having to pretend to the world that Adrian was his son. He'd ended up loving Adrian, but it'd been a nightmare.

"It's just ... I see the way they live. They talk of love and family, and I want that, too," I ended in a whisper, a whisper because to speak of such things was breaching the unspeakable. Not only was it not done in my family, but it was taboo. But I was sick of making myself small, twisting myself to fit into my father's box of what I was supposed to want, what I was supposed to be.

There was a long silence on the other end of the line.

"I see," he said gruffly.

"What?" I asked, somewhat irritated by his lack of response. It meant that he disagreed.

"Do I really need to spell it out to you, daughter?"

I pressed my lips together. A mulish look crossed my face, which I was grateful he couldn't see since we weren't using FaceTime.

He let out a sigh. My heart squeezed. I was disappointing him. I knew I was, but how could I not bring this up.

"I understand it's hard for you. It's a substantial sacrifice, but your life doesn't imitate theirs. They're women living a woman's life. You're a woman living a man's life. You cannot have it all, child," he said gently. "Look at my life. I'm a man, a *şef*, who was supposed to have it all. I didn't have to face the many challenges you will face, and I still failed. How could you possibly win where I lost?"

"But Dad—"

"But nothing," he cut me off. "You have huge goals. Huge challenges. You'll make the biggest mistake of your life if you succumb to the fantasy that you can have a family and run a clan. The respect you have is solid, almost as much as mine. Do not doubt that the Hagi clan will turn their back on you if you're no longer pure. You made an oath to them as well as to me. You cannot be a fallen queen and expect to rule."

Fury raged through me. My hands curled into balls, fingernails digging into the soft flesh, leaving marks. Here I was, on the large bed in Tatum's bedroom, with the little reading nook by the big window overlooking the Upper West Side of Manhattan, and knew in my bones that I could never let him go. I didn't want to.

"Can I not?" I whispered.

"I didn't send you there to question the very foundation of your life, Clara," he replied resolutely. "You cannot have everything."

He expelled a long sigh. "You were young when our family was ruined, but I don't blame only her, *fiică*."

Daughter. I squeezed my eyes shut. He called me daughter.

"If it'd been only her, the betrayal would've been easier to digest. It took sacrifice to build this clan. I neglected my wife and child. Contributed to the destruction of my family. Trust me, I won't stand by and allow you to make the same mistakes I made."

He breathed out a shuddering breath. I heard it through the phone, heard his pain. Knew it intimately since it mimicked my own.

"Do you understand?"

I swallowed hard. "I understand, *Tata*. Have no fear. I know where my allegiance lies."

There was a long pause.

"I'm going to send Grigore out there to check on you," he said.

Dread struck my heart. Gripping the duvet beneath me, I clenched the fabric so hard my knuckles turned white.

Grigore would figure out what was happening the moment he laid eyes on me.

"No," I snapped instantly. "I'm living in a household with four other women, one of them is underage. It's like a woman's dormitory here. No men on the premises." I was sure a bolt of lightning would shoot down from the sky and strike me dead for my blatant lie, but I was willing to risk it to keep Grigore at bay.

"He's not going to live with you. He'll be at a hotel," my father tried reasoning.

"They're under stress with fixing their house. Tatum's little sister has stars in her eyes," I rambled on as I quickly came up with an excuse. "You know the kind ... almost on the cusp of womanhood and hunting for a husband. She's looking to fall in love. He's too handsome *(gag!)* and charming for his own good *(oh, please)*. The moment she sees him, she'll fall for him and then I'll have a problem on my hands. Things will get complicated, and I don't need any drama."

I gulped in a deep breath of air and continued, "Plus, he's abrasive, what with his resentment about Simu. You do want me to resolve our differences and start negotiations again, don't you?"

"Hmm ... his presence could go either way. It could give them the shove they need," he mused.

Panic gripped me by the throat. I needed more time to figure out my next move, and I definitely didn't need Grigore sniffing around, throwing a wrench in my plans.

"I'm the one on the ground, *Tata*. Let me call the shots," I pleaded.

Another pause. He was thinking, rolling every option around in his head. My heart was breaking. I thought I could change my father's mind, but that wasn't going to happen. My head swam in a sea of confusion and turmoil, but I didn't want Grigore anywhere near me. I needed time to think, time to talk to Tatum, time to figure out a solution.

"Very well, Daughter," he finally conceded.

Closing my eyes, I let out a soft breath of relief.

"Thank you," I whispered.

Disaster averted. For now.

21

CLARA

Stunned, I got off the phone with my father and dropped backward into Tatum's plush bed. My cell phone slid out of my hand and clattered to the floor. What the hell was I going to do? I wished Tatum were here with me. I'd burrow into his broad chest and take shelter from this crazy world. Normal women didn't have to contend with these kinds of problems. Hell, not even normal *mafie* women.

Head swimming, I turned over and tucked my hands beneath my cheek and gazed outside the window, staring blindly at the clouds drifting by.

This was how Tatum found me.

I shifted my head slightly as I heard him step into the bedroom, my gaze landing on him. He was as arresting as ever. His tawny hair was tousled, likely from the brisk wind outside. I hadn't been outside today myself, but I'd watched the clouds zip by from my perch, high above the rest of the world. He'd taken off his jacket, and his periwinkle blue shirt stretched deliciously over the thick, bulging slabs of his chest and shoulders.

His dark eyes snapped to me. Instantly, he prowled onto the bed. Reaching me, he braced himself above me, bracketing me with his limbs. He stared down at me, his indecipherable gaze searching.

"What's wrong?" he rumbled out, his tone grave.

I grasped his solid biceps. "Let's run away. Just the two of us. Let's run away from our families and their insane ambitions. They're going to ruin us."

A crease notched between the two perfect winged arcs of his brows.

"What's this about, Clara?" he demanded with an edge of worry to his tone. He softened his question by grazing his lips over mine ever so softly.

I couldn't blame him, I was worried, too.

"Will you swear to leave Alex for me?" I said. Asking the question, I felt gutted and flayed open, my insides exposed to him.

His gaze bored into my face. A long pause of silence stretched out between us, the strain a taut, breathing thing between us. My stomach roiled with anxiety.

"I can't." Regret bled in his eyes. "Not yet anyway. I'm working hard to get us where we need to be, but I'm not going to lie to you, it's going to take time to get Sebastian ready. He entered this world at the age of twenty-five years old. You and I were born into it and look how much trouble we're having carving our own path through this morass."

"Ugh." I twisted my head to the side. "That wasn't what I needed to hear from you."

"What did you need to hear from me, VQ?" he asked softly.

Gazing out the window, I answered, "I needed to hear you say, 'It's going to be me and you, Clara. Me and you in power, together. We'll be a couple. A team. We will be stronger together than we are apart. And we will rule the Hagi clan as one, regardless of what your father says.'"

His eyes narrowed slightly. "Your father? You spoke to your father."

"And Grigore."

"What did your father say?"

I shook my head. "He also didn't say anything I wanted to hear. Not from him and not from you."

"That's because we're both realists. He's a boss. I'm an advisor. We live in the real world, dealing with real problems on an everyday basis," he said.

"Grrr, why do you have to be so logical right now," I snapped, my eyes swerving to give him a righteous glare. "Why can't anyone coddle me?"

"Because you're a strong woman, not a child. You might think you want to be coddled, but two minutes into babying you, and you'd demand I stop. Hell, if I kept it up for more than five minutes, you'd smack me."

Shoving him away, I scrambled to my knees, crossed my arms over my chest, and hmphed. He was spot-on, but that didn't mean I liked it, and I wasn't about to admit it to him even though my heart melted at the idea of how well he already knew me.

"I get it," he said with a soothing caress of my hair. "You want everything to come easy, but that's not the *mafie* life. It's complex on a good day and downright perilous on every other day."

Pleading for leniency, he murmured, "Listen, baby, I'm not going to lie simply to make you feel better, but this is doable. I need time to convince Alex that Sebastian is ready to replace me. You already know about the recent pressure the Bratva is putting on us, but there's more at play than I can reveal. It's not my secret to spill, but I will say that it's not just our lives on the line."

"Star?"

"And my mother. Star will turn eighteen in a couple months. I can't abandon her when I'm so close to being finished raising her. Once I've married her off, I'll have the leeway to do what I want, but even then—"

Frustration crossed his face and he balled one hand into a fist.

"There's the issue of Alex."

"If this is about honor and loyalty toward him, what about honoring me, the woman you've deflowered," I snapped. God, his omissions were only adding to my irritation.

His hand collared me, the fingers around my throat promptly making me feel better, which only added to my annoyance.

"Hey, I'd take my honor toward you over him any day, but he's my *şef*. I owe him everything, my life and that of my family. I must ensure their ongoing safety by doing this right. What he giveth, he may taketh away."

He was talking in riddles, but something penetrated through my fog of frustration.

"He has a reason to take everything away, doesn't he," I demanded.

I'd been in the game long enough to catch when someone was being vague. He was hiding something. We lived in a world where there was little ambiguity—unless something was wrong. Then everything turned murky as hell, with no guideposts to lead the way through our swamp-filled world.

He swallowed hard.

"Yes," he affirmed. "He has reason to. It's complicated,

and I won't get you mixed up in it. This is my burden alone." His voice dropped so low I almost didn't hear him. "It has been for so long."

"Will this secret compromise my ability to serve the Hagi?" I asked.

A normal woman might be more alarmed at the possibility of a looming secret, but secrets were run-of-the-mill in my world. Everyone had secrets. Hell, I was keeping a huge secret from my father and clan right this instant, but it was my duty to my clan to ask.

Offense lit up his eyes and turned them into two glittering black flames. "What do you take me for? You have a clan to lead. Barriers to break. History to make. I wouldn't ever let anyone or anything harm you. I will always protect you. First, foremost, and always. Don't you think I want to tell you, I want to share the load, but I can't unburden myself at your expense. I'd die before I tolerated such a thing."

His face was set in a fierce mask of anger.

I'd insulted him.

Sitting on his haunches, his shoulders abruptly dropped in defeat. My heart cracked at having injured his sense of honor. Tatum was one of the most honorable men I knew.

I reached out to him, grazing my fingers down his chest. "I'm sorry. I don't know what to think when you can't tell me what it is."

"It wouldn't touch your ability to rule, but it would compromise my family, and I cannot allow that to happen."

"Obviously," I repeated because I knew who he was. At his core, he was a protector. He always showed more concern for his mother and sister than he did for himself. This secret must be of epic proportions because while *mafie* men were notoriously possessive and protective, Tatum took things to the nth degree. He wasn't just normal macho *mafie* protective; he was OTT protective.

But this added another unnecessary wrinkle to an already complicated situation. Did this have anything to do with Grigore's digging? I thought for a moment but shook off the idea. This was clearly personal to Tatum's family, whereas Grigore was looking for dirt on Alex.

"You might have mentioned this to me earlier?" I pointed out softly.

Releasing my throat, he scraped the scruff of his jaw with his knuckles. "There was never the right time to bring it up, and honestly, there never will be. Either it will never become an issue, which is what I pray and work for every day, or it breaks open and destroys my entire life here."

"Fuck," I squeaked out.

A grimace passed over his face.

"Your reaction is not exactly encouraging," I said. "If there's a big secret looming over you and your family, and that's pretty much what it looks like from where I'm standing, shouldn't you tell me what it is? I know that you think you're protecting me, but if this is a big deal, then I need to know what I'm getting myself into."

"Does it matter?" he challenged.

"Of course, it matters."

"It doesn't, though, because we've already fucked. We're already blood bonded. I'm within my rights to demand we get married, if I wanted to," he countered.

My jaw clenched. "Is that a threat?"

A muscle pulsed under his skin near his jawline. "Of course not. Like I said before, I wouldn't have laid one finger on you, much less taken your virginity, if I thought there'd be any blowback on you or your clan with this."

Frustration gnawed my chest. Lips pursed, I squinted at

him in vexation. Rolling my shoulders loose, I took a bracing breath.

"What am I going to do with you, Tatum? You drive me crazy. It's bad enough I had the worst conversation with Grigore and then my father. My father insists that I stand by my oath to my clan. At one point, he even suggested Grigore come to check up on me. I barely managed to ward him off. I don't know what to do. I don't know how this will work. And then, you throw this bomb into my already crazy, dysfunctional life, and I have no idea what it is or how to deal with it."

I always prided myself on keeping my cool. Sure, I was known to be feisty, but when it came to clan politics, my blood ran cold. I was logical, ruthless. This was different. I felt like everything was careening out of control.

He yanked me into his chest. Wrapping his arms around me, he embraced me tightly.

"The reason it doesn't matter is because I'm never letting you go," he swore. "Yes, there's an old family secret. Yes, in an ideal world, I'd tell you and we'd decide together how to handle it. Maybe I shouldn't have touched you, maybe I miscalculated and made the wrong decision, but it's too late. I *have* touched you. I've pounded into that virgin cunt of yours and taken your cherry. My cock was smeared with your virgin blood. So yeah, game over. Do you hear me, Clara? Game. Over. You're mine."

He lifted my chin. "I don't care what happens. I don't care if I leave scorched earth behind to keep you safe. I'll never put my interests before yours, and I'll never abandon you. As for your father, we'll figure it out together. It hurts, I know. He raised you and made you into the fine woman you are today, but I won't stand by and allow him to ruin our relationship with his stubbornness. And I know just how stubborn older Romanian men can be—"

"Only the older ones?" I quipped with a snort. "What about you?"

One side of his mouth quirked up. "Sassy little bitch, aren't you? Lucky for you, that's how I like it." His hand cupped my pussy. "Not going to lie, it doesn't hurt that you melt under my touch and turn into my good little slut."

I moaned against his mouth. When he used those filthy words on me, I melted for him just like he said. There was no explanation for it, but it was a turn-on to have him call me bad names in a soft whisper, laced with lust. No matter how I acted, he couldn't help but want me.

"I'd never let anything happen to you, I swear," he whispered the oath over my lips. "And your father ... how is he going to be able to resist the combined power of our love? We will win him over, I know it."

I wasn't sure what the future held, but I did trust Tatum implicitly. His promise to never hurt or abandon me resonated in my heart, making me feel safe and loved and whole. Being left in the dark was a hard pill to swallow, but I loved this man to my core. I ached for him. I didn't think I could live without him. I prayed I would never have that condition tested.

22

TATUM

Alex's fist connected with my chin. My head snapped to the left, a dull thud reverberating through my skull. His punch had come close to finally snapping my jaw in two. I stumbled back from the impact, my huge frame slammed against the wall. Nausea and dizziness pounded through me, and I skidded down to the floor. Peering out through the two slivers of my puffy, black and blue eyes, I stared at him looming over me.

I wiped the dribble of blood from my mouth from the back of my hand.

My world had officially imploded.

"Get the fuck up, traitor," Alex growled. "And the fact that I learned it from that snake, Grigore, was almost as bad as hearing the truth. He was fucking cackling while he told me, his revenge complete." He spat on the ground beside me.

The door to the office of his penthouse slapped open and rebounded off the wall.

"Stop," Nina said in a breathy voice, rushing to Alex and grabbing his hand. "Stop it," she demanded again.

"Ni-na," Alex warned, his voice cracked, his gaze desolate. I knew him as well as I knew myself, and his heart was breaking. As much as my own was. I'd loved this man like a brother, but it was done. We'd be torn asunder, as I'd always feared.

"Enough," she protested. "It's enough. Find another way to handle this, Alex." Her hand came up to his hunched back, her fingers squeezing around his shoulder.

"Please. For me. For us." Her hand slipped to her belly. "But especially for your soul. You're going to kill him, and you'll regret it for the rest of your life."

He shuddered under her hand.

I raised a shaky, blood-splattered hand to cover my face, my eyes. Tears bled out of them, tears of regret, tears of deep pained remorse. The demon inside me howled in agony at being torn from the brotherhood that had bred us. It was over, and we both knew it.

I never wanted to cause him pain. I knew it was almost as hard for him to beat me up as it was for me to sit back and take it. And take it I did. I didn't raise my hand to defend myself, to protect my face.

Somehow Grigore had found out. This was the payback Grigore had been working toward, sure, but my gut told me it had as much to do with Clara. Our relationship encroached on his ambitions to continue as the Hagi *consilier*.

I got played by the worthless piece of shit.

Fuck.

Vengeance burned in my gut.

I was going to kill him. I swore it.

Alex let out a growl and gave me a swift, half-hearted kick.

"*Alex*," Nina exclaimed, tugging him away from me.

"Get off the floor, Tatum," she threw over her shoulder as she dragged him away, or rather, he allowed himself to be dragged away by his woman because he wouldn't have done anything he didn't want to.

The details of how he found out, I didn't yet know, but when he called me over to his apartment, I instantly knew something was very wrong.

He asked me if I'd always known. The game was up, and I was done with secrets, so I told him the truth.

He asked me if I'd kept it a secret because I didn't trust him to choose me as *şef*.

No. Yes. Maybe. What the fuck? I didn't know. I was scared, I'd admitted.

That's when he lost his temper and the punches began.

I struggled to my feet, holding on to the edge of the large desk in his office. My arm muscles shook as I pulled myself up. Before I knew it, I'd collapsed, hanging on to the edge of the desk and barely avoiding eating dirt. Dragging myself up to my feet, I swayed but held strong and managed to stay upright. Gingerly, I touched my jaw, testing its solidity.

Glancing down, I caught the spots of blood staining my once pristine white shirt. My sapphire printed tie was askew, the fabric of my shirt bunched up, buttons missing from where he'd twisted it as he slammed me against the wall.

My face had surely blossomed into a mottled pattern of blue and purple bruises, and my muscles throbbed from holding back from defending myself. I wanted to lay my head on the surface of the desk, floor, wherever, crawl into myself, and die. Die of disgrace from my father's sins and my part in keeping them hidden. Die of shame for failing my family, for failing Alex, for failing my clan.

And for failing Clara.

I shuttered my eyes at the thought of her, holding down the bile rising in my throat.

The door flew open again, banging against the wall in Alex's wake. Nina was right behind him, eyes wide and shining with fear. Fear of Alex's rage. Fear for my imminent death.

"What fucking kills me is that you didn't trust me enough to confide in me," he thundered.

I shook my head. "Believe me, I suffered ten years over this. Suffered from disgrace at what he had done. Humiliation that I was attached to that man in any way. What did you expect me to do?"

I knew it wasn't a good idea to poke the bear, but did he truly think any of this was easy for me?

Alex opened his mouth to respond, but before he could answer, I stampeded over him, "You would've never made me your right-hand man, you would've never made me *consilier*. At least, admit that much."

"What the fuck would you have had me do?!" he exploded.

I staggered on my feet, lunged toward him, and got in his face.

I took a deep breath and explained, "Your father had just been murdered. You needed to focus on solidifying your power and avenging his death. I had to help you achieve those goals, but you wouldn't have taken me on as *consilier* if you'd known." I shrugged and lifted my hands in a defenseless motion. "So, I took the choice out of your hands and made the decision for you. The best decision for the sake of the clan."

Alex's eyes flared into twin emerald flames.

"Without me, you may not have survived the revenge. Had you survived, you wouldn't have ruled as well without me. It wasn't like you were coming into the position of *şef* while your father died peacefully in his own bed. It was no calm transfer of power. We were in the middle of outright chaos, with a looming war on our hands. That's why we dubbed it the Summer of Blood."

"Don't fucking pretend like you didn't have your own motivations as well," he sneered.

"Yes, I did," I acknowledged. "I had a mother, who was devastated by the murder of her husband, and an eight-year-old sister whom I had to raise. She didn't deserve to be tarnished by this, and I was determined to give her every-thing my father had torn away from us with his treachery. But don't pretend you would've done any differently. Despite all of that, my primary reason was you. You saved me as a kid, Alex, and I would've done anything for you. Simple as that. You wouldn't have made the best choice if you'd known the whole truth, so I made it for you. Your father would've agreed with my decision."

"Oh, Alex," Nina murmured softly into her husband's sleeve with a sniffle.

Hands fisted at his sides, he squeezed his eyes shut. "Fuck, how did this get so fucked up?"

"I understand the difficult position I've put you in. Of course, I'll take my punishment. I did you wrong. I did the clan wrong. But I will never regret it because I had to do wrong to do the ultimate right. With your father bleeding out on the street and a clan looking to you for answers, wrong overruled right because survival and revenge were the only things that mattered. All I ask, when you make your decision, is that you take care of my mother and sister. Besides Clara, they're the only people in this world that matter to me as much as you and your brothers."

The tendons of my neck were stiff by the time I finished

my speech. I could practically feel them splitting apart like the steel cords of a collapsing bridge.

"Spare them," I pleaded. "Please, Alex, please, I beg you, don't turn them out like beggars or allow them to stay only to be humiliated. This is the only world they know. My mother will die of grief if she's turned away in disgrace or if she's made to suffer for my sins. And Star, she's an innocent. She knows nothing about this. Don't let anything happen to her. Let her marry someone good."

"You think you're in the position to ask me for any favors?" he snarled.

Nina wrapped her hand around his biceps and gripped hard. She was always a gentle soul, and I knew that Star and she had gotten close over the last couple of years. Nina grew up down the street from us, next door to Alex's family. She'd been his little sister Tasa's best friend their entire lives. When Tasa ran away and Nina got together with Alex, Star made Nina feel welcomed, genuinely inviting her into the fold. Many of the other women did it begrudgingly, only because she was married to their *şef* while bad-mouthing her behind her back.

"No, I'm not in a position to ask for a favor, but I'm asking anyway. I'm begging for mercy. Not for me. You can kill me. I'm ready to accept your judgment. But for them," I finished in a low rumble.

Despite how good and pure my mother and Star were, we inhabited a twisted, *mafie* world, where women were innocent victims of the mistakes of their men. Betrayal? Treachery? Those were automatic triggers for death and dismemberment of anyone in the family trapped in one of these scenarios.

His enraged gaze locked on mine. I held my breath as I waited for his verdict. A flicker of indecision crossed his face. He was torn. From my side vision, I registered Nina's tortured expression.

Finally, he broke the deafening silence.

"I will spare them," he pronounced. "I don't need anyone but my brothers knowing about this fucked-up situation. No one else will know of this. The secret has been kept this long. Your last job for this clan is to kill the Bratva. See, that will be your incentive. Get rid of every outsider who knows this secret, and it will remain a secret. If you can manage that, your family will be safe. If you can't, and it gets out, then let the cards fall where they may."

"That's a death sentence," Nina rasped out.

It was.

Alex had laid out his decree, and I had to respect the chance he was giving me to save my family. My mission was to kill the Bratva boss, his right-hand man, and Grigore. I could take on Grigore on my own, no problem, but the chances of killing the head of the Bratva and getting away with it were slim to none.

My heart stuttered, but I iced the throbbing, pulsing muscle, iced my feelings, iced everything. There was no room for anything other than the survival of my loved ones.

"If you want to make sure your mother and sister are safe, you better kill before you're killed."

"And if I survive?"

"If you survive, my former brother, then I will let you live. Of course, you'll never step foot in this city again."

"I could live with that," I muttered.

He barked out a harsh laugh.

"*If* you live, and that's a big if. Now get the fuck out of my face before I change my mind," he declared.

23

TATUM

Alex stormed out, and it was slow going, dragging myself out of his apartment. I fell a couple of times, crawled on my hands and knees until I found a piece of furniture to use as leverage and got back on my feet. I was sure my ribs needed to be taped. My body throbbed like one vicious aching bruise, a deep, heavy emptiness beneath the unrelenting pain.

These were the rules, and I'd broken my oath of loyalty to him the instant I'd made it by keeping silent about my father. I swiped the blood from my mouth, smearing it on my shirt as I staggered out of his apartment, down the hall, and into mine.

Mine no longer, I reminded myself. This would be the last time. I'd never return.

Struggling, I hauled a suitcase out of the closet, threw it on the bed, and tossed in personal items I couldn't leave behind. Perhaps, it was a lesson in futility since I didn't know how long I had to live.

My guns were the only items I needed. Alex was likely moving his mother and grandmother out of my mother's house as we spoke. I'd use it as my base of operations for the week I had to accomplish my assignment. If I survived, then I'd leave for LA to kill Grigore. At least, I would take pleasure in destroying the miserable wretch who'd rained down pain on me and my family.

I tore off my clothes and changed into a pair of jeans and a long-sleeved shirt, all black. Making my way into the bathroom, I taped my ribs and patched myself up as best I could. I pulled out the guns I needed from my safe, quickly finished packing, and left my suitcase at the front entrance.

And waited for Clara to return from her girls' day with Star.

Clara.

Images of her flooded my mind, and my vision blurred with unshed tears.

I was going to die, but my greatest regret was that I'd never see her again, never see my family again.

I slumped against the wall and rubbed the center of my chest, aching with sharp, stabbing pain. Sweat coated my hairline, and I swiped it off with a quivering hand. I had one last task before I went on my suicide mission.

Break up with her.

I had to convince her I didn't care about her anymore. It was the only way to protect her. Heavy emptiness, numbness spread across my chest like black tendrils of poison. It would soon engulf me in the flames of agony, but my agony didn't matter if I could spare her.

Spare her from putting her clan and her future in jeopardy in a futile attempt to save me. She'd do anything to rescue me, but I was beyond saving. She couldn't stop Alex, and once I was gone, she'd be left with nothing but the belief that she'd failed me.

I clutched my chest, my nails scraping my skin. Fuck,

this was going to hurt. I gritted my teeth. I had to do it. I had no choice. None whatsoever.

Sitting down heavily on the sofa, I must have shut down and dozed off because I startled awake to find Clara staring down at me. Abandoned bags of Prada and Hermes encircled her as she kneeled on the ground beside me.

"What happened?" Her voice turned angry. "Who did this to you?"

She reached out to touch me, and God, I wanted her soft touch so much I could've cried, but I pretended to flinch.

"No, don't," I warned.

"It hurts," she declared, settling on her heels between my splayed legs. God, she looked so good there, so right.

"Why didn't you call me so I could come home and take care of you? Were you jumped by a posse or what? There's no way a couple of guys could've done this much damage."

She had on mascara and pink lip gloss, the only makeup she wore nowadays. Her dark lashes made her eyes pop like twin spheres of the most perfect shade of cornflower blue.

So clear. So rich, deep, and strong. So like her.

My heart clenched, pounding out wave after wave of bone-shattering agony. I had to rub my chest in circles to stop from heaving.

"I have to—" My voice was harsh from clogged emotion. I cleared my throat. "I have to leave for a job. You must return to California."

She drew in a sharp breath, her gaze traveling over my face, trying to read me. My insides churned a whirling maelstrom of helpless rage and heartache, but I was a locked vault; there was nothing for her to read. For her, I had to be.

"You can't tell me what's going on," she announced.

Unable to speak, I shook my head.

"When do I come back, or will you come to me?"

"Neither will happen," I croaked out.

"What?" she said hoarsely.

"You heard me."

She dropped her hand to my knee.

I pushed it off, stopping myself from doing the opposite, from grabbing it and peppering kisses all over it.

She winced.

"What are you saying? I don't understand," she said, her expression turning stoic, determined.

Oh, no. She was going to fight for us. Faced with her formidable will, I'd crumble. I was the one who wanted to drop to my knees, take her achingly beautiful face in my hands, and beg her for forgiveness. I wanted to worship at her feet, worship her pussy with my tongue until I made the bad words I uttered disappear.

But I couldn't.

I stiffened my spine. I had to do this. For her. She was my priority.

I rallied, gathering every ounce of grit and determination inside me, wrapping myself in it.

First, I had to put physical distance between us.

Standing up abruptly, I walked past her, pushing her with my thigh, tipping her over so she slid down to the floor. My hands shook from the urge to touch her, to grab her to me, to smother her with my mouth. Instead of doing any of those things, I clenched them into tight balls and ground down on my back teeth.

Glaring at her, I said, "Why are you making me spell it out, Clara? We're done. Over. Finished."

"W-what?" she stammered over the word.

"For a smart girl, you sure are slow on the uptake," I sneered.

Her eyes blew out so wide, I could see the white around

them. Panic. I saw the panic, but then I watched, riveted, as she took control of it. Fuck, she was glorious. She locked down her emotions, but I knew her too well. I recognized her tells, like the tightness around her beautiful, lush mouth. The one I had wrapped around my cock this morning. God, I'd miss that, but it was nothing compared to how much I'd miss *her*. Her essence, her sass and spirit, her intelligence, and her magnificent, giving heart. I had to tread carefully; I had to disable her intelligence if I was going to convince her I didn't love her anymore. Even saying it in my mind gutted me.

Panic wasn't enough to make her reject me. I had to shove her over the edge into a place of fury and rage.

"You don't mean it," she declared. "Something is making you say this to me, but you don't have to protect me, Tatum. I'm a grown woman, and I can take care of myself. I'm here for you no matter what's happened. We can figure this out together."

If I could've guaranteed that I'd survive my assignment to kill Ivanov, then I would've given it a chance. But there was no such guarantee, and it was my duty to protect her against the worst-case scenario. The worst-case scenario being the most likely scenario.

I clenched my stomach into a tight knot to give me strength and winced. Damn, my ribs were definitely bruised.

God, give me strength, I prayed before slashing my hand in the air and saying, "No, there's no 'us,' there's no 'together.' You think you're a grown-ass woman, but you'll never be grown enough for me. I'm sick and tired of pandering to a pampered little princess who follows her father's every command."

She fell back, breaking her fall at the last second by

planting her hand on the ground behind her. I couldn't have hurt her more if I'd physically slapped her in the face.

"I don't love you anymore," I choked out.

If I said I'd never loved her, she wouldn't have believed me. Even this was far-fetched, but I had to do my best.

"I see."

The two words came out no louder than a whisper, but they boomed through the room like a heavy bass.

Pounding the nails in the coffin, I went on, "I don't want a woman. Relationships aren't for me. Never had one before and thought I was missing out, but after trying it, I realized I'm better off alone."

I forced my eyes down, glaring down my nose at her. She was sprawled on the floor, in shock.

The buttons of her silk shirt strained at the heaving of her big tits. Fuck, I longed to drop to my knees, haul her to my chest, press her nose into my throat and breathe her in.

But I had to push her away. It'd be easier on her once I was dead, I reminded myself. I assumed I'd die in my attempt to eliminate Ivanov, but hopefully, the attempt itself would be enough to protect my family. I was tempted to break down, confess everything to Clara, and beg her to give my family shelter, but it was too late. If I walked away from my deal with Alex, he could come after me. I'd be dead, and I wouldn't be able to protect her heart the way I could now. Protecting her, I was startled to realize, was the priority. I was willing to forgo a possible safe haven for my family to protect her from the grief of my death.

After a lifetime committed to putting them first, someone else came before them. My brows drew together. It was a strange feeling, but the urgency to take care of her took precedence over everything else.

There was one last concern adding to my sense of

urgency. Clara was crazy enough to confront Alex in a hopeless attempt to save me. While I didn't think he'd kill her for meddling, it would be an act of profound disrespect, putting her and her clan in a precarious position. I couldn't allow that to happen. For what purpose? She might be indomitable, but she couldn't change his mind. The very idea of her confronting Alex and putting herself in harm's way on my behalf galvanized me.

Curling up my lip at her, I gave her my deadliest shot. "I want to smack whose ass I want, when I want, and I want to fuck an array of women. Not just you. I want more than one subbie, and a good girl at that. You don't know how to share, and you're too much of a brat for my liking."

Her gasp of shock was so loud it bounced off the high ceilings of the living room.

Fuck, I twisted the knife so deep in my heart, I almost hyperventilated. Reeling back, my spine crashed against the wall. The Romanian embroidery hanging from the walls dislodged and showered down on me. The moment I saw my queen's heart break, I wanted to tear myself limb from limb.

Scrambling to her feet, Clara stormed up to me. Her beautiful face shimmered in front of me—hair shot with flaxen gold, eyes bright gemstones, a body worth sinning for —I longed to touch her, hold her, comfort her. My very bones hurt like they'd crack under the pressure of my lie. My fingers twitched, ready to shoot out and grab her, crush her to me, and never let her go.

But I couldn't.

"I don't believe you. Not one bit. I don't know why you're doing this, but when I find out, I'm going to give you the beating of your life," she spat out. "Until then, I'll leave you to whatever you feel you need to do without me. Don't wait too long, Tatum, because I'm not going to put up with this bullshit, and I sure as hell won't wait forever."

Defiant to the end, glorious as ever, she was my goddess. My inner beast raged at me to grab her, strip her, and fuck her on the floor. Mark her ass with my hand and the rest of her body with my come. Imprint on her the eternal message that she was mine, mine, *mine*.

Instead, I forced myself to stay rooted to my spot and watch as she lifted her chin imperiously, turned on her heels, and stomped away, slamming the bedroom door where she ensconced herself.

I slid to the floor; my legs unable to hold me up any longer.

This was for her. I'd be dead, and if I was lucky, she'd hate me so much she'd spit on my grave.

What if I fought the odds and survived? The chance was slim, but even if I survived killing Ivanov, I was now a pariah. I was no good to her in my state of disgrace. I couldn't do that to her, allow the Hagi queen to remain attached to a tainted man like me.

Hopefully, I'd done enough damage to push her away because I was at the end of my tether. My heart was shattered, hemorrhaging pain, remorse, and helplessness so fast and furious I was sure to have a heart attack. Clasping my chest, I grabbed my bag of guns and mementos, including ones of her, and walked out the door, leaving my gorgeous, injured Clara behind.

It was the hardest thing I'd ever done. Before our confrontation, I'd been prepared to die, but now, I prayed for death.

24

CLARA

I left Tatum.

I had to.

With what was left of my shredded heart, I booked the first flight out of this godforsaken place back to Los Angeles, the city of light. My city.

The plan was to go home, regroup, and figure out my next step.

Bile rose in my throat. I barely made it to the nearest public bathroom in the airport in time to barf into the porcelain toilet. I watched the vomit whirl around and around in the toilet bowl, like the leftovers of my broken heart, until it finally gurgled down the drain. Like me. I was that vomit, going through the pipes and joining the cesspool, sewer, whatever, beneath the ugly airport.

I slumped against the paint-chipped door of the bathroom, wiped my mouth with the back of my hand, and let the tears flow. I'd always considered myself strong, but it took Tatum to show me just how weak I was. I sobbed angry, bitter tears as women and girls passed my stall, likely wondering who the crazy woman was, crying hysterically and alone in a bathroom stall.

I put myself together, splashed water on my face, and made my way to the gate. I squeezed myself between two people loaded with as much carry-on luggage as they could get away with. It served me right for thinking I could have it all. My mother had shown me it wasn't possible. My father had drilled the same lesson into me. But no, I was the arrogant idiot who had to try and fly to the sky, touch the sun. Like stupid Icarus, I came crashing down on broken wings.

Sweat rolled down the length of my spine as I waited stiffly for the airline personnel to call the flight. Tatum had lied through his teeth, and as harsh and painful as his words had been, I didn't believe them.

"Subbie," I muttered to myself as my row was called to board.

Of course, I'd reacted to such a bald-faced lie. He wasn't a recovering manwhore, a bad boy who'd hooked up with innumerable women. No, the man had refrained from fucking on principle, except for the occasional release. He made it sound like he was dumping me so he could go out to sex clubs every night and rack up subbies like notches on a bedpost. That was the furthest thing from who Tatum was.

His family secret had gotten out, and he felt the need to protect me. Normally, I was all for that, but what hurt was his lack of trust in me. *To think I once thought we'd rule together.* His behavior showed how shallow our bond had been. The first time something went wrong, he shut me out.

And if he shut me out to protect me, well, that just didn't work for me. I'd concede *mafie* relationships were more traditional, with the man making most of the decisions, but he didn't know me if he thought I'd tolerate a relationship like that.

The plane ride to LA felt like one of the longest in my life. I was alone, abandoned, suspended above the world, drifting among the clouds like a lost bird separated from its flock. Whatever his reasons, his actions were what mattered, and they spoke volumes. The bottom line was that he didn't trust me, he couldn't give me the kind of relationship I needed, and that ultimately, he didn't want to be with me.

There was no fighting that trio of fuckery. Still, it tore me apart inside. I loved him, wanted to build a life with him. I'd thought it was too good to be true, but he'd proven wrong with his love—until it came crashing down around me, just as I'd feared. It only proved I was meant to dedicate myself to my family. It had taken me leaving them and falling flat on my face to learn my father had been right. Really, the man was a genius.

Finally, after what felt like an eternity, we touched down at LAX. The first face I saw as I stepped out of the arrivals terminal was my father, Adrian by his side. My heart was shattered, but I braced myself and turned up the largest, brightest smile I could muster.

Whatever my father saw on my face had him wrapping me in his strong, burly arms and swaying me from side to side. I was never able to hide my feelings from him, but with the effort I was making, he knew better than to pry.

I brought my arms around his waist, and we hugged for a long time, people streaming past us.

When I felt strong enough to break our hug without spilling tears, I stepped away and faced Adrian with a soft touch of his sleeve.

"Glad to have you home, Clara," he said.

My eyes watered, but I managed to rasp, "Same here. How was your concert?"

He beamed. "It went well. I wish you'd been there to see me, Clara. *Tata* taped it for you. We will watch it at home together."

"Yes, we'll do that." My throat was so tight it hurt to speak. "I'll never miss one of your concerts again," I swore to him. It was an oath I intended to keep.

"It's okay," he replied, nonplussed. "*Tata* explained you had to stay in New York to work."

I swallowed down the pain crawling up my throat. "Yes, but that's over with. I will never leave you again." My gaze darted to my father. "I learned the lesson I needed to learn. I'm good now."

"Glad to have you back, Daughter," my father intoned.

He meant that in more ways than one, I knew.

I LAY on my bed with the French doors open, the delicate, floor-length voile curtains billowing in the breeze. The metal finial at the end of the cord hit against the glass pane with an incessant, soft *click-clack*, but I didn't have the energy to get up and wrap it around the curtain knob attached to the wall and make it stop. The sun cascaded across the classic geometrical motifs of the Fine Serapi rug.

My muscles felt so heavy like I was pulling dead weight, although I hadn't moved an inch in hours. My cousins and friends had stopped by to catch up, but I turned them away, claiming to be sick. While technically a lie, I certainly felt as if I were on death's doorstep.

My phone buzzed.

A text.

Hope against hope, I grabbed my phone, praying it was Tatum sending me any sign of repentance.

Instead, it was Star.

Ugh, I so did not want to talk to anyone, but there was an alarmed tone to her text. She'd seen Tatum. She'd heard I'd left for LA. She wanted to know if I was okay, if Tatum and I were okay. He didn't look okay, she'd texted. She'd never seen him like this before. Never seen him this undone.

I tapped on my phone, pondering how best to respond when another text came through. Then another.

She was panicking.

She wanted to video chat.

Fuck. I didn't want to. I really didn't. I looked awful, my room was a mess, and I was thoroughly demoralized, but I also couldn't deny her request. She was more than a friend. She'd become like a sister to me, and whatever Tatum had done to me could not undo the bond between us.

ME: Sure

STAR: Thanx. Calling now

The phone rang and Star's concerned face shimmered on the screen of my cellphone.

"Oh my God, I'm so scared, Clara," she launched in without even a hello. Her golden hair and dark eyes were so familiar to me, it made my heart ache. While she and her brother shared similar features, they also looked so different. Where Tatum's face was angular and stern, Star had a soft, heart-shaped face. It was as if Tatum had decided, in his infinite willfulness, that he would deal with the hardness of life and fill her life with everything that was gentle and sweet.

"He was dressed from head to toe in black. Not a suit, mind you. It was like ... like a cross between the CIA and a ninja. He came in, carrying this huge gym bag. And his face

—" She clenched her fist and pressed it to her mouth. "I'd never seen him in such a state. He's not the type of man to get into idle fistfights. Today, he looked like ... I can't even describe it."

"I know, I saw," I told her.

She jerked in place. "You did?"

"Yes, when he broke up with me," I explained simply.

"Don't you believe him for one second, Clara," she said fiercely, her voice trembling slightly. "My brother is crazy about you. I think that's partly why he's so unhinged."

"I don't know about that," I stated, releasing a despondent sigh. "Either way, it doesn't change anything between us. If he felt the need to break up with me, his reason must have seemed more important than what we had together. He chose *that* over me, over us. There's no going back from it."

"No," she denied hotly.

My brows lifted. I'd never heard her speak like this before, but it gave me a glimpse of the same inner core of steel as her brother had. "There's only one conceivable reason he would break up with you, and it's to protect you. He'd only let you go if your life was on the line."

I didn't know what to think. Since he didn't confide in me but lied and pushed me away, there was no way of knowing if she was right. Star might believe it, might desperately want to believe it, but that didn't make it true.

Star's voice dropped as if she were afraid to speak out loud. "When he went out, I snuck into his bedroom and checked inside the bag. What I found scared me, Clara."

I sat up straight. "What did you find?"

"*Guns.* A huge bag full of *guns.* There were other things in there that made me think he wasn't going back to his penthouse. Family photos, for one thing. Then there were a few pieces of family jewelry, like my grandmother's cross, and ... a lock of your hair. More proof that he loves you. He didn't even bring a suit. I mean, why would he leave his apartment with a bag filled with an arsenal of guns and only the most meaningful things he owns? He left everything else behind, even his clothes. It doesn't make sense. Yet it scares me."

My gaze wandered away from her as I tried to process what she said. My fingers started tingling and my palms sweating. I rubbed them on the pants I was wearing. He left everything, except for his stash of guns and meaningful items, including my lock of hair? I recalled when he'd taken a pair of scissors, asked me if he could clip a strand, and carefully stowed it away in an old, antique locket that looked like it had been in his family for generations.

It had been tucked away in his nightstand, so he had to have consciously remembered it in the middle of packing only the essentials, under pressure if the guns were anything to go by.

I felt my heart beating harshly against my ribs. I feared the worst, the absolute worst. A numbness spread over me. He was going to die. All signs pointed to this scenario.

"I'm scared, Clara. Really scared," she whispered, her eyes darting from left to right in paranoia.

My brain had shut down momentarily, but her words snapped me out of my coma. I had to take care of her. She was a seventeen-year-old girl and sheltered beyond belief. She was to Tatum what Adrian was to me, and I would do everything in my power to help keep her safe because if Tatum was in the kind of trouble I thought he was in, she was also at risk. I'd do it for my love of her, but also for my love and respect of her brother.

First thing on the agenda was to calm her down. I carefully weighed my words before speaking, and when I did speak, I used my *şef* tone. "Listen to me, Star. This is why you shouldn't sneak around in other people's stuff. You know men. They must do what they must do. Guns are a part of our lifestyle, there's nothing scary about that. I have a gun beside my bed." I yanked the drawer of my night table open and tilted the phone to show her my gun. "See."

"Oh," she breathed out.

"Yeah, oh. Do you have a habit of looking through his stuff?"

"No," she exclaimed.

"Then this is probably not the first time he's carried guns into the house. He seems smart enough not to get into fights, but when shit goes down, shit goes down, and he was likely caught off guard by more than he could handle on his own. He got a good beating. It happens. Not the end of the world," I replied with a dismissive wave of my hand.

"What about my grandmother's cross, the locket with your hair, and the other stuff?"

"He's Romanian," I scoffed as if that explained everything. "Naturally, he's feeling sentimental after we broke up. You're an empath and you're bonded to your brother, so of course, you'd absorb his stress. Something's going down at work, and we broke up, but that's all there is to it. I'm sure he has a very good reason for each of the things you brought up, but because you snooped around, you don't have the whole story. Stop letting your imagination run wild and calm down."

Putting up a brave front, I inhaled deeply and insisted, "Nothing is going to happen to your brother."

Probably a lie, but there was no need for the girl to get hysterical over something she had no power over. If this had to do with his secret, which I was almost certain it did, then

Star and her mother might be in danger. And I needed her remaining calm and thinking clearly.

"Listen, Star, this gives me the opportunity to tell you something I've been meaning to say for a while. You're like the little sister I never had, and your mother is like the mother I never had. I care for you both, and if you're ever in trouble, you come to me. I'm your woman. Don't worry. If anything should happen to Tatum, which it won't, you can always count on me."

"Why are you saying this right now?" she asked hesitantly.

Guiding her away from her fears, I said, "Because your brother and I broke up, but it doesn't mean you and I should break up as well. I'm powerful enough to protect you if you ever need to seek sanctuary here. I just want you to know I love you, and if you should ever need me, I'm here for you."

"Umm, thank you, Clara. I love you, too. You're like the big sister I never had," she said softly. "I trust you. It's the reason I called you when I saw the guns. I didn't want to worry Mama. I guess, you're like family."

"You can tell me anything," I assured her. "You can visit me. You can live here if you want to get away from New York. You can start a new life in California. You can do anything you want. I'm here for you."

"Okay." She paused. "You're sure this isn't coming from Tatum's guns?" she asked tentatively.

"No," I replied firmly. "I'm giving you options. I'm a great believer that women should have options, and I'm your number one supporter. And if you're ever troubled about anything, you call me. I know you have your brother, but sometimes you need the guidance of a woman who's not your mother. That's where I come in."

I was trying to coat my message to something benign, yet

hoped my words resonated with her. If her world blew up into smithereens, as I feared it might, she'd remember my promises, and she'd come to me.

Star was such a proper young woman, so well-behaved and polite. Courteous as ever, she said, "I love you and thank you, Clara."

I didn't know what kind of trouble Tatum was in, and I didn't know how he was going to get himself out of it, but I wanted his sister and mother to know they had a place here with me.

"Anytime, Star. Seriously, call me anytime. Now that we've got your worries and my confession out of the way, I have one last piece of advice to give you. Stop sneaking around your brother's bedroom and let him focus on the job in front of him. Focus on being a teenager, on your schoolwork, and your friends. He wouldn't like knowing you're worried about him."

I was stooping low, using a guilt trip to get her out of worrying about her brother, but it was my job to worry about him. God knows, I would do enough worrying for her and me combined.

25

TATUM

I was prepared to die.

In the afterlife, because there sure as hell wasn't a heaven for me, I'd miss my loved ones. I'd miss Clara. There were so many things I missed about her. Holding her. Telling her I loved her, that she'd given my world a new meaning, more than I thought possible. I wanted to marry her, breed her, rule beside her. If I'd lived another life, had another kind of father, it might have been possible. My stomach clenched into a tight ball, the pain of my sacrifices slicing through me. Clara had been the hardest loss, but did I have a choice?

If I had, I wouldn't be lying on my belly on the asphalt-covered rooftop of a brownstone, sniper in hand, peering through the scope aimed at the entrance of the building across the street. The cold early-December morning seeped into my bones. The sun rose behind me, but it had little warmth to give.

Suddenly, shadows fell on either side of me. Instantly, I rolled to my back, rifle up, swinging it back and forth to the two men looming above me.

Luca and Nicu.

They stood still, with their arms crossed over their chest.

"Fuck, if it's that easy to creep up on you, it's a good thing we showed up. Right, Nicu?" Luca tilted his head to the left and threw his younger brother a little smirk.

Squinting up at them in the brittle winter sun, I asked, "What the hell are you doing here?"

He cocked his head, arched a brow in the way only Luca could, and retorted, "If you think we'd let you die, then you never knew us."

Nicu dropped to a crouch beside me.

"Besides, what's Clara going to do without your ass? She's a hellcat, that one. Without you to control her, she'll go back to being a pain in my ass."

My heart thumped hard against my ribcage. These men. My brothers. I didn't deserve them, but I was hella grateful to see them. I might very well have a chance at life.

"What about Alex? He know you're here?" I asked.

Nicu shook his head. "Best not to ask questions you don't want the answers to."

Fuck, I felt the stab in my heart. It shouldn't have hurt. It was expected, except it did hurt. More proof Alex had repudiated me forever. At least, these two men were my true brothers. They wouldn't let me die an ignoble death, even if it got them into trouble. Assuming we survived this mess, we'd never fight on the same side again. Hell, we might never see each other again, but at least I knew they were my brothers in arms. Brothers of my heart.

"Please, motherfucker," said Luca. "Cat may have reformed me in some ways, but I'm still the black sheep. I do what the fuck I want to do, regardless of the consequences."

He turned to me, his normally silver eyes a flat, gunmetal gray, and said, "I wouldn't be alive if it weren't for you. You saved me the day you found me in that closet. Before that, he was determined to kill me. Slowly, but surely, he would've succeeded. You thwarted him when you discovered me. And knowing I always had a place to escape to helped me survive the rest of it."

He spoke the truth. Luca spent half his childhood at my house. Got along with my father better than I did. The man must've looked like a saint to Luca.

As if reading my mind, which knowing Luca wasn't a far-off possibility, he continued, "Your father was a dirty bastard, but I'll always be grateful to him for opening his house to me and for killing Mihail. He might've been dirty, but he wasn't a monster."

He paused, his gaze far off into the distance, past the roofs of the buildings across the street, past everything. "Alex's hands are tied, and he's hurt by your betrayal, but you know how he is. Rules are rules. Everything is either black or white. My truth is different, Tatum. Your father saved me by killing my father because eventually, I would've had to off him myself."

"Not only are you my brother, but you saved Luca," piped in Nicu. "I'm not about to repay you by letting you die for your father's sins. I understand why you kept his secret, and considering the secrets our father kept from us, I don't fault you, Tatum."

"You can never be seen with me again if we get out of this alive," I declared.

What they were doing for me, defying their *şef*, was too much as it was.

"Let's get through this first, shall we," Luca quipped.

I looked around me. "How did you find me?"

The roofs on this side of the street covered the entire row of houses in Brighton Beach, the Bratva enclave on the

Brooklyn seaside. I'd broken into a building half a block down, come up the roof, propped the door open as an escape route, and made my way over the roofs of half a dozen buildings to stand on the one facing Ivanov's girl's apartment, where he slept most nights. My plan had been to shoot him as he left his girlfriend's apartment for the armored car idling on the curb, waiting for him. Wasn't much of a plan, but it was the best I could come up with on short notice.

Nicu chuckled. "You're a fool if you think it was hard for us to follow you. We know you, know how you think." He gave a little shrug. "Followed you from your mother's house. When we saw you break into the building down the block, we figured out what you were up to."

I handed Nicu the sniper. "Glad you're here. You're the best in the family. If anyone can clip the bastard, it's you."

Giving a little snort, he pushed my rifle away and lifted the Striker 40 grenade launcher in his hand, a personal favorite of Nicu's.

I shook my head and grinned at him. We weren't going to risk firing at Ivanov and missing. No, we were going to wait until he settled in his car, and then Nicu would launch an airburst smart grenade and blow the whole thing up. There'd be nothing left of Ivanov to identify afterward, unless one counted bits and pieces of him splattered on the stoops and façades of the brownstones on either side of the blast.

This was going to be phenomenal. It was deadly. It was bloody, but hey, we weren't nice guys. Never would be. Blood and sin were seared on our hearts for eternity.

"Yeah, we're gonna survive this, aren't we?" I said.

A big, wide smile spread over his face, his ice-cold blue eyes dancing with glee. "Yeah, we are."

He patted it. "I'll have to abandon her here so we can make a run for it afterward, but it's a worthy sacrifice."

I wasn't one for cracking smiles, but how could I abstain with fortune on my side? Now, we could kill two birds with one stone. I stowed away my weapon, and we waited, crouched and hidden. We were done talking. It was time to hunt. A cold, brisk wind picked up, skating over our hoodies. Anticipation zipped through me, through us. The scent of the imminent kill permeated our nostrils.

The minutes passed one after the other, boredom and alertness two sides of the same coin. A pigeon landed on the edge of the roof, walking with its wonky bob and head thrust a few feet away from us. With a coo and a strut, it pecked at the asphalt.

We could be there for another minute or a few hours, there was no way to know. As it turned out, about ten minutes later, they came down together. Perfect.

"Here we go," muttered Nicu softly.

An edgy excitement thrummed through me as Nicu set up his little army-grade toy, and when the two men were sealed into the Range Rover, I tensed. He pulled the trigger.

The explosion sent us scrambling backward, covering our heads. The noise from the blast rang in my ears, and it felt like someone had taken a sledgehammer at my head. We clambered to our feet, booked it at a full run, and hurdled over the low walls separating every building, pounding the black tarmac of the roofs. Reaching the door I'd left propped open, we flew down five flights of stairs and sped down the street to our individual cars.

Still in full-sprint mode, my hands shook as I dug out my keys and clicked the door open. Slamming it shut behind me, I revved the engine and tore down the street, Luca and Nicu behind me. Making a sharp turn onto Ocean

Parkway, I nodded to Nicu as he ripped past me, and that was it. The last time I'd ever see the men I'd spent every day of my life with since I was a kid.

Once I was out of Bratva territory, I slowed down, turned onto a random street, and turned off the engine. I dropped my head and sputtered out a stunned breath. I was still alive. It was over. The first thing I wanted to do was text Clara, but I forced my hands onto the steering wheel and gripped it hard to stop myself. She was better off without me and my stained reputation. I was alive, but I was still no good to her.

I abandoned the car and made my way to the subway, texting one word to Alex.

Done.

The deed was done, but so was my life as I knew it. My mother and sister would remain in the Lupu clan, but I would roam the world like the lost soul I was. They'd be cut off from me. Sure, I might get the chance to see them on a rare occasion, but my daily life with them evaporated like a puff of smoke.

Waiting on the subway platform, I looked around me in wonder. I was alive, but I'd never step foot on a concrete New York City sidewalk again. Not after today.

When you've lost almost everyone and everything you loved, when you've almost lost your life, you don't have any fucks left to give. I couldn't sacrifice *more.* I'd done my best for others, and my best came around to bite me in the ass. I was done doing for others. In this new reality, I only wanted one thing.

Clara.

I was a man carrying the equivalent of a scarlet letter A, a man with a target on his back. I should leave well enough alone, but I knew, deep in my bones, that even if she was better off without me, I couldn't let her go. Not without a fight.

Considering I was talking about Clara, it would no doubt be a fight.

Thinking of her, I checked the tracking app I'd installed on her phone.

What I saw brought the sensation of fire ants spawning on my skin. I scratched, leaving jagged red marks on my arms and chest, raw and bloody.

The dot of her phone on the GPS had moved from LA to Malibu—where Grigore lived.

Fuck. No.

26

TATUM

I switched to the 7 train, got off the subway at the 46th Street-Bliss Street station, walked down Queens Boulevard, and took a turn onto my street. Pausing on the stoop of my family's home, I took in a deep breath. This was probably the last time I'd walk down my street, the street where I was born, the street where I grew up, the street where I met Alex and became the *consilier* of the Lupu clan.

I walked through the door to find Star sitting on the living room sofa, wringing her hands. Jumping to her feet, she flung herself at me. I caught her and hugged her tight. I didn't generally tolerate much physical affection, but this would have to last a lifetime.

"Thank goodness you're okay," she muttered into my black hoodie.

"I'm okay," I said, choking back tears.

"I didn't think you were coming back. I don't know why, but this time I was afraid."

"I almost didn't," I confessed.

She dropped to her feet, stepped back, and blinked up at me.

This was the first time I'd revealed anything about what I did. She knew, of course, but it was an unspoken rule that we'd never address it out loud.

"I have to go away," I grated out, my eyes drinking her up, memorizing every detail of this girl who'd turned into a stunning young woman in the blink of an eye.

"Will you be back?"

I shook my head once.

"Mother?"

I looked left and right. "Is she here?"

"No, she went grocery shopping. She'll be back soon."

"I have to leave before she returns."

Her lashes fluttered in distress, her hands coming together and clinging to each other. "You won't say goodbye to her?"

"It's better if I don't. It'll be easier on her. Less drama. Less crying. Fewer questions. You'll have to be the one to take care of her now," I said. "I know it's a big responsibility."

Star's big, beautiful chocolate eyes enlarged with fear. I gripped her trembling hand and dragged her to the sofa. Sitting beside each other, I realized this was the first conversation we were having as equals. She'd have to rise to the occasion and take my place. She'd have to become me, and there was nothing I could do to save her from this fate.

"Starlene," I began. "You're my baby sister. I took care of you from the beginning." We both knew the story of Mama's postpartum depression after Star was born, and my father wasn't the kind of man to take care of babies. "I've tried to protect you. I've done the best I can." I spread my arms wide. "This is it. This is where I get off the train, and you keep riding on your own."

"What does that even mean?" she whispered.

I clasped her hand. It didn't come naturally, but I did it anyway because this might be the last time I touched my sister, and I wanted her to feel my love for her, I wanted to imbue her with my strength. She was going to need it.

"I did what I thought was best. Whether it was right or wrong, I don't know. I'll tell you everything, and you decide whether Mama should know the truth because from now on, you'll be making all the decisions."

Holding her gaze, I squeezed her hands tighter and blurted out, "*Tata* was involved in Mihail's death. He saw the way Alex trusted me, relied on me, and believed I'd become the next *consilier*. To speed up the process, he schemed with the Bratva to take a hit out on Mihail."

Star inhaled sharply.

"I found out because I'd snooped around on him like you did to me when I left the house earlier today," I said.

"How did you—"

"Never mind how. Ivanov killed *Tata* as well, seeing him for the weak link he was. During the Summer of Blood, I had a choice to make. Tell Alex or keep quiet. I thought the best choice for everyone involved was to keep quiet. That decision came home to roost when Grigore somehow found out and used it as revenge for Simu's death."

"For that and for you and Clara getting together," she quickly added.

Huh, I always knew Star was quick, but she'd seen or heard more than I thought.

Her fingers curled around mine in solidarity with me and my pain. It took some effort, but I didn't pull away. I only wanted Clara's touch. I loved my sister, but only Clara could make the pain go away.

"Alex tasked me with killing Ivanov as the only hope for you and Mama to remain in the clan. There was little chance I'd make it, but Luca and Nicu came to my rescue and helped me kill Ivanov. Alex agreed to keep this a secret. Only he and his brothers know. He won't hurt you or Mama, but I have been cast out of the clan, never to return," I concluded firmly.

"Never?"

Now the tears started flowing. My own throat felt sore, my chest burning with impotent rage and grief. My demon beat his chest, howling, feeling as if his heart was being torn out. He wasn't wrong. It was. His and mine both. I loved my sister, my mother, with every ounce of me. Our family was torn asunder, but this was our new reality.

"Never."

"Where are you going to go? Are you going to Clara?" she rushed out.

"Yes," I confirmed.

"Let me come with you," she pleaded with an edge of desperation. Her grip tightened further on me.

"I can't. I still have Grigore to kill, as part of my agreement with Alex. Apart from that, I honestly don't know if Clara will take me back."

"And if she doesn't?" she inquired.

"Then I will roam the earth like a ghost, I suppose," I replied with a wry smile.

"I'll roam with you," she replied fervently, tears spilling down her cheeks. Her nose had turned red, running a little. She let go of my hand to use the sleeve of her shirt to dab her eyes.

"No," I sternly countered. "This is your home, your

world. You will stay here and take care of Mama. She's not strong like you and me. She wouldn't survive the humiliation alone, much less being cast out."

"But I want to be with you. I want to roam the world with you," she complained softly. "I don't want to be separated from you, Tatum. You're like my other half. You're the only one who understands me and makes me feel like less of a freak."

I jolted in surprise, the breath punching out of my throat. What the fuck was going on, and why was I hearing about this just now, when I couldn't do anything about it. "Why would you feel that way?" I asked carefully.

She pulled away, drawing her hands back to her lap. She cast her gaze down, shrugged, and said, "You know how it is ... how kids can be ...."

"Why do you only speak of it now?" I pressed. "Is it because of our father?"

It was a softer way of asking if it was because of our ethnicity, the way I'd been mocked and bullied as a kid.

She shook her head and said resolutely, "Nothing like that."

Another breath escaped me. It was adolescence. "Listen, being a teenager isn't easy, but you will graduate soon, you will get married, you will continue with your life. Most importantly, you will be safe here. You have people who love you. Once you're married, it will be in your husband's best interest to protect you, and your position will be further solidified. Alex has acted with mercy, and it's not something I take lightly. I suggest you don't either. Finally, never breathe a word about this to Gabby or anyone else. If Alex wants it to remain hidden, then leave it be. Do you understand me, Star?" I asked sternly.

"Yes," she assented in a whisper. Her gaze jumped to

mine and held. "I understand, and I will take care of Mama, but if I can't leave with you, then I want you to do something for me."

"What?"

"Go after Clara. Put yourself first for once."

"It's not that simple, Star."

My heart felt like it'd been shredded in a meat grinder when I thought back on the horrifying lies I'd told Clara.

"I know you broke up to protect her. She's a reasonable person, and she understands how things work. You did what you had to do, not what you wanted to do."

I dropped my chin to my chest, suddenly exhausted. After blowing Ivanov up and running for my life, the amount of adrenaline rushing through my blood was in freefall. I was crashing fast.

"I don't know what she'll do, Star. You know me so well," I said sorrowfully.

I'd always treated Star like a child, and having just realized she was an equal, I would never have the chance to develop this new possibility. Even if we talked every day, it would never be the same.

"I was on a death mission, and if I told her the truth, I was afraid she'd confront Alex."

I flicked my fingers to my chin by way of explanation as I went on, "Look what he did to me. He was enraged and wouldn't tolerate any backchat, Hagi princess or not. Then, I reasoned that if she hated me, she wouldn't grieve me so much once I was gone. Gone is where I would've been if Luca and Nicu hadn't found me. The idea of her in pain is like thrusting a knife in my throat. I couldn't save you and Mama, so I went all-in with her. Surely, it's too late."

Star grasped my hands, brought them to her lips, and

kissed the bruises on my knuckles from the few times I covered my face to soften Alex's blows.

"Keep the faith, Tatum. Kill Grigore. Go to her. Then grovel. Grovel like you've never groveled before. I know it's a new concept for you, but do what you *must*."

Grovel? Star was speaking of herself, of what she would need to forgive such a trespass of the heart, but she didn't know Clara. I'd never win her back by groveling. She had no interest in a man that showed signs of weakness. Forcing her into submission, forcing her to forgive me, those I could see working, but grovel? No, that was the wrong plan of action for my dirty girl.

Of course, I couldn't explain this to my sister. She might be stronger than I'd first assumed, but she had no idea about the kind of appetites I had, the games I played with my love.

A smile tugged at the corner of my lips. "That's the plan, huh? You're my sidekick now?"

"I would've been earlier, if you'd let me in," she shot back succinctly.

Ouch, little sis.

"I'm never going to be a Clara, but I'm stronger and sharper than I look. Clara saw it in me immediately. You're slower on the uptake." There was a strain of sorrow in her tone.

"Oh, so you're all grown up. You don't need me anymore, huh?" I teased to distract her.

"I'll always need you," she said fiercely.

Her dark eyes blazed, and I saw some of the strength of which she spoke. It struck me that I'd been blind, and a bit sexist. If she'd been a boy, she'd have been inducted and fighting by my side at her age. I would've confided in her, expected her to help carry the burden of my secret, work beside me, and share in fixing it once it exploded. But, she'd been born a girl, and I felt it was my sole responsibility to protect her. I'd never really seen her in her glory. My sister would become a formidable force, and I would never see it.

My eyes grew soft. "I only wanted to protect you from this awful world, but I see I've underestimated you."

"You did. It made you feel safe to coddle me, keep me hidden away and wrapped in bubble wrap, but you're not all-powerful. And stop doing that," she chided me.

"Doing what?"

"Looking at me like this is the last time you'll ever set eyes on me again. We *will* see each other again. We *will* talk. I don't care where you are, as long as there's phone reception, we will be in each other's lives. I will never be ashamed of you, I will never hide you, even if this secret comes out to wreck everything for me."

"For your sake, I hope that never happens," I said forcefully. "Don't taunt Alex. It won't end well. He feels betrayed, and his pride is hurt. Not a good combination."

"I won't provoke him on purpose, but I'm sick of keeping myself small, Tatum, and I refuse to be kept down any longer."

"Is that what I did?"

"You did it, but I allowed it to happen." She waved her hand in dismissal. "I wasn't ready to shine. Regardless of how we got here, here we are. Secrets do not scare me. Yes, you've been cast out, but it has no impact on our relationship. If anything, I'm happy for you because you're free to pursue your woman and create a new life and family with her. You deserve every happiness in the world, brother. Grab it with both hands and never let go."

She'd rendered me speechless.

To think I'd deprived myself of the comfort and succor

she gave me, like a salve to my stained and broken soul. I cleared my throat and switched the conversation back to her, wanting to know more. Desperation clawed at me to know more of this new sister, flowering before my very eyes.

I leaned forward, my forearms braced on my knees, and asked expectantly, "What about you? What are your hopes and dreams? I always assumed they were to get married."

"They are, of course, they are," she said. "But being tainted saves me, too."

"How do you mean?"

"Because you won't expect me to marry for anything less than what you have with Clara. I saw how you two are together, and I won't settle for anything less. If I can't have that, then I won't marry. I'll figure out something else to do instead. See, I too have been freed by the prospect of being cast out one day."

Fuck.

I hadn't expected that. My aim was for her to get married so that her husband could protect her from whatever vagaries life threw at her. Again, my sister surprised me. Not only was she being realistic, as opposed to terrified like any other *mafie* girl would be in her place, but she already had other plans, more thoughtful plans.

"You will never have to worry financially. I will always provide for you," I stated. I'd created banking and investment accounts in their names. I'd have to teach her how to take control of them, but I had no intention of stopping there. I'd find a way to continue working with my unique set of skills. Hopefully, for Clara.

Dryness laced the inside of my mouth. My heart started pounding loudly in my chest at the thought of her and the challenge facing me. Jesus, I had no idea what kind of chance I had of winning her back.

"Even so, life is precarious. I've been lucky to have you to take care of me, but I'm better off learning how to take care of myself and Mama. I'll figure something out. I have one more year of high school, and then we'll see. Luca's wife, Cat, has started college. She's been trying to get us to continue our education, even after we get married. She can guide me."

I let out a deep sigh, a tinge of nostalgia to it.

"I see that I'm leaving a sister behind who's a full-fledged adult, and an intelligent and resourceful one, at that," I acknowledged.

"And don't worry about Mama. She's my responsibility from now on. I'll tell her you went on a trip, for starters. It will give me a couple of weeks to come up with something else. If you work things out with Clara, it will help me craft a story with a happy ending for her."

"Oh, you're a storyteller now, I see," I joked.

"I'm a woman of many talents," she shot back.

I looked deep into her eyes, eyes which suddenly looked older and wiser than their years. Did my sister have experiences I didn't know about? Had I missed entire aspects of her life and character while I treated her like a little girl? Did she have secrets? The thought worried me. She wouldn't be taking this so well if she hadn't had difficult experiences, but I was running out of time to probe into her soul.

"God, I hope you'll be okay."

She held my gaze steadily and promised, "I will be okay."

I nodded once.

"Then I should go...."

"Yes, before Mama comes back."

"Clara could reject me." I spoke low, the admission almost too much for me.

She kissed me on the cheek. "Don't underestimate her like you did me, Tatum. You're a warrior, and she's your warrior queen. Go get your queen."

27

CLARA

My father gave me a day to stew in my self-pity and then forced me out of my bed to listen to the details of his newest plan, which included Grigore of all people. If I hadn't been so depressed, I would've immediately told him I'd have nothing to do with it. Even thinking of it made me nauseous. There was only so much I could handle at one time, and unless I wanted to have a total meltdown, I had to compartmentalize. In this case, it meant stuffing his words to the back of my mind and going about my business of the day.

And the business of the day was making the rounds to visit clan members or risk insulting them, which of course, included Grigore.

After procrastinating the day away, I finally pushed myself to drive to Malibu. Parking in front of his white, angular modern house by the beach, I stepped out of the car to find him waiting to greet me personally with a kiss on each cheek. His hand lingered on my forearm. *Yuck.* I barely stopped myself from shaking it off. His touch made my skin crawl, triggering reminders of my father's latest scheme.

Grigore wasn't awful, I chastised myself. This was my father's idea, even if Grigore profited most from it. Mostly, it felt plain wrong for any other man to touch me. But Tatum was gone. And Grigore wasn't a man to insult. There was no point in offending him when I was in a weakened state with secrets to hide.

I took a seat on a minimalist turquoise couch. There were two more sofas, both striped white and beige, and the three sofas framed a fireplace made of blue granite. I stared down at the fabric of the one I was sitting on. It was supposed to give a pop of color to the place, but good God, what an ugly color. The only Romanian elements in his house were the intricate, lavishly colored rugs on the light gray hardwood flooring.

I could see waves rolling in on a perfect, sunny California day through the open doors. I took a calming breath. I'd always have the glorious sun, practically every day of every year. I may have warmed up to New York, but California would always be my home. After years of living here, it still felt like a miracle to me.

Georgina, his maid, a dark-haired beauty who I was sure was his mistress, came to me with a small crystal glass of *vişinată*, a sour cherry brandy I knew she made herself. I'd been to his place enough times for her to know my preference.

Grigore sat back against one of the sofas. He was a handsome man, older than I was but younger than Tatum. Completely different in almost every way. Not nearly as tall. Fit, but rangier than Tatum with his bulky muscles. Tatum was so tall and big. He'd made me feel safe and cared for. I gave a little sigh; reminiscing about his splendid body so did not help my state of mind. Perhaps there was some irony in the fact that I found solace in a big guy who ordered me around, but that was how it was. I felt like I could let go, shed every mask I wore, and just be me. He loved me exactly as I was, not as a Hagi princess soon-to-be *şef*.

He preferred me best sans makeup, wearing a pair of sweats, my hair in a top knot. Most Romanian men liked their women dolled up. Even as a boss lady, I was supposed to utilize my sexuality to manipulate men. I'd certainly done it with Grigore, used it in a dance to entice him while keeping him at a sufficient distance.

With Tatum, it was the opposite.

He liked me best, lounging on his bed, in the privacy of his own space, where I could relax and be my authentic self.

No guises. No façades. No dances. Only playing.

Those days were over with. I was expected to buck up, return to duty, and get on with it, even if my heart was cracked and spewing anger and grief.

"So ...," began Grigore, taking a sip from the glass of *ţuică* Georgina deposited on the small table beside him. "How was New York?"

"Average," I said, feigning disinterest. "You've seen it, having visited Simu. It's dirty. Cold. Crowded."

"Hmm," he answered cryptically.

"Don't see yourself living there, then?"

I sat up straight, on the alert. "Of course not. What kind of question is that, Grigore?"

"Just making conversation," he lied.

"Let me assure you, I have no intention of living anywhere but my father's house until the day I die. Clear enough for you?"

"Quite clear," he said with a wide, cold smile. Too many teeth. He was showing far too many teeth. I pulled in a deep breath, my tummy clenching in an unfamiliar tug of fear. He seemed more predator than human. Why had it taken me so long to see his snake-charmer smile? Cold. Fake.

"Good," I replied pertly, taking a small sip from my drink.

He set his own drink down and sat beside me on my sofa, taking my hand in his. I stiffened my body to prevent myself from instinctually flinching away from him. The surface where his fingers touched mine prickled in disgust.

"I'm glad to have you back, Clara. It's been so boring without you. There's no one I can talk to like you. I've been on my own at weddings, celebrations, gatherings. Usually, you were there to help pass the time. We'd mock the various ludicrous things we'd see people do. How silly people are," he murmured.

There was a dangerous edge to his comment. Silly? Like me. A shiver sped down my spine. There was an underlying threat behind his comment. I felt it in my bones. Did he know about me and Tatum? It sure as hell felt like it.

I pulled my fingers out from his grasp, patted his hand, and put space between us.

"I'm back, so you will be lonely no longer. How are the other clans?" I asked, redirecting the conversation, although my father and I had been in constant contact, and I was up to date with everyone.

Ignoring my question, he said, "I was worried, to be honest. I didn't know if they would bring you over to the dark side. They're a wily bunch. Charming, but devious. Especially that Tatum. He's truly a brute inside."

Better a brute than a snake, I almost bit out. The retort sat on the tip of my tongue, but I swallowed it down.

His eyes turned sharp. He was so transparent, clearly taunting me, but I wasn't about to fall into his trap. Tatum and I hadn't been excessively careful, and while we thought no one besides Alex and his brothers knew, Grigore could have potentially spied on me. He may know nothing, or he may know we lived together, but he could only presume the rest. Not knowing must be killing him.

"I didn't like him from the beginning," I stated, keeping it vague.

He gave a disbelieving little huff. "That changed in New York."

"Somewhat," I conceded while maintaining ambiguity.

"Then it's a good thing I got him out of the way—"

Brows slamming together, I swiveled in his direction. "*What?*"

One side of his lips cocked up in a mocking smirk.

"My dear, don't you know?" he asked with an edge of disdain I did not appreciate.

I shook my head in confusion.

"His father was involved with the Bratva in the plot to assassinate Alex's father. Tatum knew and kept it from Alex all this time. Naturally, when I found out, the only proper recourse was to tell Alex."

My heart slammed against my ribs, pounding as if attempting to escape. What the fuck? This was the reason Tatum broke up with me. My eyes narrowed on Grigore. Because of *him*. My world imploded, my heart was ripped out of my chest, my relationship with Tatum severed because of *him. I fucking hated him.*

His hand snaked over mine, and this time, it was his turn to give me a patronizing little pat. "You look pale. Something wrong?"

My skin flashed hot, cold, hot. Goose bumps burst over my skin like red-hot flames, searing me. Goddamn the fucker. Somehow, he'd dug up Tatum's secret and thrown it in Alex's face as revenge for Simu. Tatum was a dead man, and he'd purposely tried to make me hate him.

My mind reeled. Oh God, he could be *dead*. Dread gripped me by the throat. *No, no, no.* I breathed through the sharp stab of pain. I had no proof. Locking down my panic, I refused to unravel in front of Grigore.

Until I learned otherwise, Tatum was alive.

I gulped.

Alive, but excommunicated, for sure.

This wasn't the time or place to dissect my feelings. Throwing up a mask of disinterest, I refused to allow this snake to get the better of me. He dropped this bombshell to get a reaction out of me, but I'd outsmart him if it killed me.

Giving him a megawatt Hollywood smile, I said, "Not at all. If anything, I'm impressed by your slyness. You got your revenge in the end. Just as it should be, Grigore. Congratulations for a job well done."

You putrid, sewage-loving snake.

His face faltered for a split second before he regained his balance—he always was quick on his feet—and bent his head in false modesty, maintaining his pomposity.

"Only doing my duty," he murmured.

You scheming, conniving snake.

"You did well," I commended him. "I assume my father has rewarded you."

"I haven't spoken to him of this, actually. I thought it would be my special gift to you," he said falsely.

Gift, my ass.

"I'll be sure to put in a word of your good deed. Anything for the family, I know that was your intention, of course," I feigned.

Of course *not*. I seethed with fury. He hurt Tatum. Ruined his life. Destroyed his relationship with Alex and the Lupu brothers. Tore him from his clan, his mother, and his sister. *Star.* I promised to watch out for her, and my right-hand man was the one responsible for tearing her world apart. Shaking with bottled-up rage, I fantasized about eviscerating this man, slashing him from his throat to his cock, tearing out his intestines, and stuffing them in his mouth.

Today, he would live. *Enjoy it buddy, because your days are numbered.*

"Of course," he replied smoothly. "Anything for the Hagi clan."

I had to get out of there before I throttled him to death.

Checking my cell phone, I exclaimed, "Oh, it's getting late, and I've been gone all day visiting people."

I drained my drink and stood up. "What a great ending to a long and tiring day, but I must get back home."

We kissed each other on the cheek, and I gave a shout of goodbye to Georgina, who hurried into the foyer to see me off, standing beside Grigore like the couple they were.

Knowing he could be watching from the window, I maintained my expression until I turned around in his driveaway and had my back to his house.

The instant I was out of sight, I let out a string of curses. I was going to kill both men. Grigore, for ruining the lives of his mother and sister. And Tatum, if he was still alive, for the way he handled this situation. Instead of confiding in me and letting me help him, he'd sacrificed our relationship to protect me. Stubborn man. I wanted to kiss him and strangle him at the same time. Hopefully, I'd get the chance to do both. But first, I had to find out if he was still alive.

28

TATUM

I stared down at Grigore in the dark gloom of his bedroom, my knife to his throat. His security system was top-notch, so it took some doing to get through it. In the end, I had to make a call to Luca to help disable it from New York.

But here I was, the monster in the shadows, ready to finish this job. After the Summer of Blood, as *consilier*, I didn't have to do much of the dirty work, but staring down at Grigore, I realized I didn't mind it too much. Brought me back to my roots. Reminded me of where I came from. The bottom.

I smacked Grigore on both cheeks till he startled awake and instantly froze the moment he felt the cold blade of the knife against his jugular.

"You thought you could fuck with me, motherfucker? You thought you could get revenge on Alex and the brothers through me? Use me like a filthy whore and then let Alex do the dirty work for you, hmm?"

I felt the slight movement of the knife as his Adam's apple moved up and down.

I shook my head, tsking him. "You dumb fuck, rule number one to any plan of revenge: make sure to kill the target yourself, Grigore. No one teach you about loose ends?" I jeered. "Word to the wise, never leave any loose ends." I paused. "Oh, wait, that lesson's come too late for you."

"Fuck you, you piece of shit Lupu trash. You've been cast out like the mongrel dog you are. I spit on you and your family," he sneered.

"Big words for a man about to die," I taunted, pressing the knife deep enough to slice skin.

Blood oozed from the cut.

Hissing, Grigore pushed down into the mattress, but I kept the pressure steady to remind him who was in control. It wasn't so easy to trash talk once you realized the man holding a knife to your throat was willing to use it. Idiot thought I'd dragged myself out here to threaten him. Miscalculation on his part. But then again, everything had been a miscalculation from the moment he thought he could use me.

"Yeah, so you're going to murder me, and then what? Cause a war?" he taunted. "Because that's what's going to happen. Coming in here, on Hagi territory, and killing a *consilier*. Alex will kill you for creating this clusterfuck."

I laughed, nice and long. "Who do you think ordered this?"

His eyes flared wide with fear.

"He wants you dead."

Moonlight streamed in through the floor-to-ceiling windows off the terrace I'd hopped onto, illuminating his expression. His gaze turned sharp and calculating as he pivoted in another direction.

"Don't do it for him," he argued. "The fucker rejected

you. If you spare me, I'll make sure you have a place here with the Hagi. We could use a smart man like you."

I barked out a dark, humorless laugh. As if I would trust a man who'd ruined my life by stabbing me in the back. He must think me an idiot.

"So you could use me to learn everything you want about the Lupu clan to continue your vendetta? Might have considered your offer if I didn't want to kill you myself so fucking badly. But if there was a pissing contest between Alex and me, I'd win by a long shot," I assured him. "No, you're not getting out of this."

Back to his first argument, he nervously muttered, "If you touch a hair on my head, the Hagi will seek out who did it and will take vengeance on you. Clara, especially. She fucking loves me, sweet-tasting little thing—"

Possessiveness ripped through me. My brain exploded with fury, my knife pressing deep enough to cut him off with a frightened little whimper.

"Don't you dare speak her name, much less talk about how she tastes, you fucking prick," I thundered. My hand trembled with rage. Fear trickled down my spine. Had I goaded her to turn to this prick for comfort?

Praying I hadn't, I spat out, "You have no fucking clue what she feels like, do you now? What her tight cunt feels like wrapped around your cock, all that snug, wet flesh massaging your shaft like a thousand tiny digits. Her nails scoring down your chest as she loses control. Her screams in your ear, so loud you could go deaf."

Grigore's face contorted and I saw my answer. For a moment, I was terrified I'd driven her into his arms. Seeing her car parked at his Malibu beach home on the tracking app, I had no idea how far I'd pushed her. Seemed like I'd made it in the nick of time.

"But I do," I continued. "And you never will. I'm here to make sure of that."

"She won't ever take you back. She loathes you."

I let out a derisive laugh. Of course, he was right. I'd hurt her, I'd shoved her away at a critical time, and Clara wasn't a forgiving woman, but he sure as hell wasn't a reliable source. I'd find out for myself how Clara felt, what she would or wouldn't do, and go from there. And I had weapons of pleasure and pain in my arsenal. I was going after her, armed and dangerous.

I beat my fist on my chest, desperation tearing at my lungs. "Mine. She's mine. You will never have her. Even if she doesn't take me back, she'll always and forever be *mine.*"

"If she was yours, what the fuck was she doing in my house this afternoon, huh?" he goaded.

"That ends today," I bit out.

"You're like a rabid half-breed dog that needs to be put down," he snarled.

"Try me, motherfucker. Because you have something to lose, but me? I have no clan. No family. *Nothing.* Fucking try me. I beg you."

His right eyelid flickered.

A sign of fear, of weakness.

In a standoff between *mafie* men, you never show a sign of weakness.

I should've taken the eye tick as more than what it was because a second later, he grabbed my shirt and shoved me off him. I laughed. The bastard was fool enough to think he could win in a physical fight against a man like me. He wasn't wrong when he'd called me a rabid dog, I was rabid, but more like a rabid berserker, bloodlust thrumming through my veins.

He jumped off the bed, his hand scrambling to open the

drawer of the nightstand, scrambling for a gun. I was hoping to play with him for a bit, but a gun would change the odds significantly in his favor. I wrapped my arm around his neck, pulling him back into my chest.

"I'll fucking destroy you," I gritted out.

He struggled viciously. We wrangled, toppled to the floor, and the knife flew out of my hand and bounced under the bed. Sprawled on the floor as one, I saw his outstretched hand reach underneath the bed.

Slamming my balled fist on top of his hand, I heard a crunch.

He screeched.

Wrestling him beneath me, I blindly tapped the pitch-black space beneath the bed until my fingertips grazed the cool handle. One hand on his nape to keep him in place, I lunged and got a grip on the knife. I grasped his hair, brutally yanked his head back, and sliced a perfect arc across his throat in one swift, efficient move.

Blood gushed everywhere.

Black moisture splashed onto my gloved hand and forearm. I felt a spray of wetness across my face. From the incoherent gurgling sound he made, I'd severed his windpipe. There were a series of harsh gasping noises as he shuddered his way into death.

Blood soaked the floor. Goddamn, I must have slit his carotid artery and jugular vein, two powerful jets, because blood seemed to spew out endlessly.

I released his hair and his head plunked down, his temple hitting the ground with a loud thud. My shoes squelched in the pale-colored wooden flooring, the pool of black wetness spreading beneath my feet. Adrenaline pumped through my veins, leaving me with a rapid heart rate and heightened senses. The shadows seemed to sway back and forth, like live beings, as I bent down and wiped the knife clean on his sleeve before returning it to its holster.

The cursive of blood etched on my face was cooling, coagulating on my skin, pulling it taut. I stumbled around in the shrouded darkness toward the bathroom, closed the door, and flipped on the light. The blood had dried enough that it took a little effort to rub it off. Without taking off my blood-stained leather gloves, I cleaned it off with a small, spotless white hand towel, which I stuffed into the back pocket of my dark jeans, to dispose of later.

Stalking back into his bedroom, I kicked him a few times. There was no need for confirmation, but it was an old habit of mine. With one final scan to make sure I'd cleaned up, I stepped out onto the terrace and texted Alex.

The surf was loud, breaking over the shoreline, each wave crashing and receding, only to roll up and crash again. The sound wasn't half bad. California might take some getting used to, but I was willing to make the effort. I drew in a deep, bracing inhalation of cool, salty air. The last part of our bargain had been completed.

My phone vibrated.

Alex: I will take care of them. Good luck with the rest of your life brother. *La revedere.*

Farewell.

It was bittersweet. Mostly bitter. A tinge of sweetness in his nostalgic acknowledgment that, till the end, we'd be brothers. Separated till death, but perhaps we'd reunite in the afterlife.

I swung over the wrought-iron banister of the terrace and jumped down a flight to land on my feet.

It was time to go get my woman back.

29

TATUM

I came through the open window and landed inside Clara's bedroom. It had been easy—way too fucking easy—to get through the paltry security around the parameters of their home. That was a Romanian for you. Grigore had been the exception, which only proved to show he knew how shady he was and that he needed protection. Everyone else was cocky to a fault, thinking they didn't need souped-up security like the cartels.

I heard movement in the en suite bathroom. *Clara.* My insides vibrated with nerves and a keen desire, knowing she was so close. Positioning myself by the entryway, I cut off any chance of escape. Leaning my shoulder against the door, I gazed around her bedroom.

There were stuffed animals piled high on her bed, which was a bit alarming. Not something I expected of her. She was soft, but all woman, and I simply couldn't imagine her in bed cuddling those things. Doing other, naughty things, yes, that I could clearly see.

Other than that, her bedroom was no different from the rest of the house, meaning it was cluttered with more furniture than necessary. Besides her bed, there were rows of waist-high bookshelves, a vanity, a messy desk, a couple of armchairs with adjoining tables, and a small piano. The last one seemed supremely unnecessary in a mansion with a dozen other bedrooms.

But I didn't have time to contemplate it any further because Clara stepped out of the bathroom at that moment.

She startled, let out a gasp, but recovered quickly.

Fuck, she was gorgeous. It hurt to look at her, but I couldn't turn away if I tried. My gaze devoured every inch of her.

Her face was clean of makeup, her luxurious hair tucked into a chignon at her nape. She wore one of her killer suits, minus the jacket. Her tight-fitting skirt, black with white piping, stopped midthigh, flashing me with the lace top of her sheer thigh highs. Son of a bitch, I wanted to drop to my knees, sink my teeth in the lace, and tear it down her leg. My gaze flicked back up. Her sheer indigo shirt showed enough cleavage to get my fingers twitching with the urge to rip it open so I could feast on her delicious tits.

Our eyes locked.

Silence reigned.

The electricity zipping between us charged the air.

A band tightened around my chest, leaving me breathless. Dizzy. I ached for her so bad, it took every ounce of control I had not to attack her like an animal.

Anytime I was around Clara, it felt normal to want to touch her, to take her, and our little hiatus viciously amped up my desire to dominate her, to fuck her like she was a rag doll. After what I'd been through, I was seriously unhinged.

Folding her arms over her chest, she glared at me and said, "What are you doing here?"

"I have no clan," I declared, getting to the root of things without preamble.

"I know," she retorted quickly. "Although I didn't find out from you. Thanks for that, by the way."

The lump in my throat doubled in size. It was hard to speak, but speak I would. She deserved the truth, the whole, unvarnished truth.

Sweaty hands clenched in fists, I swallowed hard and began, "Grigore told Alex my father had conspired with the Bratva to take out a hit on his father. He tried to kill me." She inhaled sharply. "Nina stopped him at the last moment. I was given an ultimatum. Kill the man who killed his father, and I would live. It was a chance to redeem my name and give my mother and Star a chance to remain within the clan, but it was a death sentence. Luca and Nicu came to my rescue, and Nicu blew the fucker up."

I squeezed my eyes shut for a moment and then snapped them open again. "I know I failed you, but I—" My throat cinched tight and I couldn't speak.

I cleared my throat and redirected my speech to the heart of the matter.

"I can't do it anymore, Clara."

"Do what?" she whispered, her voice breaking.

"This." I flicked my fingers between us. "Us not being together. Yeah, my world imploded. Yeah, I'm separated from my mother and sister forever. Yeah, I should be crushed. I am, but I'm also grateful. Grigore told Alex, hoping to destroy me, but it freed me. I accomplished my mission, I'm alive and free and *alive*. But do you know what I couldn't stop condemning myself for?"

"What?" she rasped out.

"For ruining *us*. I was free from this secret that shackled me for over a decade, but it didn't matter because you were gone."

Her beautiful eyes were wide with unshed tears. "Why Tatum? Why didn't you confide in me?"

"I was thinking of you. You think it was easy to break up with you, to say the hurtful lies I said? It fucking killed me inside, but I was convinced I was going to die. If I told you, you would've confronted Alex—and he was fucking enraged. Any challenge to his word would've blown back on you and your clan. I also thought if I hurt you bad enough, you'd hate me, and you'd be glad I was dead," I confessed. "That I'd spare you the grief."

"I could never hate you," she whispered.

That one phrase made my heart soar with unadulterated hope.

"H-how are your mother and sister safe in New York?"

God, this woman was beautiful, inside and out. The first thing she worried about was my family.

"They can come here," she continued. "I will give them my protection."

Gracious, always so damn gracious.

"I might take you up on that offer if things don't work out," I replied. "But for now, for my mother especially, they're better off staying where they are."

She lifted her chin regally, eyes flashing as she stared down on me like I was dirt beneath her shoes, which wasn't far from the truth.

"The offer stands, but only for them," she clarified, drawing a line in the sand.

A line I had every intention of disregarding.

I took a step closer.

She took a step back. Fuck that. Time to lay down the law and get my woman back.

Hardening my tone, I declared, "We're back together, Clara. I'm going to marry you, and then I'm going to make your belly round with my babies and put any questions of who owns you to rest, do you hear me?"

She jerked, backing up further. I followed her, step by step, until her spine hit the wall. Her eyes raked me over from head to toe. Her gaze raked me over from head to toe. It roved over my features as if memorizing them for the last time. I was hers. She was mine. Why the look of stark desolation on her face?

She swallowed. Looked away. Returned her gaze to me like the queen she was. "God, you can't imagine how much I've wanted to hear that, but too much has happened." She gave a harsh bark of laughter, her eyes bleeding agony.

"It's too late," she announced.

Over my dead fucking body. I'm not taking no for an answer.

"Come here," I demanded.

She vigorously shook her head.

"It's too late, Tatum. You're too late, don't you understand? You can never own me. Never." Her voice ended in a pained rasp, the words *own* and *never* hovering out of my reach.

But I refused to accept it. Never was a word meant to be torn apart with my bare hands. When it came to this woman, *never* was a word to be banished from my vocabulary.

"On your knees," I ordered, my tone turning vicious.

I scoured her with my eyes. Every inch of her was mine, dammit.

Other men groveled, as they should. As should I, except this was my version of begging for forgiveness. And if she didn't follow my command, if she didn't forgive me, I didn't know what I'd do. I fucking loved her, was madly in love with her, but if I'd permanently severed our bond, I'd shrivel up into a ball and die.

She shifted on her feet, uncertain.

She licked her lips.

Then she dropped to her knees.

Thank Christ.

"Crawl to me."

She didn't dare shake her head, but her mesmerizing eyes begged me to release her.

I would not.

"Never," I replied to her unspoken plea. "Now. Fucking *crawl now.*"

I heard her slight intake of breath. I avoided cursing in her presence, until now. Breaking us had broken me. I wasn't the same man. I'd gone ahead and done everything in my power to wreck the beautiful thing that was *us*, and I'd spend the rest of my life building it back, giving her whatever she wanted, worshipping her pussy until my last dying breath.

She might be the one physically kneeling, but I was the one figuratively on my knees. I might be the one commanding her to crawl to me, but I'd crawled back to her, tail between my legs. I'd fucked up, and I would not rest until I owned her and bound her to me for all eternity. They would speak about us and about our rule over this goddamn sun-drenched land she loved so much.

She slapped the parquet floor.

The tight skirt bunched and tightened around her wide hips, but she didn't dare tug at it to give herself space to move more comfortably. Not without my permission, she wouldn't, and I wasn't about to give it to her. But that was the reward of owning a submissive treasure like Clara. I didn't have to be perfect around her, I just had to be me. It was so simple, yet damn monumental. She didn't love me perfect. She loved me as I was.

I released the breath strangled in my throat and praised her with a *good girl.*

Her lips opened, and I feared what would come out of her mouth. Perhaps a plea to release her. Or a declaration that it could never work between us. I couldn't allow those words to be said. I didn't know how much more restraint I had, but I couldn't stand to hear any denials coming out of her mouth.

Hands clenched to my sides, I growled, "Not a word. Come here now. Unless you want me to tan that sweet ass of yours before fucking it raw."

I was at the end of my rope, a rope so frayed from the distance I'd built between us, it'd snap in a second if she didn't start moving.

My power over her was only, and always would be, an undeserved gift she benevolently granted me like the fucking queen she was. Realizing my desperation, and deciding to show mercy, she planted one hand in front of her and began to sway those sexy hips of hers.

The time it took for her to cross the floor was excruciating, the silk thigh highs catching between the planks of wood.

The instant she was within arm's reach, I seized her by the bun, unraveled her hair, and dragged her to me. I dropped onto a gilded chair near the door, spread my legs open, and hauled her close.

Once she was trapped between my legs with her cheek resting against my inner thigh, I leaned back. Releasing a pent-up breath, I gazed down at her beautiful face lifted toward mine, her gaze a whirlwind of emotion. Excitement, adulation, apprehension.

Caressing her hair, I said, "That's right, my queen, this is where you're supposed to be. Now say whatever bullshit you have to say."

She licked her lips and stared up at me. Worry bled through her gaze and trepidation prickled at my nape. But with her near me, bracketed between my thighs, eyes on me, I felt like I could conquer anything.

"My father arranged for me to marry Grigore," she breathed out.

My stomach dropped down to the floor.

Instinctively, my hand twisted in her hair, pulling her closer to me. Fury ricocheted through me. Not because of Grigore. Grigore was dead. But the arranged marriage part. Her father could easily replace Grigore with another Hagi man.

She swallowed, but never backing down, she continued, "He knows. I'm not a virgin anymore. To get in front of the scandal, he's put out rumors that Grigore and I have fallen in love."

My entire body stiffened.

"Like hell he has," I ground out.

Tears beaded at the corners of her eyes, falling indiscriminately as she went on, "There's nothing I can do. He's furious with me. He feels I betrayed him and our clan. Ruined his plans for my succession. It's part mitigation strategy, part punishment. Okay, mostly punishment. You know how Romanians are when they feel betrayed."

A brittle smile spread over my lips.

"It's fucking perfect," I said, my voice harsh and guttural. My mind was racing, flipping through the different scenarios of how I could use this to our advantage.

Her jaw dropped.

"What?" she hissed, gaze turning deadly.

"If he's willing to marry you to that bastard, then he's opened the door to marriage, period."

"He means for me to marry *him*. I already explained, it's a punishment."

I clucked confidently. "No one punishes you but me."

I smoothed my hand over the veins of golden honey streaking through her thick mass of hair. Dipping my hand underneath it, I massaged the base of her skull. Despite the tension in her body, she melted under my touch. A little sigh of pleasure slipped between her lips, and my heart swelled at the proof that I could give her comfort during the worst of times. I was her haven, as she was mine.

"He hasn't declared your engagement yet," I stated.

"Not yet, no. But any day now. There's a wedding in a few days. The entire clan will gather for it. I expect he'll do it then."

She sniffed and her eyes darted away from mine.

Taking her by the hair, I hauled her up as I leaned down and smashed my lips against hers. Our tongues met, and I inhaled her taste, sweet as ever. Everything about her taste spoke of home and hearth. Our tongues entwined and then dueled for dominance. As always, I won.

When we finally broke away, breathing heavily, I stared deep into her eyes and said, "First off, Grigore is dead. I slit his throat. As for your father, he'll have news to declare alright. He'll be declaring *me* as your husband."

30

CLARA

I blinked up at Tatum. A rush of vindictive pride surged through me, gleeful to hear of Grigore's death at Tatum's hands. I was as bloodthirsty as the next *şef*, and to hear Tatum had wiped out his rival made me wet with lust.

I felt his striking eyes like a hot brand on my face, scrutinizing every flicker of expression. Gaze searching his, I tossed my head. Instantly, his grip tightened around my hair and regained control. Hmm ... that felt too good for words, him controlling my movements, however slight they might be.

I paused for a moment to just stare at him. God, he was so beautiful. The expression of determination lining his face made my panties wet. Jaw set, one fine muscle flickering with willful intent. His beautiful, sculpted lips pressed together, another sign of his persistence. There was no moving this man.

An errant blond lock of hair fell across the bruise that had blossomed around his eye. Each time I looked up at him, I was reminded of what he'd survived, and I wanted to weep. But I knew that I was a comfort to him just as I was, lying at his feet, thigh-high torn at the knees, ironed skirt wrinkled, and my tight chignon wrecked by his hand.

Tilting my head back, he said, "I want to fuck you, but I want to marry you more. Get a bag packed. We're leaving for Vegas."

Now he was babbling nonsense. The shock of losing his clan and life in New York must have addled his brain.

"We're going to be a force to be reckoned with," he promised. "An unstoppable force. This is checkmate. We take the game back with this killer move."

"I'm not fighting my father," I replied. That was never going to happen. "My father didn't do anything wrong." Okay, even if he was in the wrong, I wasn't about to tear the Hagi clan in half and ruin his life's work.

"I beg to differ. He manipulated you with this 'remain a virgin' thing, tangling you up in this mythology he's spun around the Virgin Queen. Once he learned you lost your virginity, he reverted to the old, patriarchal ways and planned to marry you off, giving Grigore the keys to your kingdom. He should be thrilled when he hears we are married. Unlike Grigore or any other man who panders to your family, I will always have your back."

I shook my head. This was madness. I mean, he'd come back contrite, but he hadn't even declared his love for me. Was I simply to assume it? I mean, I kind of did, but still. And then, there was the assumption that my father would automatically accept us. While Tatum made a good point that if he was going to allow marriage, then Tatum was a dead ringer for a contender, but ...

Tatum went on, "I followed Alex. I never wanted to be first. Not as an equal or a peer, but you make me want to be more. You inspire me to become the greatest version of myself. I will earn the right to be by your side, rule alongside you, throne to throne. No other man could ever give your father that guarantee."

His dark eyes turned flinty. "But make no mistake about it, Clara, I'm not giving you a choice. There's no scenario in which you are not mine. You will never belong to another man. *Ever.*"

I did like the sound of that. The idea of being with anyone else made my skin shiver as if the temperature had dropped to zero. Almost every *mafie* man I knew had ice in his veins, cold and calculating. Tatum included, except when it came to me. With me, his blood ran hot.

"If you're so sure he'll be happy, why don't we get his blessing?"

"I can't risk that," he stated curtly. "Because I fucking love you, and I can't risk anything getting in the way of *us.*"

Okay, that did it. Something about hearing the words that he loved me tore down the last wall of resistance. I was all in.

"I love you, too," I murmured.

People always underestimated Tatum. He was the quiet one, happier working in the background, in the shadows. But for me, he was like the blinding sun on a hot summer beach. His light shone as brilliantly as a clear LA day.

There was nothing as magnificent and all-consuming to me as Tatum.

His nails scored down my scalp in a delectable manner that had my eyes rolling back in my head. It was hard concentrating with him so near me. Something about being surrounded by Tatum's larger-than-life aura affected me like a drug. I inhaled the faint remnants of his earthy, warm cologne. The leather notes of his scent triggered something in my subconscious, and my body went limp. It was the recognition that I was home, protected, and free.

Returning to reality, I started, "But you said—"

"That he should be happy for you, for us. He should be, but it doesn't mean I'm going to leave the decision in his hands. We have a better chance of getting his approval if it's a *fait accompli*. From the instant we're joined together in holy matrimony, we'll adjust and deal with whatever's thrown our way. Best-case scenario, he sees it the way we do. Worst-case scenario ..."

He shook his head and looked down on me with a little smirk tilting one side of his lips upward. "There's no worst-case scenario because we'll be together, and no one can tear us apart. I'll marry you and put a huge rock on your finger. I'll fuck you. Breed you as soon as possible. I'll leave my come to dry on your skin, my bite marks on you, bruises to show everyone who you belong to. Any man who looks in your direction will know, without a shadow of a doubt, that you belong to *me*."

I shiver of lust coursed down my spine. Rubbing my cheek against the fabric covering his inner thigh, I shifted where I was sitting. "You're sure you don't want to ... you know?"

"Fuck?" he supplied helpfully with his signature smirk.

I batted my lashes at him. "Mm-hmm."

"Right after I marry you. Now pack a bag. We're leaving."

"Bully," I griped.

I left a note on my bed for my father, packed a little bag, changed into something more befitting for clamoring down the side of my house, and slipped out with Tatum. I couldn't believe I was eloping. I prayed my father would accept our marriage, but Tatum was right. Either he accepted us, or we'd figure out something else.

After fearing he would die, after his marriage proposal and his declaration of love, I was for Team Tatum. There was no going back. If I was meant to be the Hagi queen, I would be, virgin or not, married or not, baby or not.

Killing Grigore turned out to be the perfect move because helping me crawl down the trellis beside my balcony was a highly skilled *consilier* who just happened to be available.

"Your security is shit," he muttered with disgust as we crept away. "Jesus, you don't even have guard dogs. I brought meat and sedatives with me, but there was no need. Tossed it in your trash. Your father deserves this scare to learn what it's like to lose you." He grabbed my hand and stalked toward the entrance as I skipped to keep pace with him. "Believe me, that's never happening under my watch."

We jumped into his car and sped away toward Vegas. I googled 24-hour wedding chapels and found plenty, surprisingly enough. Five hours later, I was a married woman.

Tatum steered me into the Waldorf Astoria as night seeped into twilight, beckoning to dawn.

The suite was surprisingly masculine, with rich brown, burgundy, and deep wine reds, but it wasn't the simple, angular modern decor I hated on so much. Whisking a glass of champagne off the table, I drifted toward the expansive view and looked out onto the Vegas strip, the mini– Eiffel Tower glowing a bright gold below me.

Tatum placed our bags on a small red velvet bench and came up behind me. His shadow fell over me. A second later, I felt the delicious heat of his large body pressed against my back. Desire curled in my belly.

My breath shuddered out of me when he said the word *wife* before wrapping his arms around my waist and dropping kisses on the side of my neck. A dreamy, marvelous wave of rightness flooded me.

Leaning back into his chest, feeling his strong arms enveloping me, his enticing scent swathing me, I said, "Who knew it would be such a sexy sounding word."

"The sexiest. Wife, wife, wifey," he repeated.

"Husband," I murmured.

"Hmm, you're right, it does sound good. Almost as good as you screaming my name when you're in the throes of an orgasm."

I tilted my head back, giving him a mock-angry look. "It should sound better."

"Nothing sounds better than you screaming my name when I'm balls deep inside you and your tight cunt is palpitating around my cock," he said.

"That's because you haven't heard me scream 'husband' when you're balls deep inside me and my tight cunt is coming on your cock," I shot back.

He buried his face in my hair and snuffled out a choked laugh. "You're the only woman I know who would dare repeat what I said and sound hot doing it. I'm the luckiest fucking man alive, swear to God."

"Why are you cursing so much?" I asked curiously, snuggling deeper into his body.

I felt him shrug behind me. "Because I've labored and struggled to be perfect most of my life, and it didn't save me. All that toil and sweat, and what do I have to show for it?"

"Me," I retorted.

Gently taking my flute of champagne, he pressed it to my lips for a sip before placing it on a small table alongside his own.

"Oh no, that had nothing to do with my constant striving to be perfect. I'm nowhere close to behaving around you. I let my demon loose on you, and yet you love me still. That's nothing less than sheer luck. A goddamn miracle is what you are."

I turned into the tight cove of his arms. My hand drifted to the rough scruff of his jaw, fingernails scraping against the bristles. He was always clean-shaven, every morning. This was the scruffiest I'd ever seen him, and I loved it.

I lifted onto my tiptoes and slanted my mouth over his, engaging him in a slow, languid kiss. I wanted to savor the taste of him, like honey, leather, and smoke intertwined in a taste that was uniquely Tatum.

He hoisted me up, grinding his stiff rod against my clit. Giving me a sharp slap, he let go of me. My feet made contact with the ground, and I frowned up at him.

Smiling down on me with a little shake of his head, he turned me around.

Taking my hand, he pressed it flat against the windowpane. Then, he did the same with the other. I dropped my head forward, staring down at the sunlight hitting the concrete of the strip laid out before me.

He whispered across my nape, and a little whine hummed in my throat. I bit my lip to stop myself.

"Don't stifle the needy sounds you make, sweetness," he commanded, his big hand smoothing down the side of my white dress. I'd chosen one of the few flirty summer dresses I owned, and this one was white to boot, which came in handy for our shotgun wedding.

He palmed my ass, and I arched my back to give him as much access as possible.

"I miss having your mark on me," I confessed as I looked over my shoulder at him. He'd taken a step back and dragged his gaze down to my feet and back up as if he couldn't believe I was there. The feeling was mutual. I could see the outline of the bulge of his cock and itched to touch it, pull it out, but I stayed still, knowing he wouldn't let me.

"I like casually touching your bite," I told him. Touching it, I'd feel the ghost of his teeth on my skin. It was as if he were always with me, but the bruises and marks had faded fast. Like flowers, they needed watering and attention.

"Hand back on the window," he ordered.

I put my hand back. He leaned over and dug his straight teeth in where my shoulder met my neck.

"I miss seeing them," he confirmed, as he scraped his teeth across the tendon and then gave it a long, smooth lick to make it all better.

"I wanted to suck on this since I saw you in your bedroom," he ducked his head and nuzzled my neck. His large palm soothed over one buttock. "But I knew if I touched you, I'd fuck you, and I swore to myself I wouldn't fuck you until I got my ring on your finger. I'm getting you the biggest diamond ring in existence."

I lifted my hand, staring at the simple gold band we'd purchased at the chapel. "I love my ring."

"That's sweet," he said with a snort of disbelief. "But I'm getting you a huge one anyway. It's a message to every man who lays eyes on you."

"So possessive," I quipped.

He languidly suckled and nipped at my neck until he was satisfied. "Lift your dress. I'm going to fuck you right here, against the window. I want the whole world to see my slutty little wife getting railed against the window."

"Yes," I groaned, yanking my dress up to my waist, the cool air conditioning whisking over the crackling heat of my skin before I brusquely pushed into his hand. His hand slipped down and a thick finger tapped lightly on my clit before pressing in between my pussy lips.

My belly tightened in excitement. Oh, God, that felt good. I missed him so much, and my body shuddered in anticipation, in desperation to have him penetrate me. There was a flutter between my legs, begging, pleading, supplicating.

His other hand slammed down beside mine, followed by his forearm as he pushed against me. I felt his arousal against my lower back, his fingers spearing me.

It was good, but not nearly enough. I needed to feel the stretch and burn of his shaft parting my silky, wet flesh, pliant and ready for him. Feel him thrusting deep, his body surrounding me, his cock dominating me, satisfying me.

My pussy pulsed as my hips twitched from side to side, seeking more friction. His breath gusted out harshly against the side of my neck. Ahh, he liked that. I did it again and he nipped the side of my throat. I gave a little moan, and he laved the bite with his wet tongue to soothe the pinch of pain.

Attacking my mouth, he yanked my panties down my legs. I stamped my feet to get them free.

Spreading my thighs, I displayed myself.

I heard a groan, followed by the sound of a zipper.

"Fuck, baby, you know how to torture a man," he murmured.

"I'm presenting myself. Isn't that what you want?" I asked, angling my head so he could see the flutter of my lashes.

His breath hissed as his hot, stiff cock prodded against my wet slit. I pushed back against him, attempting to rush him. His large palm smacked across one ass cheek as a warning. I bit down to stifle the sound of surprised pain mixed with pleasure.

"Don't do that," he threatened and then gave me a hard

kiss. "I told you, every fucking sound you make is mine. Fucking mine, and I want them. Every single one of them."

To emphasize his point, he shoved inside hard, splitting me in two. I loved the burn of that stretch, the first time he entered me after our hiatus. It wasn't like the night he took my virginity, but it was a tight fit.

I glanced over my shoulder and watched as he pulled out of me slowly until only the fat crown of his thick cock was lodged inside, his face going slack as he riveted his gaze to the point where our bodies merged.

"Fuck me, look at this pussy, spread tight around me, and my cock, baptized in your fucking juices," he growled as he sank back into me.

His hips punched into me, his cock sliding into my soaking wet hole.

I moaned in gratitude. I needed it hard and fast, but Tatum chose this moment to tease and torture me with slow thrusts. Thankfully, after a few minutes, his control frayed, and he slammed into me, again and again.

"Why does this cunt have to be so fucking good?" he growled.

Thrust.

"Wet."

Thrust.

"Tight."

He gave a few short thrusts.

"Tight. Fuuuck," he moaned.

My thighs began to tremble. My nails clawed down the glass, having no purchase, and I didn't know how much longer I could stand it. I bucked against him, tilting my hips to take more of him. Groaning, he flexed his hands around my hips. His breath labored behind me, wafting over my shoulder as he worked himself in and out of me. His fingers slipped in front of me, and he pinched my clit, just the way he knew I needed it.

"Come for me, baby," he demanded, and I exploded. Detonated. Throwing my head back, I cried, *"Husband!"* My inner walls clamped down on him, suctioning his cock. I heard his feral growl and wet slaps of flesh on flesh through the rapture of my climax as he pumped into me, rutting hard, and then he flooded my pussy with his come. I fucking loved the hot jets of seed as he filled me to capacity, my womb teeming with his seed.

I angled my head back to watch him. His teeth were bared. He was sensitive, but he couldn't stop pummeling into me. I leaned into the window. My cheek connected with the cool glass, my breath fogging up the glass.

His lips ghosted over my other cheek.

"I didn't think you'd come for me," I mused out loud, floating on the afterglow of a good, hard manhandling fuck.

"As long as I was alive, I was coming," he replied against my skin. "If it had been my secret, I'd have given it up immediately. But I was torn. Been like that for practically my entire life, and I didn't know any other way. Now that I'm free, there will be no more secrets between us. Now, I can be your everything."

"You already are," I declared.

"And one day soon, we'll have our own family," he replied casually.

My heart tripped over itself. This. Man.

His chest heaved against my back. "Please tell me I'm breeding you right now."

"You're breeding me right now," I whispered back with an upward curve of my lips.

"Thank fuck."

EPILOGUE
TATUM

I walked into the church for the christening for the baby of Marku—a loyal Hagi solider—and his wife, with Clara at my side. I'd deflowered her, married her, killed the competition, and had her in my bed every fucking night since I stepped foot on LA soil. She was mine, all mine, and mine alone. Being magnanimous, I chose to share her with her clan and family because of who she was. A daughter. A sister. A leader. A queen.

But now, also a wife. Hopefully, soon to be a mother. I missed my mother and sister, the Lupu brothers, even Alex. But something fundamental shifted inside me. The roiling, gaping hole in my chest had been stitched up. I was free, and my heart and soul were filled and overflowing because of my beautiful, loyal wife.

And in the darkness of our bedroom, I filled her up. Gave her the dominance she craved, and in exchange, she ruled over her world. At first, I tried ruling by her side, but I found myself sliding back into the shadows, where I felt most at home. I could've ruled on the throne alongside her, as I had promised, but I didn't like the limelight. I much preferred to melt into the background, the strength behind the throne. I was better able to protect her from there, and protecting my queen was my primary concern.

We gathered around the white stone baptismal font at the west end of the church. I'd given the clan time to get used to the concept that their queen had a partner. Thank fuck, her father came around eventually. They'd had a few ugly arguments, which I barely withstood. But when I slid back into the shadows, showing no interest whatsoever in co-ruling with her, he became more amenable to me.

I moved into her home, with her father, no less. Ostensibly, it was because she couldn't leave Adrian, but her concern about her father was evident. I'd fit in well enough, Adrian and I bonding over music, his father and I bonding over soccer matches.

Soon after moving in, Clara and I took over a separate wing of their mansion because I needed privacy with my woman to smack her and torment her without anyone being bothered by her screams of ecstasy. She was a screamer, my woman.

I grabbed her hand, dragging her to me, unabashedly nuzzling the little love bite I'd left for everyone to see. As I bent my head, I felt a twitch from my new tat, the one purging the tat of the Lupu wolf baring his teeth over my heart.

It was now covered by a lynx, the symbol of the Hagi clan. The big feline devoured the heart in its claw, blood dripping off its chops. The heart in her claw was mine. My love for Clara overrode everything in my life, and I shamelessly flaunted my obsession with her.

Turned out, without other obligations to distract me, my obsession went pretty deep. I liked to creep, stalk, hunt my woman. Watch her back, make sure no one so much as touched her without my approval. All I saw was her. All I wanted was her. All I felt was her.

I was consumed.

Even though we were in a crowded church, with eyes on her, Clara leaned into me. Her lips grazed over mine in a gentle kiss, her hot beach fragrance whisking over me, drawing me in. As she pulled away, I grabbed the tresses on the back of her head and held her still to deepen the kiss. My heart filled with pride. *My* fucking woman. God, she glowed with happiness. I broke off and hugged her into the side of my body.

The baby cradled in her godmother's arm was sprinkled with water when I caught sight of Clara's hand instinctually gliding down and resting on her belly. My heart stilled; my breath stuttered.

My hand slipped from around her waist and joined the hand over her belly. She lifted her face to mine and gave me a brilliant smile. Nodding once, she confirmed my aspirations and dreams.

She was pregnant.

Over the droning of the priest's incantations, I leaned in close, rumbling in her ear, "My woman is fucking gorgeous, and now with her belly growing full with our child, I don't know how I'm going to stand it."

"So, you're happy then?" she teased.

I gave a little snort of disbelief. "Happiness doesn't begin to express how I feel."

"It's too early to tell people," she warned.

"So we don't tell people," I replied with a shrug. "And you're so stunning, it makes my teeth ache. You're intelligent, sweet, and submissive, although that part is only for my eyes, which I love even more, wrapped up in one hot as fuck package." I pounded my heart with my fist. "You make me so fucking happy it hurts to breathe."

She snuggled into me, and I wrapped my arm around her, securing her against me, breathing her in. Knowing she was growing a life inside her made me want to fuck her, to mark her again and again. Leave the scent of my come embedded in her skin. Since being with her, I sloughed off any vestiges of civilization. I was a fucking animal when it came to her.

The baptism finished and everyone started converging toward the new parents to congratulate them, and in that moment of quiet, she cupped my cheek and gazed up at me, her eyes hungry. My heart exploded with pleasure, as it always did.

Desire was sweeping through her—right into me. We were in church, surrounded by people, and I could barely keep my hands off her, could barely refrain from dragging her behind the screen of icons separating the nave and fucking her over the nearest table.

"Same here. I was worried you'd miss them too much, miss New York," she confessed, her tone laced with concern. "That you'd have remorse ..."

"I miss them, of course, but I talk to Star and my mother a few times a week." I pressed my cheek into her hand. "You speak and text her more than I do. I miss New York and the Lupu brothers, but that's life. I had to pay for my sins, and I'm fucking alive, Clara. Not only alive but living with the woman I'm fucking in love with."

My hand slipped down to her belly. "Going to have a child with said woman." I pressed a kiss to the side of her mouth. "Honestly, I couldn't have dared dream of having it so good. I fucking love you, Queenie, from the depths of my heart. I'd do it all over again to stand here, right beside you.

Every damn miserable moment made this—us—possible. I have no regrets. *None.*"

A tear slipped out of the corner of her eye, skipping down her cheek. My heart burst open with feels. I bent down and lapped up her tear.

"Damn pregnancy hormones," she muttered.

"I can't wait to take you home, tie you to our bed, and feast on your pussy for hours. I'm not going to let you come. I'll give you a reason to cry. And then when I do, when I thrust into your sweet heat, I'm going to brand you as mine, from the inside out. I'll spend the rest of my days proving to you how damn lucky I am to have you." I rubbed her belly. "Sound good?"

She giggled. "Sounds divine."

I placed my hand possessively on her lower back and prodded her toward the crowd, whispering in the shell of her ear, "Come on, the sooner we congratulate the parents and you make the requisite toast, the sooner we can get the hell out of here and I can start my adoration of your cunt."

I felt her shudder of arousal under my hand, giving me the answer I was looking for.

I'd had to lose everything, rise from the ashes of hell like a phoenix, slay dragons to get to my woman, but I'd go through every single moment again because the life we'd forged together was worth it. She was worth it. Life was a fucking merry-go-round, and I was only grateful she let me hop on to ride it beside her.

THANK you for reading THE PERFECT HEIR! I hope you loved Tatum and Clara. I'm working on Star's story next, a Mafia High School Bully novel. If you'd like to get snippets of my work in progress or hear more about me, check out my newsletter, https://bit.ly/SteamyReadNewsletter

Or start with Book One of The Lupu Chronicles.
Get THE CHOSEN HEIR Now!

"Sexy Mafia read! Monique Moreau knocks this one out the park. Alex is what dreams are made of. He command's the room and doesn't back down from anyone, but her." – 5 Star Review

Here's a taste...

"Fucking hell," I gritted out as I read the text over my grandmother's shoulder. Tasa was safe and she begged us not to look for her. *Really, Tasa?* As if I'd leave my baby sister to hang out to dry, regardless of whether she'd run away. Oh, and had she conveniently forgotten about her fiancé, Cristo? And what part of the term "dangerous enemies" had not penetrated her thick skull, despite my relentless repetition of that threat?

Bunică gave a nonchalant shrug of her skinny shoulders and a grin that showed off her gold tooth. That woman could get her teeth fixed a thousand times over, but she wasn't one to put on airs. As she always said, "I was born a peasant girl, and I'll die a peasant girl."

Peasant girl, my ass. She was as sharp as they came, and while she loved to ham it up with her country ways, she'd graduated from Romania's finest medical school. No lie, she could dig out a bullet and sew up the wound in under half an hour. It had come in handy on more than one occasion, when the doctor on our payroll didn't arrive quickly enough.

"What is she thinking?" I spat out. "She's roaming the country doing God knows what. No protection, no body-guard, no—"

"Oh, hush, you act as if Tasa's an invalid instead of a smart young woman who can take on the world with one hand tied behind her back. She'll be fine. And you best leave her alone," she warned, poking at my chest with her bony finger.

I stared down at her, incredulous. Leave my sister to roam the country unprotected? *Is she insane?*

"Christ, *Bunică*, she's a female. Alone."

My eyes rolled up to the kitchen ceiling, seeking patience, as I took a seat on one of the stools scattered around the island in the kitchen of our family home. This was where *Bunică* practically lived so this was where family members came to talk to her. Was I the only rational one in this conversation? It wasn't like she didn't know who we were. It's not like she wasn't acutely aware that our enemies would start crawling out of the woodwork to kidnap Tasa.

"A *lone* female," I reiterated, emphasizing the word "lone" in hopes of getting through to my grandmother. "Of the *Lupu* clan." My gaze passed over the midnight-blue double oven range my father had imported directly from Italy when he busted out the back wall and extended the kitchen to please his mother and wife. The chrome from the state-of-the-art appliances gleamed under the bronze farm-house lights.

We are the Lupus, the Romanian upstarts who quickly rose to the top of the New York City mafias. The speed of our rise was a point of embarrassment for the Bratva, the Russian mafia, and the main reason why they're so intent on destroying us. As for the Italians, they were a shadow of what they were before the takedowns and trials of the '90s. Which had left a vacuum for my father to fill when he arrived in New York, solidifying our foothold in Sunnyside, Queens. Better known now as "Little Bucharest."

Returning my attention to *Bunică*, I reminded her, "Enemies? Remember them? Why do I need to mention this? It's not like you don't know what I'm talking about. She's in real danger."

She let out a cackle as she whipped out a bottle of *palincă*, a traditional Romanian spirit from the region she came from. Plunking down two small glasses, she poured two shots and pushed one over the kitchen island to me. The other, she threw back like a pro.

"What's obvious to everyone but you and your mother is that Tasa is her own woman. She's smart, and she's not going to get caught by some two-bit *mafie* idiot. She'll be fine."

I narrowed my eyes at her. She was too relaxed by far, considering her youngest grandchild had just run off to god-knows-where.

"What do you know?" I demanded.

Fluttering her wrinkled hand weakly in front of her chest, she lied without a shred of remorse, "Who? Little old me? Why, nothing!"

"You're as deceitful as the day is long," I snapped, my patience finally fraying.

"Back off," she warned, her innocent features turning dark. *Ah, there's the real* Bunică. "I don't happen to know anything, but if I did, you bet your last dollar I wouldn't tell you. I won't help you drag her back here and keep her prisoner until she marries that worthless *tâmpit*, Cristo. *Uck.* He's barely a man. And he has a little two-bit hussy of a side piece. Each of you must marry in the *familie*, but why him? *Bah!*"

"You're unbelievable, you know that, right? Come on, out with it," I insisted, flicking the fingers of my open hand at her.

"Like I said, my lips are sealed." She made a gesture as if locking her lips together and flinging away an imaginary key.

My jaw clenched. Women. The bane of my existence. And those two stuck together like super glue. It was hopeless on my part to try to sever the unbreakable.

"Fine, then," I replied, releasing a long, exhausted breath. "You're not the only person I can press for information."

Her hand nabbed the sleeve of my jacket, crushing the fine wool between her bony fingers. "Leave that poor girl alone. You know she's in love with you. Don't you dare take advantage of her."

My grandmother was talking about Tasa's little best friend, the beautiful, supple Nina, of course.

Nina.

Damn, that girl. Smelled like jasmine and a hard fuck waiting to happen. Just the thought of her brought crackling heat to my skin and a stiffness to my cock. That woman was my Achilles' heel, if ever there was one. Sweet as could be, with large brown eyes and a chest I could face-plant in and suck on for days on end. Annnd...

And she's also like a sister to you, asshole.

Not.

There wasn't a shred of brotherly feelings toward that little minx. Unless one included the taboo kind.

Laying my forearms heavily on the smooth wood of the kitchen island, I warned, *"Bunică*, it's Tasa we're talking about here. My little *sister*. For some insane reason, you don't think she's in jeopardy, but I happen to know exactly what our enemies are capable of. I know exactly what they do during a torture session. Once it's out that she's gone, finding her and using her to get to us will be at the top of their list. This is like a nuclear arms race, during the Cold War." I tapped the watch around my wrist. "Time is ticking, and I can assure you that this won't finish well. Least of all for Tasa. Who's going to want to marry her if she's tarnished? Think about that and come talk to me when you've regained your common sense."

"Băieţel, don't speak to your *Bunică* like that. I wiped your bottom when you couldn't even feed yourself. Any man should be grateful for the chance to marry my little girl."

I snorted out an exasperated sigh. I hated it when she called me *little boy*. Deciding it was in my best interest to pretend I didn't hear her last comment, I bent down low and dropped a kiss on the crown of her head. "Do you think I enjoy this? Do you think I enjoy having to lay down the law and act like an enforcer with the people I love?"

"You *do* enjoy it," she shot back. "You always think you're right. In that way, you take after your father. Regardless of what everyone in this family thinks, he wasn't a saint, you know. He was human, and he made his fair share of mistakes."

Yeah, right. She always said that, but it was never quite believable. The man was a brilliant businessman and strategist. He loved his family and was the paradigm of how to behave in our twisted world. He was honorable to his core. If I could live up to half of the man he'd been, I'd die content. Which brought me back to the issue at hand: Tasa's marriage.

"I've been negotiating with Nelu on this marriage contract between Tasa and Cristo for *years*. It's more than a simple wedding, as you well know. What's going to happen when he finds out his future daughter-in-law ran away? It will be perceived as a stain on his honor. It could legitimately lead to war when we've only just begun our truce. Not only is business booming, but Tata would be disappointed in me. I gave him my oath that I would do everything in my power to make this happen. There's too much on the line," I finished with a frown.

The responsibility of taking care of my family fell heavily on my shoulders, but on days like today, the weight was crushing. Although *Bunică* was whip smart, the truth was she couldn't relate. She'd always been taken care of. First by my grandfather, then my father, and now me. She could afford to focus solely on the personal, not the big picture. No, that fell on me.

"Pfft. And so you had to sell Tasa to do this? Of all people, you chose to sacrifice your little sister?" Reproval shimmered in her eyes at me.

"*Tata* would've commended me for it. *He* would've thought it was a brilliant move. With the Popescus, Tasa will be taken care of. She'll be protected. And it would solidify a peace that's eluded our families for decades."

Bunică stared at me like she was about to spit on the ground. "Don't make it seem like you're doing this for Tasa, Alex. It's beneath you to lie."

"I *am* doing it for her," I ground out, fists balling at my sides. Christ, this old woman was never satisfied. She was spoiling the girl with notions of love. Our life was based on duty and, for women, that included the duty to marry a man chosen by her family. As the boss or *şef* of this family, I might be given a leeway regarding this rule. But for a princess of marriageable age like Tasa, it was unthinkable.

"She's the baby of the family. The Popescus, curse their name, are worthless mongrels. Animals. Unlike the Lupu clan, they didn't gain power until the fall of Communism. That's a blink of an eye in the span of history, and you sold your precious sister to those heathens?"

I snorted. "They're powerful enough now; I can tell you that much. We can look down on the Popescu clan all we want, but only a fool would underestimate their potential to do damage. They're *vicious*. Ruthless. You know this as well as anyone." It was also common knowledge that their tempers were like hair triggers. One wrong move and *kapow*. I made a dismissive wave. "In any case, it's done. My hands are tied. There's nothing I can do but retrieve her and make sure her marriage goes off without a hitch."

She stalked up to me. Barely five feet tall, she went toe to toe with me and spat out, "Then, you will get no help from me. I will do everything in my power to thwart you. The marriage be damned."

"You're impossible," I heaved out, throwing up my hands. "You know the situation."

When Tata was bleeding out in the ambulance roaring through the quiet streets, his dying wish had been for me to take care of the family. I'd already failed on that promise, with Tasa stranded somewhere out there, alone and vulnerable. Possibly hurt. My back teeth ground together at that last possibility.

The second oath had been to reconcile our family with the lowbred Popescus. I didn't disagree with *Bunică* that every one of them was a bottom-feeder. No education, no class, no nothing. Violence was their greatest attribute. The

two families had been at each other's throats for generations, clawing their way to the top by throat-punching the
other. We may be at the pinnacle, but they came in at a close
second.

Nelu, their *șef*, and Tata were always vying to be the top
dog. Tata often said that it was too late for their generation,
that there was too much bad blood. But at his death bed, he
declared, "There needs to be a marriage. It's the only way."
Those last words were the proverbial nails in my coffin.

"Go back to your fancy apartment in Columbus Circle,
Alex. I don't want you under my roof until you come to your
senses."

Goddamn, this woman was impossible. She refused to
acknowledge the possibility of a looming war. Instead, she
was banishing me to the penthouse floors of the two towers
of the Time Warner Center building in Manhattan, where
my brothers and I lived.

Tasa had moved in with Nina a few avenues over, in a
nice high-rise building overlooking the Hudson. Of course,
Tasa, always with the rebellious streak, couldn't share an
apartment with her twin, Nicu. Oh no, our building was too
snooty and fancy for her. And Tasa was as opinionated as
the day was long. Thank Christ, she had her little best
friend living with her.

My back teeth ground down harder, my fists flexing by
my sides, but there was nothing I could say when *Bunică* got
into one of her fits. Turning on my heel, I marched out of
the kitchen, grabbed my coat from the hallway closet, and
stalked out of the house. What in the ever-loving fuck?

Tasa gone.

Contract in ruins.

Potential war on the horizon.

Everything I'd worked for gone.

Gone.

I was an abject failure. No, I refused to let that stand. I didn't care what it took to make this right. I'd fulfill Tata's oath. I'd drag Tasa back by her hair to marry the Popescu if need be. I'd make my father proud if it fucking killed me.

GET THE CHOSEN HEIR NOW>>>

MORE BY MONIQUE MOREAU

The Lupu Chronicles

The Chosen Heir (Alex's story)
The Recluse Heir (Luca's story)
The Savage Heir (Nicu's story)
The Perfect Heir (Tatum's story)

Coming Soon!

The Bastard Heir (Sebastian's story)
The Princess Heir (Emma's story)

Fans of sizzling hot alpha bikers and the sassy, strong women who tame them will love Monique Moreau's steamy MC series.

The Demon Squad MC Series

Kingdom's Reign (Book 1)
Cutter's Claim (Book 2)

Loki's Luck (Book 3)
Stanton's Sins (Book 4)
Puck's Property (Book 5)
Whistle's War (Book 6)
Her Hidden Valentine, A Squad Novella (Book 7)

Learn all about my books at moniquemoreau.com